WHATEVER HAPPENED TO BETSY BLAKE?

DAVID B. LYONS

Print ISBN :- 978-1-9160518-1-2

❀ Created with Vellum

WANT TO STAY UP TO DATE WITH DAVID B. LYONS'S NOVELS?

Visit David's official website

TheOpenAuthor.com

Or

Sign up here to become a David B. Lyons insider and receive exclusive information on his latest novels.

www.subscribepage.com/dblinsider

For Lola

10:00

Gordon

I DON'T KNOW WHY I'M SMILING WHEN I'VE JUST BEEN TOLD I have a fifty per cent chance of dying today. But I am smiling. I can feel it; my cheeks high and wide on my face. It must be the shock. Or perhaps the prospect of death is appealing to me; the thought of my mind finally shutting the fuck up.

'Do you understand, Gordon?' Mr Douglas asks.

I feel my cheeks fall back down to their resting position, then let out a little sigh and nod my head.

'I understand, Mr Douglas.'

'Well, we're going to prep the theatre as soon as it's free. In the meantime, Elaine here,' he says pointing to a young nurse dressed in purple scrubs, 'will be available for you to talk to anytime you want. She'll be positioned outside at the nurses' station. Just press this button and she'll be with you in no time.'

He hands me what looks like a Nintendo games controller from the early nineties; one red button in the middle of it. Then he purses his lips at me before spinning on his heels. They all follow in unison, like a synchronised swimming team. I count them as they head towards the door.

1

Seven. I'm waiting on them all to leave so I can sink the back of my head firmly into the pillow and yell obscenities. But Elaine turns back, walks towards me.

'Mr Blake, are you sure there's nobody I can call... nobody who can come up to see you?'

'It's Gordon, please,' I tell her, my forearms propping me up on the bed. 'And eh... no, there's nobody. Not yet anyway. I may call my wife a little later.'

'Your wife?' she says, her eyebrows twitching.

'Ex wife.' Elaine makes an 'O' shape with her mouth. 'There's a few things I need to iron out in my head before I call her.'

Elaine places the palm of her hand on top of mine and then purses her lips before turning around and walking out the door to catch up with the rest of her team. They must master that in medical college; how to purse your lips before spinning on your heels. As soon as she has closed the door I push my head firmly into the pillow.

'Fuuuuuck!' I screech, clenching my fists; my fingernails stabbing into the palms of my hands. I allow the reality of the situation to wash over me as much as it possibly can. A fifty-fifty chance of survival. That's what Douglas said. Fuckin hell. I reach out to grab my phone and hold my finger against the screen so I can check the time. 10:03. Douglas told me the theatre would be ready at three p.m. I twitch the top of each finger on one hand to count upwards. Five hours. Jesus Christ. I might only have five hours left to live.

'Fuuuck!' I don't screech it this time. I scream it. I tilt my head; stare over at the door handle in anticipation of it being pushed downwards. But it remains upright. Nobody's coming to soothe me.

My breathing grows heavier. Flashes of Betsy's pretty little face consume me. At first she's smiling. Then crying. Gagged. Suffocating. I shake my head to get rid of her. This is nothing new. I've been doing this almost daily for the past seventeen years. I consciously try to slow my breathing, then rest my head back on to the pillow.

I remember a college lecturer – many years ago - asking me a question that relates to the situation I seem to have found myself in right now.

'If you had just hours left to live, what would you do?'

I think I answered by saying 'sex' or 'bungee jump' or some other adrenaline-filled piece-of-shit activity. She was trying to get across the concept of bucket lists and positive thinking. But that's a load of bollocks. I've never had a bucket list. Unless finding your daughter is applicable to being on a bucket list. That's the only thing I want in life. To see her face again. To hold her. To apologise to her.

A tear squeezes itself out of my left eye. I shake my head again. Not to remove the tear, but to remove the image of Betsy from my mind. Then I grip my mobile phone; scroll into my contacts list until I see the name Ray De Brun and stare at it. I picture his chubby little face; bet he's all fat and old now. Useless prick. I touch his name and then hold the phone to my ear. That annoying high-pitched tone you get when a number is out of use pierces through me. I grip the phone firmer in frustration, let an audible sigh force its way out of both nostrils. I scroll through the screen of my phone again, into my Internet browser and search for 'Kilmainham Garda Station'. The phone number appears instantly. I press at it, bring the phone back to my ear.

'Hello, Kilmainham Garda Station.'

'I need to talk to detective Ray De Brun.'

'Just one second, Sir.'

I chew my bottom lip while I'm on hold. What I've been told this morning is too mammoth to fully comprehend. But I've just realised I'm not my greatest concern. Betsy is. And always has been. My greatest fear may play out today; I may very well die without ever knowing what happened to my daughter.

'I'm sorry, Sir, Detective De Brun is not on duty today. Is there anybody else who can assist you?'

I speak slowly.

'My name is Gordon Blake. Betsy Blake's father. De Brun knows who I am. I have his mobile number but it seems out of action – has he changed it?'

'Oh, I'm not aware of that, Mr Blake. Detective De Brun is in semi-retirement now. Our lead detective is Detective Marshall, shall I see if she is available to talk to you?'

I fall silent. Marshall. Never heard of her.

'It's an emergency. I need to talk to De Brun right now. Please pass me on his mobile number. He won't mind. I'm dying... may only have hours to live.'

'Eh... hold on just one second, Mr Blake.'

A tipple of piano music plays. Doesn't last long.

'Hello, Mr Blake – this is detective Marshall. How can I help you?'

'Marshall... De Brun was the lead detective in the case of my missing daughter over seventeen years ago. You may be familiar with it.'

'I am indeed, Mr Blake. But you are fully aware that case is closed, right?'

I turn my face away from the phone and gurn. Nothing annoys me more than being told the case is closed. It's not fucking closed! It won't be closed until I'm holding my daughter again.

'Mr Blake, the case was closed in 2009. Elizabeth was announced deceased and—'

'Listen, Marshall,' I shout, my patience already stretched. 'Firstly, her name isn't Elizabeth okay, it's Betsy. And secondly, she's not fuckin dead. How can she be announced deceased when you and your colleagues never found a body?'

'Mr Blake, I can call up the files for you later and—'

'I don't have *later*, Marshall!' I snap. 'Listen, can you please just get me in touch with De Brun. I need to speak with him as urgently as possible. I'm in Tallaght hospital. I have to undergo emergency surgery in a few hours time and there's a huge chance I won't wake up from it.'

The line falls silent. All I can hear is my own breathing reverberating back at me.

'Please,' I say, sounding desperate.

'Mr Blake, Detective De Brun is in Galway – he's semi-retired, has a home out on the west coast and spends an awful lot of his time there. He—'

'Please.' I say it even more desperately this time.

'Tell you what. I'll give him a call and let him know you are looking for him. I can see your number here on the screen. I'll ask him to ring you as soon as possible. But... I must inform you, Mr Blake, Detective De Brun goes to the west coast to get away from phones, to get away from work. He may not have it switched on. There's no guarantee I can reach him imminently.'

My eyes twitch, flickering from side to side. Maybe I'm going mad. I've been seventeen years searching for Betsy, with possibly only five hours left. What makes me think I can get to the bottom of this today? I allow a long sigh to force its way out of my nostrils.

'Just ask him to ring me as soon as he can. It's an emergency.' I hear my voice crack as I say that. Then I hang up. The tear that dropped out of my left eye is now hanging from my chin. I swipe it off with the palm of my hand, almost cutting my fingertip against my sharp stubble. Then I lie flat back down on the pillow.

Maybe I should ring Michelle. Tell her my terrible news. Though I'm not quite sure what that would achieve. Douglas said it's imperative I relax ahead of my surgeries, says that having a positive mind-set could be key to success. Having Michelle come up to me will only cause me stress. *Us* stress. She gets more worked up than I do. She can't stand the fact that I can't let go; that I haven't accepted that Betsy is gone. And I can't stand that she gave up; that she's happy to accept the cops' theory.

And that's all it is; a fuckin theory.

No. Fuck her. There's nothing I can achieve by ringing Michelle.

But I can't lie here and do nothing. I pick up my phone, scroll into the Internet search browser again.

10:00

Lenny

LENNY CAN FEEL CLAIRE'S KNEES VIBRATE AGAINST HIS. IT isn't a shivering of her knees that is causing the vibration. It's the constant swiping of her palms against her thighs. She's trying to rid them of sweat; is all too aware that she's about to receive an answer to the mystery that has engulfed her for the past six months.

They're both sitting at Lenny's tiny desk, inside his tiny office. Calling it a desk is exaggerating; it's no bigger than the type of table you would find on a train. And calling it an office is probably exaggerating too; it's no bigger than a laundry room in a modest home. But it's all he can afford. The office just about has enough space for the desk, two chairs and one tall, skinny filing cabinet, which can't fully shut due to the amount of paperwork desperate to jump out of it. Most of the paperwork is redundant, but sorting it out isn't high on the list of Lenny's priorities. It's not as if the day doesn't afford him ample time to sort it out, he just couldn't be bothered. He's more interested in finding new assignments than poring over the contents of old ones.

He finally stops typing, then turns his laptop screen to face Claire. She sucks in a sharp breath, then holds a finger to the tip of her nose; her attempt to halt the tears from loosening their grip from the tips of her eyelashes.

'He's... he's my line manager at work,' she whispers into her finger.

'Have you any idea why he would be doing this to you?' Lenny asks.

Claire begins to drum the tip of her finger against her lips as she sinks into her thoughts. Then she shakes her head slowly.

'I mean... he tried it on with me at our Christmas party last year,' she says, finding volume. 'But... that's about it. I can't think why... Derek! Derek Murray. I don't believe it.'

Lenny closes the lid of his laptop and looks up sympathetically at Claire. He's been in this position many times before; not really knowing what to say next. The job she offered him had reached its conclusion, yet he understands Claire will have a thousand questions racing around her head right now.

'Do you know why... why he is doing this to me?' she asks.

Lenny scratches at his temple. He always feels awkward when he has the opportunity to upsell.

'Well that's another job. If you would like me to confront Derek, get those kind of answers for you, I can indeed do that but...' Lenny shrugs his left shoulder.

'I eh... I eh,' Claire stutters, 'I don't really know what to do next.'

'Tell you what. Now that we've found out the who, why don't you take a step back and think it all through. If you want to find out the why, get in touch. I'll be here for you. For now, I recommend going home, having a nice hot cup of tea and thinking all this through before contacting me again.

I'm at the end of this phone anytime you need me,' he says, picking up his clunky mobile from his desk. 'Y'know, perhaps you have enough information now to see if the cops would be interested – now that you know who has been stalking you they may look at it differently.'

Claire throws her eyes towards the stained ceiling, then stares back down to her fidgeting fingers on her lap. She'd taken that road before. The cops didn't want to know; they didn't even hide the fact that such a complaint was beneath them either.

'I'll think it through, Lenny. I'll go home, have that cup of tea, and eh… thank you so much for all of your help.'

Both Claire and Lenny stand up at the same time. Lenny holds his hand out for his client to shake, but she squashes it between them both as she drags him in for a hug.

'Allow me,' Lenny says after they release. He pulls his door open, then steps aside so Claire can squeeze her way out.

'I'll send my report on to you by email, but eh… just so you know, there'll be no H in the report. This old thing,' he says, slapping the lid of his laptop, 'it's getting old. The H key came off and…'

Claire offers Lenny a thin smile and then nods her head once before turning around. She's still in a sterile state of shock as she slumps down the corridor, her head bowed. Lenny doesn't watch her leave. He's too bothered chasing the sheet of paper that has floated into his office. He tuts, picks it up and then paces down the corridor himself, turning left before he reaches the stairs Claire is now making her way down. He walks past two doors, all equally battered as his, then knocks on the third one he comes to.

'Sorry, Joe,' he says, after opening the door himself. 'Any Blu Tack?'

'Again?'

Lenny holds the sheet of paper towards Joe as an answer.

'Fuck sake, mate… can you not get a proper sign? Won't cost much.'

'I keep meaning to, it's just…' Lenny shrugs his shoulder again, then blinks his eyes rapidly.

'Didn't you have a client in with you just there? She was alright lookin' wasn't she?'

'Yeah, nice girl really – job's all done.'

'She paying you?'

Lenny nods.

'Well then buy a fuckin sign,' Joe says as he lobs a marble-sized blob of Blu Tack towards Lenny. 'Or at least buy some of your own fuckin Blu Tack.'

Lenny looks around Joe's office space. It's not much bigger than his; probably longer. It's more rectangular in shape, but still only fits a small desk, two chairs and one filing cabinet – though Joe's filing cabinet is a little chunkier than Lenny's.

'Thanks, man,' Lenny says before closing Joe's door and plodding back down the corridor. He grips the sheet of paper between his teeth while pulling at the blob of Blu Tack, dividing it into four separate smaller blobs. Then he removes the sheet from his teeth, stabs a blob onto each corner and slaps the paper to his door before rubbing his thumb repeatedly over each corner firmly. He knows that no matter how many times he rubs his thumb over the corners, the sign is still going to fly away again. But he might at least try. He stands back, stares at the sign as if it's the first time he's ever read it.

Lenny Moon – Private Investigator.

It's written in black felt-tip pen on a blank A4 sheet of white paper.

Pathetic.

He closes the door behind him and sinks back down into his Ikea office chair. Aside from the laptop, the chair is the most expensive thing in the room. A hell of a lot cheaper than the chair on the other side of the desk; a fold-out seat his mother used to use in their old home to help her reach the top shelf in the kitchen.

Lenny opens a Word document on his laptop labelled 'Claire Jennings' and types the word 'complete' at the bottom of it, all in capital letters. Then he highlights what he has just typed and changes the font colour to red before slapping his laptop shut and resting the back of his head on to the top of his chair. He always pictures his wife when he does this. Imagines her staring at him; her lips turned down. It's almost impossible for him to picture her smiling anymore. When he's intent on picturing her smiling, he has to close his eyes even firmer. By the time the lips in his imagination have turned upwards, Sally's face will have turned into something else. Somebody else. He barely tries to imagine her smiling anymore anyway. He's just content to picture her. To know she's still around. Still alive.

The noise of the phone vibrating on his desk brings him back to the real world. But he knows it's not a massive deviation. The person ringing is most likely the person he has just been thinking about. Either that, or someone is ringing about work. The chances of that are slim, though – about twenty-five per cent. Only one in four phone calls are work related; the rest of the time it's Sally calling. She rings three times a day.

'Hey, sweetie,' he says.

'Busy?' she asks. She always asks this. He always answers the same way; by sniffing a short laugh out of his nose.

A silence rests from both ends of the line. This is not unusual. Sally mostly calls for no reason, other than routine.

'You okay?' Lenny asks.

'Yeah – today's a good day. I think. Been cleaning the house; put another load of washing on. Jesus, Leonard, do you have to change your boxer shorts so regularly?'

Lenny sniffs again, but then stays silent. She's often asked this question. It's best he doesn't answer, best he doesn't try to justify that he changes his underwear every morning like most people do. Like most people should. Because if he did try to justify it, he'd get barked at. It would turn Sally's 'good day' into a 'bad day.' And that's the last thing he wants.

'Spoke with Jared's teacher this morning when I dropped them off… says he's been doing well in class lately.'

'Oh… good, good,' Lenny replies. 'Was that the classroom teacher or the SEN one?'

'Eh… the short one.'

'Yeah – Ms Moriarty,' he says, 'it's Mrs Morrissey we need to get information from. She's the one who keeps track of him on a daily basis. We must arrange a meeting with her soon.'

'You're always saying that.'

Lenny nods his head. He's well aware that he's always saying that.

'Okay – just thought I'd see how you were doing,' Sally says.

'Thanks, sweetie, talk to you later.'

Sally hangs up after repeating the word 'bye' seven times, like most Irish women do when finishing a phone call.

Rather than rest his head onto the top of the chair Lenny opens his laptop, scrolls down to the Solitaire icon at the bottom of his screen and opens up a game he had begun playing when he first entered the office just before nine o'clock this morning. He's good at Solitaire is Lenny; gets lots of practice at it. But his meeting with Claire Jennings consumed his mind this morning and he didn't get a good enough start at the game. And getting a good start at Solitaire is everything. He checks the clock ticking away at the bottom corner of the screen. Thirty-eight minutes.

'Pathetic,' he whispers. And he's right. It is pathetic. Especially for someone who plays the game almost every day. His meeting distracted him. He wasn't sure how Claire would react when he revealed to her that it was her line manager at work – Derek Murray – who had set up two fake online accounts to stalk her. The poor girl has been on edge for the past three months, even left home to live with her sister because of the fear it was causing. She turned to the cheapest Private Investigator she could find after the Gardaí told her there was nothing they could do about the fact somebody was bullying her online. Lenny liked Claire, felt sorry for her. He'd be intrigued to follow up the investigation, to confront Derek, ask him why he was reducing himself to such juvenile behaviour. But he won't follow it up until Claire instructs him to do so. He needs the upsell. Needs the money.

The phone vibrates again.

Fuck sake.

'Yes, sweetie,' he answers.

'Sorry?' a man says.

'Oh... no, no, I'm the one who's sorry.'

Lenny sits upright, resting both of his elbows on his tiny desk. 'I thought you were my wife. Eh... Lenny Moon, Private Investigator – how can I help?'

'Is this Lenny?'

'It is, Sir.'

'Oh, good. I thought I'd get your secretary.'

Lenny's head pivots around his pokey room, wondering where a secretary would even sit. Atop the filing cabinet perhaps.

'My name is Gordon Blake. My daughter went missing

seventeen years ago. I'm dying. May not have long to live. How soon could you get to Tallaght Hospital?'

Lenny squints his entire face; his eyes, his nose, his lips. When he started up his Private Investigating business, he had wishfully thought he would be inundated with calls such as this one. But none had ever come. Not one in the past six years. This is such an unusual call that Lenny immediately feels he is being played. Having a Private Investigating business listed in the Yellow Pages opens you up to a whole world of prank calls.

'Eh... Gordon Blake, that's B. L. A. K. E. – am I right?' Lenny asks, tapping the name into a fresh Word document.

'Yes... my daughter's name was – is – sorry, *is*, Betsy Blake. She went missing in 2002. Was snatched from our street.'

Lenny sits even more upright, his mouth slightly ajar.

'Betsy Blake. I remember,' he says.

'Yeah – she's my daughter. Please tell me you have time to give me today. I can give you one thousand euro for the next five hours of your life. If you can give me some answers, there's more on offer. A hell of a lot more.'

Lenny stares over his computer screen at nothing in particular. He's trying to soak in the surreality of the call.

'Let me, eh... let me just check my schedule, Mr Blake... it seems... eh...' Lenny slaps away at his keyboard, just randomly typing nonsense into the Word document in an effort to sound busy. 'I can push some things aside. And eh... that's cash is it – the one thousand?'

'I can transfer it into your bank account as soon as you get here. I'm in St Bernard's Ward, Tallaght Hospital. Are you in your office? It's close by right? You're in Tallaght village...'

Lenny takes the phone from his ear. Checks the time on the top of the screen. 10:19. Then he lets out a long, silent breath that almost whistles through his lips.

'I'll be with you just gone half past,' he says.

SEVENTEEN YEARS AGO

Betsy

DADDY TURNS AROUND AND LOOKS AT ME.

'Don't go far, Betsy.'

Then he smiles. I like when he smiles. It means he is happy. When he is happy we play games. When we get back to our house we can play hide and seek or football. I like hide and seek best but most times I play football because I know Daddy will play that for longer with me. Football lasts longer than hide and seek. A lot longer. Sometimes we play until dinnertime. But that's only on days when Daddy is happy. Like today. We'll probably play football until Mummy calls us in for some stew or pasta. Today is Wednesday. It might be pasta.

I smile back at Daddy and then he turns away. That is okay. Maybe he is busy thinking about work. When he can't play with me he says it is because he is working. But normally when he is working he is on the phone or on his computer. But now he is just looking out onto the road. I don't know what he is doing. I do some dancing while I wait. I'm a good dancer. There is no music. But sometimes I don't need music. Then a man puts his hand towards Daddy and

Daddy puts his hand in his. I don't know who the man is. It is somebody Daddy works with I think. They just stand there talking. And talking. And talking even more. I'm bored. Too bored to even dance anymore.

I see a little wall at the end of the road and skip towards it. I am good at walking on walls. Mummy and Daddy say I should hold their hand if I'm ever walking on walls but sometimes I do it when they are not looking. I'm a big girl now. I don't like holding Mummy and Daddy's hands. Not all the time. My cousin Ceri doesn't hold her Mummy's hands anymore and she is five. I can't wait to be five. But June seems a long way away. Even though Ceri is a bigger girl than me, I don't think she is happier than I am. She doesn't have a Daddy. I would hate to not have a Daddy. It would make me sad. Really, really sad. I would cry. A lot.

I put one foot in front of the other and spread my arms out. I have seen somebody do this on the TV when they were walking on a rope. I don't know how you can walk on just a rope. But this man did it. Way up high. Almost in the sky. He walked on a rope from the roof of a building all the way across to the roof of a other building. Mummy says the man must have gone to school for lots and lots of years to learn how to do that. That seems like a fun thing to do at school. I wonder when I am going to start learning how to walk on ropes at school.

I put the other foot in front and then the other. Slow. I try not to look down because when I look down I feel a bit dizzy. The wall is big. It is about the same size as me. Mummy measured me with a measuring tape before. I think it was in the summertime. She said I was three foot, three inches. She said I was going to be a big girl soon. That made me happy. I can't wait to be a big girl.

I put the other foot in front. Then the other. I am getting close to the end of the wall. I turn back to see if Daddy can see me. I want him to smile at me again. But he is too far away. He is just like a small spot at the end of the road. There are two small spots. He must still be talking to the man that works with him.

'Daddy, Daddy.' I wave.

He doesn't look. I am too far away. I should shout loud.

'Da—'

A man's hand is on my face. He picks me up off the wall and then down behind it. He has one hand across my mouth. His other hand is around my legs. He's holding me really hard. It hurts.

'Don't scream, Betsy.'

I don't scream because I am scared. But I want to.

10:20

Lenny

LENNY SNATCHES HIS BUNCH OF KEYS FROM HIS DESK, THEN pauses in the doorway. He's trying to work out whether or not it's appropriate for him to drive to Tallaght Hospital from here.

It's one of those in-between decisions most of us have to make on an irregular basis; take a fifteen-minute walk or be a lazy bollocks and take the car for a three-minute drive. The hospital is less than a mile away from Lenny's office, at the far end of Tallaght.

It's a shared office block Lenny works from; nine small business all renting space within it. There is an array of 'entrepreneurs' operating here; two start-up tech guys, two freelance graphic designers, a photographer, a jeweller whose sewing machine can be heard stuttering throughout the building, a stationery designer, a copywriter – which is what Joe does when he isn't being distracted by Lenny asking for Blu Tack – and, of course, a private investigator.

Each of the office spaces are cramped; though cramped in different ways. Some of the rooms are square – like Lenny's – some more rectangular – like Joe's. But they're all dingy, echoey and almost always cold – whatever the season. They are solitary though; allowing those who rent the spaces the opportunity to work undisturbed for most of the day and – more importantly – they are as cheap as chips to rent. Lenny pays two hundred and fifty euro every month for his space. A pittance in Dublin, even if it is for a room the size of an under-the-stairs bathroom. It's fine for Lenny though, because aside from his advertising costs – which consist of an annual fee for his appearance in the Yellow Pages – Lenny's overheads are minimal. He just has to make sure he brings in at least one-thousand four hundred euro every month to cover his outgoings; two hundred and fifty euro to pay for his office space, eight hundred and fifty to pay the mortgage on the family home along with utility bills, plus the three hundred he and Sally calculate they need for groceries each month to feed all four Moons.

For the most part he just about manages to sneak in the required amount, but there are months when the family have to live on reheated stews and coddles for days on end when he comes up a little short.

Lenny has tied himself to two insurance companies who use him on a regular basis to find out whether or not they are being scammed by people making claims from them. The money from these jobs is decent enough – about two hundred euro a go. But Lenny needs to ensure he picks up at least seven of those gigs a month. Sometimes he does, sometimes he doesn't. There's no projecting it. Though a new wave of clients seems to have evolved for Lenny over the past year; those who hire him to find out who's anonymously bullying them online. This type of 'crime' is a growing concern in the modern world; but it's not much of a concern for Lenny – it puts an extra few quid in his coffers. He likes this type of job, it's less boring than sitting outside somebody's house, waiting on them to come out so he can take a photograph of them that may prove their back injury isn't as bad as they are claiming.

Though neither of these gigs have anything to do with the reason Lenny became a Private Investigator in the first place. He assumed he would be playing detective; solving proper crimes; murders, kidnappings, thefts, larceny. But that was slight delusion, borne from reading too many crime fiction thrillers over the years. He never got a call asking him to solve such a crime... until three minutes ago.

He nods his head, decision made. He'll drive over to the hospital. That way if he needs to get on with the job immediately, he'll have his wheels close by. Lenny grabs at his yellow puffer jacket and Sherpa hat, then pulls the office door behind him and sets off down the rickety stairs.

During the months of October through March Lenny always wears a Sherpa hat; he needs the fur inside to protect his bald head from the elements. Lenny lost his hair in his early twenties. Aside from the fact his head is always freezing during these months, losing his hair has never bothered him. He has the right shaped head to carry it off. He offset the baldness by growing out some stubble on his face. The stubble irritates Sally – she finds it discomforting to kiss her husband – but they both agree that a full beard doesn't suit him; it hides his jaw line, while a fully-shaved face makes him look like a twelve-year-old. And that's not a good look for somebody who wants to be taken seriously as an investigator. So they both decided stubble was the best option for him. Even with the stubble, Lenny still looks much younger than his thirty-three years, but at least he has the maturity to pass himself off as a man in the middle stages of life.

He thumbs his dated mobile phone as he paces his way to the car, trying to remember the images of Betsy Blake that were plastered all over the media many years ago. The most prominent picture used was a school portrait; her beaming a gummy grin at the camera dressed in her navy-blue uniform. The nation was obsessed with the story of Betsy Blake. Lenny was only a mid-teen when the story blew up. Over half his life-time ago. His memory is letting him down. If he had a smart phone, he'd be able to recall that image now. But what would it matter? Betsy isn't four-years-old anymore; she'd be twenty-one now. A woman. Lenny shakes his head and puffs out his cheeks as this reality hits him.

He throws his phone on to the passenger seat of his car, turns the key in the ignition and pulls out of his parking space without hesitating. He sings along to the Little Mix song that blasts from his stereo. This is always a tell for Lenny that he's in a good mood. He's excited about this job. The one thousand euro on offer from Gordon Blake is definitely playing a part in dictating Lenny's positivity, but it's more the job that has him buzzing. Trying to find a girl who's been missing for seventeen years. That sure as hell beats filling in paperwork for an insurance company.

He drums at the steering wheel, imagining the press he would receive if he were to somehow make a breakthrough in the Betsy Blake case. Though Lenny's not stupid; he's aware he's day-dreaming. He's a decent private investigator – more often than not his clients are pleased with his work – but he has never achieved anything of note that would suggest he's capable of making even the smallest of dents in the highest-profile missing person's case the country's ever known. Anyway, he assumed Betsy was dead. Was certain the Gardaí closed the case about ten years ago.

Soon he's turning right into the hospital grounds and circling the parking lot. When he finally finds a space he can fit his tiny Nissan Micra in to, he leaps out of his car, trudges down the brick staircase and finally across the zebra crossing that leads to the hospital entrance.

He takes in the stench of antibacterial soap immediately, can almost taste it on his tongue.

'St Bernard's Ward?' he asks the man sitting at a rounded reception desk.

'Floor three.'

Lenny sprint-walks towards the elevators and then pauses after pushing at the button. He watches the digital numbers above the doors click upwards, from three to four, then eyeballs the staircase behind him. He knows he would get to Gordon quicker if he used them. But he can be a stubborn fucker sometimes, can Lenny. So he stares back at the digits, taking seconds to will them to count downwards. But they don't. Both lifts are now on floor five. He huffs, spins on his heels and makes his way to the stairs, striding up them two at a time. He's almost out of breath by the time he reaches a sign that reads St Bernard's Ward. The hospital corridors are overly bright, the yellow glare constant, regardless of the time of day. Lenny knows the hospital quite well. Has spent many hours in here, sitting next to Sally.

'Gordon Blake?' he asks a young nurse dressed in purple scrubs.

'Oh... Mr Blake is in room number thirty-two,' she replies. She stares at Lenny after answering, but he doesn't say anything. He just nods a 'thank you' at her and then paces in the direction she had pointed, staring at the numbers on the ward doors as he goes. When he arrives outside number thirty-two he pauses to catch his breath. Gordon Blake had asked him to be as quick as he could possibly be. Lenny removes his mobile phone from the inside pocket of his coat, notices it's 10:36. Fourteen minutes since Gordon Blake called him. Not bad. Then he blinks and pushes at the door.

A pale face turns towards him, then the man in the bed sits up, pushing his back against the railed bed post.

'Lenny Moon?'

'Yes, Mr Blake. I got here as quickly as I could.'

Lenny stares at the man. He looks as if his death is imminent alright; the face gaunt, the veins in his neck trying to poke their way out of the skin that covers them. All of his limbs are thin and long; even his fingers. Strands of his balding black hair are matted to his forehead.

'Lenny. I may only have a few hours left to live. I need you to find out who took my daughter.'

Lenny nods his head as he walks closer to the bed.

'I've been trying to recall Betsy's case on the way over here,' he says. 'What is it you would like me to find out for you, Mr Blake?'

'Gordon... please. And eh... I need you to find out who took her.'

Lenny sniffs out of his nostrils, then points his hand towards a blue plastic chair. When Gordon nods an invite for him to sit in it, Lenny takes off his hat and coat, hangs them on the back of the chair and then sits in it, crossing his right ankle over his left thigh. He reaches into the back pocket of his trousers, pulls out a small note pad that has a pen attached to it, and opens it up to a blank page.

'Okay, Gordon,' he says, clicking down on the top of the pen, 'what makes you think I can find out what happened to your daughter in the next few hours?'

SEVENTEEN YEARS AGO

Betsy

IT'S DARK. DARK FOR A LONG TIME. A LONG, LONG TIME. EVER since the man put me in the back of his car. I don't know how long I've been in the back of his car but I don't like it. I'm hungry. And thirsty. And tired. Really, really tired. But I can't go asleep. Even though I want to. It's been too bumpy and wavy. I lifted up the flap that is under me earlier. There's a big wheel underneath it. That's why I can't lie down nice and go asleep. I'm really scared. But I'm not crying. I stopped crying a long time ago. I don't have any tears left inside my eyes probably. I just want to go home. I want my dinner. Want my Mummy. My Daddy.

It smells really bad in the back of the car. A bit like Daddy's old socks. But maybe the smell is my wee wee. I did two wee wees in my Dora the Explorer pants. My pants aren't wet anymore. But it still smells. He opened the door one time. He threw me in a apple and a bottle of water. But that was a long time ago. It's gone really cold. It's not as cold when he's driving. But when he stops driving it is really cold. Really, really cold. And he has been stopped driving for a long time now. I wonder what Mummy and Daddy are doing. They have probably called the police. The police might be looking for me. But maybe the man will let me go soon. If he does, I'll stop a man or woman on the street. Tell them my name. Who I am. Who my Mummy and Daddy is. I don't know the name of where I live. But if Mummy and Daddy have called the police then they can come and take me home.

Daddy will be crying. I'm not sure if Mummy will. I've never seen her cry before. Daddy cries all the time. Even when he is watching telly. I saw him cry watching Coronation Street one time. I sometimes think I love Daddy more than Mummy. But then other times I think the other way round. Sometimes Mummy is my favourite. It can be different. But I know they love me because the two of them buy me sweets sometimes. And the two of them play games with me. Wish I was playing a game now. Maybe next time I play hide and seek with Daddy I will hide in the back of his car. Because it would be a good place to hide. Nobody can find me in here. Oh. Nobody can find me in here. My eyes do still have tears inside them. I can feel one come down my cheek. Then another one. I wipe them away. But my nose is making tears too and I can't stop it. I don't want to cry. But I'm making the crying noises now and I can't stop it. My body is shaking. I'm scared again. I had forgot I was scared.

'Twinkle, twinkle little star,
How I wonder what you are.
Up above the world so high,
Like a diamond in the sky.'

Daddy sings that to me when I cry at sleep-time. It helps me stop crying. But it's not helping now when I sing it to myself. My nose still has tears coming out. I should keep singing anyway. It might work. Might help me stop if I keep singing it. I haven't sung Twinkle, Twinkle Little Star in a long time. I told Daddy I was becoming a big girl and didn't need that song anymore. I told Daddy I didn't like it. But I do. I wish he was singing it to me now. If he was singing it to me now I would stop crying. I know I would. I miss my Daddy singing. I miss hearing my Daddy's voice.

Twinkle, twinkle little star,
How I wonder—

I hear him. He is close by me. Maybe he is going to give me another apple. Another bottle of water. He is definitely going to open the door. I can hear the keys. The door lifts up. But I can't see him. It's too dark.

'Shhh.' I think he is holding his finger to his mouth. I blink my eyes loads of times to try to see him. I think it's getting brighter. I can see him a little bit now. He reaches in to me and grabs me around the shoulders and around the legs. A bit like when he carried me off the wall earlier. I think that was yesterday or maybe today. I don't know. But I do know it's night time now. I can see the light on the other side of the street on. That's the only light I can see. Everything else is dark. Really, really dark.

'It's okay, Betsy.' He drops me to my feet. Then he reaches up and puts a key in the door. I think it's a purple door. Or maybe it's black. After he opens it, he picks me up again. I don't want to go into his house. Maybe I should scream. But I don't want him to hurt me.

He carries me past two rooms. I try to look inside. But don't see anybody. I don't see anything. Then he kicks open another door and carries me down some steps.

'There ye go, Betsy.' His voice is all funny. He has a different voice. It sounds funny. Not like my Mummy's or Daddy's. Not like Ceri's Mummy or anybody I know. I think he is from a different country. I saw somebody on the television one time from a different country and he had a voice like this man. But his skin was brown. This man's skin isn't brown. He has the same kind of skin as me and Mummy and Daddy.

He walks back up the steps. He opens the door then walks out. It's dark in here too. But not as dark as in the back of the car. I can see a few things. I can see walls. Can see the floor. It's all very hard. Like stones. I try to walk around but my legs are tired I think. They won't let me walk. So I sit down on the cold floor. I wonder why I'm here. What the man wants me to do. I just want to go home. Maybe I should scream. My lips shake a little bit. Scream. I want to scream but my voice won't let me. Scream, Betsy. Go on.

'Ahhhhh.'

The door opens. He runs down the steps.

'Didn't I tell you to be quiet, Betsy?'

I think he looks angry. It's the first time I can see his face. It got lighter in here. Because the door up the steps is open. And it's really bright up there. He is about the same age as Daddy. But more scary looking. 'You scream out loud again, Betsy, and I will hurt you. Do you understand?'

I look down at the stone ground. Then I nod my head. I don't want to make him angry.

'Good girl.' He puts his finger under my face.

'Look.' He takes a teddy bear from behind his back. It's brown. 'You like teddy bears don't you, Betsy? This is yours. It's called Bozy.'

I look at the bear. That is an odd name. I nod my head again because I don't want the man to hurt me. Then he holds Bozy to me and I take it. The man runs up the steps again. I just look at the bear. I used to have a teddy bear in my bed with me. But it wasn't brown. It was white. And I didn't give him a name. Just teddy bear. But I better call this one Bozy, because the man might hurt me if I just call it teddy bear. Then the man comes back down the steps. Not running this time. Slowly. Real slowly. He is carrying something big. He throws it down in front of me.

'This is your bed tonight.'

I look down at it. Then I look at him. I don't want to cry. But I can't stop it. Another tear comes out of my eye.

'Why do I need a bed?'

10:40

Gordon

He doesn't look like a private investigator. He's too short. And his beard – if anyone would call it that – is a mess, like he just hasn't bothered to shave for the past week. Not that I'm in any position to judge someone's appearance. It's just... I assumed a private investigator would look more like... more like... well... I'm actually not sure what I expected a private investigator to look like. Maybe I've watched too many movies down the years; expected this guy to turn up in a trench coat and fedora hat, not a fuckin plastic yellow jacket that makes him look like the Michelin man and a stupid furry-muff hat.

He points towards the blue plastic chair by my bedside and I nod to welcome him to sit in it. Though he shouldn't be sitting for long. He needs to be out there; out there finding Betsy.

He sits, removes a pad and a pen from his pocket, and then crosses his legs as if he's getting comfortable.

'Okay, Gordon,' he says. 'What makes you think I can find out what happened to your daughter in the next few hours?'

That's a hell of a question. A question I don't have an

answer to. I've been looking for her for seventeen years. I don't expect this guy to find anything in the next few hours, but I have to at least try. I can't lie here and do nothing.

'The police have never done a good enough job,' I say, not wanting to pause too long, in case he realises I don't have an actual answer to his question. It's the first thing that came into my head. But it's also the truth. They didn't. They fucked up the investigation on day one. They took too long to ignite their search – concentrating on me as if I had something to do with it. It meant whoever took my daughter had time to get away; time to get Betsy hidden in whatever place he wanted to hide her.

'They questioned a few suspects, but not intricately enough. I know she's out there, Lenny. And I—'

'But what makes you think *I* can find her in the next few hours if nobody has found her in the past seventeen years?' he says, interrupting me.

I take a deep breath as I push myself back into the steel bedpost to sit more upright.

'There're a few things that have niggled at me for years, things I couldn't push too far because the cops wouldn't let me. But now that I'm dying... or probably about to die, I need a new perspective on this. I can't lie here in the final hours of my life and not... and not...' A tear drops from my eye. Lenny stands up, turns towards the bedside cabinet and pulls two tissues from their box.

'Here,' he says. I fold the tissues in half, dab at my face.

Then I turn to him.

'One thousand euro to try your very best over the next few hours, but,' I say, pausing. 'If you make any breakthrough I'll make you a rich man.' Lenny blinks. Repeatedly. About four little twitches. He looks like a fuckin idiot. But I know he's totally tuned in. He's intrigued. 'Listen; I have no family, no friends. Not anymore. I've got nothing. My life is my home. It's all I have,' I tell him. 'If I don't make it through the day and you do your very best for me in my final hours... I'll leave you my house. I have a lovely home on the South Circular Road. Y'know those red brick Victorian houses?' Lenny nods, but he looks perplexed. As if he doesn't know what to make of me. 'They're worth close to a million,' I say. 'A neighbour sold his at the tail end of last year for nine-hundred and forty grand. And he didn't have the kitchen extension I have.'

Lenny squints his eyes, circles his tongue around his mouth.

'Gordon, let's start with the one thousand promised. Can you – as you suggested – transfer that into my account? I think we're both keen for me to get started. Then I'd like to talk to you about the leads you said you had.'

I take my phone up from my lap, log into my online banking app and within seconds I'm punching digits into the screen.

'What are your bank details?' I ask him. He scoots one bum cheek up off the chair and removes his wallet from his back pocket. Then he slips out a debit card and hands it to me.

'Account number and sort code are on the bottom,' he says. I type them into my screen, then turn the phone to face him.

'Press transfer,' I say. And he does. Without hesitation. Maybe he's desperate for the money. Maybe I've chosen the wrong private investigator. If he's not very rich, he mustn't be very successful. I just plumped for the nearest private investigator I could find on the Yellow Pages website. I was surprised to even find one based in Tallaght. I needed someone here as quickly as possible.

'Transfer complete,' I say, turning the screen back to Lenny.

He blinks rapidly again. It's really weird.

'Thank you, Gordon.'

He sits back in his seat, reopens his notepad and re-crosses his legs. He has the same tics every time. He's meticulous. Perhaps he is a good investigator after all. I guess we'll find out.

'In terms of leads—'

'You only have until three p.m.' I interrupt him. 'I'm having emergency heart surgery then. May not wake up from the procedure.'

He flicks his eyes up from his notepad to stare into mine.

'My heart's a mess. The hiatus hernia I've had as far back as my late twenties has grown and torn my main aorta. I have to have an open aortic valve replacement as well as some other procedure... a eh... triple-A something. I can't pronounce it. The two surgeries have to be done at the same time. If they're not carried out as quickly as possible, I'll have an unrecoverable major heart attack. My heart's basically a ticking time bomb, Lenny. Doctors said if I hadn't come into the hospital last night, I'd already be dead. They're just waiting on a couple more members of the surgical team to get here, and for the theatre to be cleared and set up. Said everything will be ready for three o'clock.'

Lenny gets up from the chair, walks slowly towards the foot of my bed.

'Do you mind?' he says, nodding towards the clipboard hanging on the bed rail.

I shake my head.

'An abdominal aortic aneurysm repair,' he says, his eyes squinting.

'That's the one.'

'So this could literally be your last roll of the dice. You want to throw everything into your final hours to find Betsy and you're hiring me to do it?'

'Ah – you *are* a good detective, huh?' I say. I laugh as I say it. But the laugh isn't reciprocated. Probably because it wasn't funny.

He hangs the clipboard back onto the rail, then paces to the blue plastic chair and sits in it again. But he doesn't cross his legs this time; instead he leans forward, eyeballs me.

'Gordon. It's admirable that after seventeen years of looking for Betsy and all that you've been through that you would dedicated the final hours of your life to continue looking for her... but...' he pauses, then blinks rapidly again. 'What, eh... what do you think I can actually achieve in such a small amount of time?'

Monkeys see as monkeys do. I blink too, mirroring him.

'Barry Ward,' I say. 'Police interviewed him. Dismissed him too early for my liking. I've spent a lifetime digging around, following him, getting information on him—'

'So you think he took Betsy?'

'Him or Alan Keating.'

'Hold on,' Lenny says, scribbling down the two names I gave him on his pad. 'Just so I can be clear now... you are paying me one thousand euro to speak to a Barry Ward and an Alan Keating to see what they know about Betsy's disappearance? Is that what you're hiring me to do?'

'I'm hiring you for more than that. I'm hiring you to find Betsy,' I say. I know it sounds ridiculous. I know I sound like a madman; like the madman Michelle has often told me I am. But what else am I supposed to do? Lie here and die without giving it one last go?

Lenny's eyebrow twitches, as if he is trying not to blink. I swing my legs over the side of the bed, wait for him to look up at me, to meet my eyes.

'You make a breakthrough in this case today, Lenny, my house is your house. While you're out investigating, I'm going to write a new draft of my will. It'll include you getting my house if I die today. I'll leave it in an envelope there on that cabinet with your name on it. I'll send a picture of it to my lawyer. But you'll have to make a breakthrough for that will to be sanctioned.' I grip the top of his hand; the one he has resting on his notepad. 'It means everything to me that you try your hardest to find Betsy; that you give it your all. You have until three o'clock.'

I take my hand off his, reach it under my pillow and take out the note I spent the last fifteen minutes writing.

'Here you go. Everything you need to know is on here.'

SIXTEEN YEARS AGO

Betsy

I LIKE LOOKING AT THE PICTURES ON MY WALL. DOD LET ME hang the pictures with something called Blu Tack. They are pictures from the magazines he buys me. Some pictures are of girls. Some pictures are of boys. I like the picture of a girl called Christina Aguilera the most. She looks pretty. She has yellow hair and orange skin. I put that picture over my bed. I look at it when I wake up in the morning and then look at it before Dod puts the light out at night and I have to go asleep. My bed is nice. I remember the first night I slept here. I only slept on a small bed with a cushion and a blanket. It was really cold. I cried all that night. I don't cry so much anymore. Sometimes if I can picture Mummy and Daddy in my head and they almost become real I will cry. But it's hard for me to picture them as if they are real anymore. When I close my eyes I want to see them. I want them to become real. But it is not easy. Most times when I close my eyes I see the people who I read about in my books. Dod brings me lots of magazines and books.

I have fourteen books now. I counted them yesterday. One book I have teached me how to count. One book teached me all about shapes. One book teached me all about the farm. One book teached me all about the park. I used to go to a park with Mummy and Daddy. It had swings and a slide in it. Just like the park in my book. But I haven't been to a park since I got here. I haven't been outside at all. Haven't been out of the house. Haven't been out of this room. I did go up the steps once when Dod left the door open but when I got in to another room he just rushed me back down the steps. It was bright up there.

Sometimes people come to Dod's house. He says I have to be very quiet when they come. He says if I'm not quiet he will hurt me real bad. So I just read my books. Sometimes Dod reads them to me. He hugs me on the bed and puts his fingers in my hair and reads to me. I like that. Sometimes I am scared of him. Sometimes he is really nice. I always know when he is coming. There is a small light that I can see under the door. And when he comes to the door the light goes away a bit. It's gone away now. He's coming.

> 'Happy birthday to you.
> Happy birthday to you.
> Happy birthday, dear Betsy.
> Happy birthday to you.'

He has a cake and there are light sticks on it. He brings it over to my bed. Then he sits on the bed and smiles at me. He is being nice today.

'Blow out the candles.'

I look at him.

'What is candles?'

He makes a blow on the light sticks and the light almost goes away.

'Go on, blow.'

I do the same. I blow really strong and two of the lights go out. Then I do it again and the other three go out.

'Happy birthday, Betsy.' He kisses me on the cheek and then puts the big cake on the bed. I read the cake. It says 'Betsy'. And then a big number five. Dod walks back up the steps and then comes back down carrying a box.

'Am I five?'

'Yes, Betsy. You are five today. It's your birthday.'

'Am I a big girl now?'

'Yes, Betsy. You are a big girl now.'

'Does it mean I don't have to hold Mummy and Daddy's hands anymore?

Dod doesn't say anything. He just hands me the box. It has red paper all over it. I should be happy. But I am thinking about holding Mummy and Daddy's hands instead. I told them before that I didn't like holding their hands. But I want to be holding their hands now.

'Open it.'

I look at Dod.

'Rip the paper off... here, let me help you.'

Dod begins to rip the red paper and then I help him. The box has pictures of a slide on it. It is a yellow slide. With a blue ladder. Dod is smiling. He must really like this slide. I smile too.

'A slide?'

'Yes. A slide that you can have in here. You can pretend it is like being in the park in your book.'

Dod pulls the box open and then takes out the big yellow slidey bit. Then he takes out the blue ladder bit and gets down on the stone floor. He tries to put them together so I can climb up the three blue steps and slide down the yellow slide. I should be looking at him and being really happy. But I am looking up at the door. Dod has left it open.

'Don't look up there, Betsy.'

I look back at Dod. He is not smiling anymore. He is just trying to put the slide together. Maybe I should be happy that it is my birthday and Dod bought me a cake and a slide. But I am not happy. I am thinking about Mummy and Daddy. I am thinking about what presents they would get me for my birthday.

'Ah for fuck sake!' Dod seems really angry. He throws one of the blue steps against the wall. 'My fucking thumb.' He kicks the slidey part. 'Stop fucking looking up there. Didn't I tell you, Betsy? Never look up those steps when the door is open. You little shit.'

Dod picks me up and throws me on to the bed. The cake falls off.

'I'll hurt you, Betsy. You do as I say.'

Dod puts his thumb in his mouth and sucks it. Then he turns around and runs up the steps really fast and closes the door. It gets all dark again. I put my hands all around the bed until I find Bozy. Then I lie back under the covers with Bozy and we hug each other. This is what I do when Dod is angry. Hug Bozy. Bozy is my best friend. When we are scared, we sing.

'Twinkle, twinkle little star...'

10:50

Lenny

LENNY STABS AT THE BUTTON. SIX TIMES. AS IF IT'S GOING TO make the lift come any sooner. He doesn't eyeball the stairs behind him this time. He just waits; transfixed on the sheet of paper he's just unfolded. Gordon rushed him out of the ward; told him to concentrate on the note he'd written and to call him when he needed to ask any questions.

Suspects

Alan Keating. Keating is a well-known criminal, nicknamed The Boss in the newspapers. I had some dealings with him before Betsy went missing. Underhand dealings. Illegal. I'm sure he had something to do with Betsy's disappearance. But Keating keeps his hands clean. Knows he is always being watched by the cops. He's now living up in Rathcoole. His seventh house in the last seventeen years. He has a sidekick freak who does all the dirty work for him...

Barry Ward. Keating's sidekick freak. I think he was a traveller. Certainly sounds like one. Would do anything for Keating – including killing people for him. He's more than capable of kidnapping a four-year-old. I've no doubt about that. He's a scumbag. Lives in Drimnagh still. Be careful with him.

Jake Dewey. Slippery fucker. Thinks he's ex IRA – but he's not. He's deluded. Lies for a living. Came into my wife's life just as Betsy went missing. Never trusted him. Cops sounded him out but didn't dig far enough. Has a restraining order against me, so I can't go near him. Need you to dig deep today.

You make an impact today, Lenny, my house is yours. This is literally a million euro job for you if you get it right.

Lenny takes a deep inhale as the lift door pings opens into the hospital lobby. He hadn't even realised he had gotten into the lift. Then he paces out the door, over the zebra crossing and towards the car park. He stares upwards just before he enters the archway, after the first drop of what looks like many today drips onto his shoulder. The clouds turned from off-white to dark grey in the fifteen minutes Lenny had been inside the hospital.

'The fucking Boss,' Lenny whispers to himself as he slides his parking ticket into the machine. He's lost in thought as he waves his debit card over the reader, not even noticing that he's paying ten euro for leaving his car here for just a quarter of an hour. If he noticed, he'd be furious. Ten euro can go a long way in the Moon household. Goose pimples begin to bubble up on his arms; and not because the temperature has dropped. He smiles to himself as he paces up the steps and towards his car.

'Fuck it!' he says as he swings his legs inside. 'This is why you became a private investigator, Lenny boy.'

He turns the key in the ignition only to be met by a loud hissing of white noise. The radio doesn't work in here. He reaches for the standby button, knocks it off. Then he stares at his own eyeballs in the rear-view mirror and winks to himself.

'You can do this.'

His orange Nissan Micra pulls out of the car park and over the speed bumps. It's a 2005 Micra Lenny has. He can't afford anything more modern. With the temperature dropping, and the car heaters not working, Lenny flicks the collar of his yellow puffer jacket up to cover his bare neck, then reaches for his Sherpa hat and pulls it on. A small part of him – the conservative, weak side of him – is beginning to wish he was back in his pokey office, playing Solitaire, waiting on one of the insurance companies to ring him with another boring job. But another part of him – the adventurous life-is-too-short side that he used to be filled with until he married Sally – is excited about what lies in store. He became a private investigator because he wanted to solve crimes. And it's pretty impossible to solve crimes if you don't deal with criminals. Though, he must admit, criminals don't come more notorious in Dublin than Alan Keating. The whole of the country knows Keating's the head of one of the biggest crime gangs in Dublin – but the cops can't do anything about it. He keeps his nose too clean; controls his men from the comfort of his own homes.

Lenny knows titbits about Keating – like most people in Ireland do. It's no secret Keating was involved in the attempted murder of crime journalist Frank Keville back in 2003. Keville was shot in the back outside his child's classroom during a routine school pick up one Friday afternoon. The Guards still haven't found the man who pulled the trigger, but they know the instruction came from Keating. They just can't prove it. Keating was on holiday in Portugal when Keville was shot. He always hid himself well. It was actually Keville who first coined the nickname 'The Boss' for Keating. He was obsessed with Keating; wrote about him at least once a month in his weekly column for the *Irish News of the World.*

Lenny squelches up his mouth, then sucks his teeth. While he's aware just how dangerous Keating can be; he can't see a reason why he would have abducted Betsy without there being financial gain for him and his gang. It doesn't make sense. He drums his fingers against the steering wheel as questions whizz around his mind.

'Where'll I even start?' he says, eyeballing himself in the mirror again.

He reaches into his pocket, pulls out his phone and when the traffic halts his progress, he presses at buttons on his cheap mobile phone and goes into his call history, straight to the last dialled number. Lenny can't quite afford a hands free kit for his car, but he's mastered the art of gripping the phone between his thighs with the phone's loud speaker turned on. A horn beeps from behind just as the tone begins to ring and Lenny steps on the accelerator and pulls off with his wheels spinning.

'Hello.'

'Gordon, it's Lenny Moon.'

'Good. Where are you now?'

'I'm on the N7. Heading to Rathcoole to see if I can have words with Alan Keating. You wrote on the note 'Peyton Avenue' – where is that exactly?'

'It's up off the village, a left turn before The Baurnafea House pub. You can't miss the estate.'

'Estate? What number does he live in?'

'I have that information at home. I can't think of it. You'll have to ask somebody when you get there. I think it's on the second row of houses.'

Lenny rolls his eyes, then blinks them. The surreality of the whole job begins to consume him.

I'm off to question The fuckin' Boss about the Betsy Blake disappearance.

Lenny stares at his eyes again in the rear-view mirror as he pulls off the N7 at the Rathcoole exit.

'Lenny,' Gordon says, startling him back to the call.

'Yeah.'

'What are you gonna ask him?'

Lenny blows out his cheeks.

'I'll just start off as if I'm interviewing him for a routine investigation. I certainly won't be accusatory. I'll just say that as an associate of Gordon Blake at the time I'd just like to ask you a few questions.'

'Lenny...' Gordon says, then pauses. 'Ye have to tell him I'm dying. We used to be mates once; ask him... please, if he knows *anything* about Betsy. Anything at all. I don't have much time. No pussy-footing around. If you're happy with one-thousand for your day's work, fine, pussy-foot. But if you want serious money – and I mean if you want to become almost a millionaire in the next few hours – you gotta get me some answers. Answers I've never heard before. Please. I'm almost convinced that fucker has something to do with Betsy's disappearance. He's gotta know something. I'm begging you to figure it out!'

'Hang on, Gordon.'

Lenny scratches at the stubble under his chin, then pulls into a parking spot outside a bungalow at the entrance to Rathcoole Village.

'You wrote on the note that you had illegal dealings with Keating. You're gonna have to give me the details.'

Lenny hears the sigh on the other end of the line.

'I was his accountant. He practically forced me to handle his books; ran all his dealings through me. In simple terms I cooked his books... what can I say? I was doing it for about five years. I was probably a bit afraid of the fucker... but I... y'know... I was earning great money doing it and then... And then we just had a falling out. He kept wanting to push it too far... I was wary of getting caught. At one point I told him 'no'. And he... he threatened me.'

'Threatened you how?'

'Y'know... he just held me up against the wall, said I'd regret fucking with him.'

'Did he ever threaten Betsy?'

The line goes silent. Then Lenny hears a woman's voice in the background.

Gordon's tone turns different. More mature. More pronounced.

'Sure, Elaine. That is no problem. Whatever if it is you need to do, my love... Lenny,' he says, returning to the call. 'I'll have to ring you back. A nurse is here to run some tests.'

Lenny stares at the phone in his hand after Gordon's hung up.

'What the fuck am I doing?' he says. He laughs after he says it too, then shakes his head.

I'm off to question The fuckin Boss about the Betsy Blake disappearance.

The million pound house on South Circular Road crosses his mind. Not because he's dreaming about living in it – nor is he even considering the possibility – but because it's added to the craziness of his morning. He then runs back through the moment he held Gordon's medical chart in the ward; just to remove the possibility of being bullshitted to. He's been pranked well before, but this'd be some world-class award-winning pranking. He picks the phone up from his lap and presses in to his call history before pressing at the button beside 'home'. It was at moments like this, when he had to ring Sally to check something on the internet, that Lenny wished he had a smart phone.

'Hello.'

'Sweetie, sorry to bother you, But could you just check the online banking? I wanna see if money was put in this morning. Somebody was supposed to pay me today for a job.'

Sally hid her sigh well, but Lenny still caught a hint of it. It didn't bother him. He wouldn't have expected anything less. The fact that her sigh was so subtle was actually a sign that she was having a good day. The slight humming of a tune from her lips while she typed away at the home computer confirmed it. Today was a good day for Sally Moon. Normally that'd be enough to make Lenny content, but he's still staring down into his lap, scratching at his bald head with confusion when Sally sucks her lips; signalling she's about to talk.

'Yep. One thousand euro exactly. About half an hour ago. Who's that from – that's a big payment?'

'Oh a client I did a couple of jobs for a while back. He's owed me that for quite a while.'

'Gordon Blake?'

'Yeah – he's a guy I met through one of the insurance companies… asked me to look into a number of old clients of his he thought was scamming from them. I had to look into each of them. Turned out to be very little in it, but eh… yeah, he said he'd pay today, so I can scratch that off my list.'

Lenny wasn't concerned Sally would take the conversation much further. She'd been bored by his job for quite some time. Nothing exciting ever happen to her husband.

'Okay,' she says. 'Nice few quid. We need that coming up to Christmas. How is your—'

'I'm so sorry, sweetie. I'm gonna have to go. I got a spate of calls from insurance companies this morning and... eh... give me a call at, y'know, the usual time. Love you.'

Lenny hung up. It was unusual he'd hang up on Sally, but her feelings, unusually, aren't at the forefront his mind right now.

'A grand,' he says to himself. He's chewing on the edge of his rubber mobile phone cover when it buzzes in his hand.

'Yes love.'

'Sorry?'

'Oh sorry. Eh... Lenny Moon – Private Investigator.'

'Lenny... it's Gloria Proudfoot, Excel Insurance.'

'Gloria – how are you? Sorry... miles away.'

'Listen, I have a job for you. A Delaney Griffith. Claims she injured her back in a car crash back in August. But we've just had somebody tell us she's off down the gym lifting weights this morning. Can you get out to Coolock now, get confirmation and a photograph for us?'

'Now?'

'Yeah.'

Lenny brings the phone back towards his mouth to bite on the edge of his rubber case.

He normally jumps on anything an insurance company offers him. In fact he lives for it. But he never had the option of comparing the taking of a standard photograph of somebody in a gym over the interviewing of Dublin's biggest gangster about the most intriguing missing persons case to ever hit Ireland.

'Can't, Gloria. I'm sorry. I'm on a job at the moment.'

'Ah... okay, no probs, Lenny. I'll hit you up next time.'

'Sorry, Gloria,' he offers once more before the line goes dead. Then he stares at his eyes through the rear-view mirror again and laughs; his laugh fogging up part of the mirror.

He rolls down his window and points his index finger towards an elderly lady pushing her trolley along the narrow pathway.

'Can you tell me how to get to Peyton Avenue?' he asks.

The lady twists her body, to look in the opposite direction.

'That's one of the new estates,' she says, rolling her eyes, as if new estates are bothersome to her. 'Next left, then you'll see it when you get to the first roundabout. Sure, ye can't miss it.'

Lenny winks a thank you back at the lady, then winds his window back up and pulls out from the curb.

The woman was right. You couldn't miss it. Even before Lenny got to the roundabout he could see a massive sign reading 'Welcome to Peyton'. It was like one of the signs you'd see in America for a new housing estate; he even had to drive through a pointless archway to enter it. He blows out his cheeks while driving towards the first row of houses.

'There must be a hundred gaffs in here,' he mumbles to himself. He rounds the first bend, to get to the second row of homes just as Gordon instructed, then pulls over to stare at the front doors. They're big enough gaffs. Red brick, three storeys. The homes of people who make comfortable money. He couldn't quite work out why Alan Keating, who must rake in millions a year, was living here.

Lenny pulls the zip on his puffer jacket all the way up to his chin and yanks at the two strings of his hat, as if those actions are going to protect him from the rain. Then, without hesitating, he walks up the pathway of the house he pulled up outside and rings the doorbell.

A middle aged woman greets him with a confused smile.

'I'm looking for the Keating house. Do you know what number they live in?'

The woman drops her smile, narrows the gap in the door so just half of her face is showing.

'Number forty-nine,' she says. 'You'll know he's in if his black Merc is in the driveway.'

The door is fully closed before Lenny has finished his thank you. He walks back down the pathway, begins to stroll past the row of houses, counting the numbers on the doors as he goes. Then he stops dead, stares at the front of a black Mercedes that's taking up way too much space on the driveway of number 49. He takes the mobile phone from his pocket and then brings it to his mouth; not to ring anybody, just to chew on the rubber case; the rain falling around him.

Go on, Lenny Boy – grow some fucking balls!

He swivels, stares up and down the estate for no reason and then, almost as if somebody pushes him, he paces confidently, as if he isn't intimidated one iota by the infamous figure who lives behind the door.

It's only when he holds his thumb against the bell that his stomach flips itself over.

11:05

Gordon

THERE'S A FUMBLE AT MY DOOR, A CLANGING. THEN ELAINE walks in, wheeling a small machine in front of her; leading it towards me. She purses her lips at me again, but I don't mind this constant sympathy gesture coming from her. She's nice looking. Not good looking. There's a distinct difference. And I'd take nice looking over good looking all day long.

She notices I'm on the phone, mouths the words 'heart rate'. I stretch the phone away from my mouth.

'Sure, Elaine,' I say. 'That is no problem. Whatever it is you need to do, my love.' Then I bring the phone to my mouth again. 'Lenny. I'll have to ring you back. A nurse is here to run some tests.'

Elaine opens the Velcro strapping on a small rubber tube and then releases two blue suction tabs. She motions towards my T-shirt and without hesitating, I lift it over my head. Then she places the two tabs on my chest and turns to twizzle at some nozzles on her machine.

'Sorry to disturb your call. Won't keep you long,' she says. 'We just need to keep checking your rate.'

I'm about to tell her the call wasn't that important when

Elaine makes a strange sound; almost as if she's sucking her own tongue.

'Heart rate's gone up significantly, Gordon,' she says staring at me.

'I'm not surprised. After the news I was told an hour ago.'

'Have you been resting as we suggested?' she asks, while walking to the end of my bed to pick up the clipboard. She scribbles some notes on it while I try to find the words to phrase my lie.

'Yes. Just as you said. Haven't really done anything... Was just ringing a friend of mine there to—'

'That the same friend who was in with you half-an-hour ago?' she asks, staring at me over the clipboard.

'Yeah – an old friend. My best friend. The only person I could think of to call on to be honest.'

Elaine purses her lips again. She hangs the clipboard back on to the rail at the foot of my bed and then walks around to sit her pert bum on the edge of my mattress.

'Gordon... Mr Douglas spoke to you about the need for relaxation today. I can't stress how important that is.'

I roll my eyes. She catches me. It wasn't difficult – my eyes are about two feet from hers.

'I can't fully understand how difficult it is to digest the news you've been given, Gordon,' she says, 'but your best chance of surviving these procedures is to keep your heart rate steady.'

Douglas had already mentioned this to me; he told me my ability to keep my mind-set consistent over the next few hours would be just as important to my success as his steady hands during the procedures. The medical team are mostly afraid of blood clots; there's a high risk that multiple clots will form during my operations that can swiftly make their way to my lungs, to my brain. If that is the case; I'll never wake up. That's why Douglas – and now Elaine – are keen for me to relax – they want my heart rate to remain consistent. The more relaxed I am, the less chance there'll be of blood clots forming. But blood clots aren't their only concern. My heart's a ticking time bomb. I could have a massive heart attack while I'm cut open, could even have it before then, which is why they're trying to get me to the theatre as quickly as they possibly can. Two more of Douglas' surgical team are flying in from London as I lie here and the theatre will be prepped after the surgery that is going on in it right now is complete. It's why they've been very specific about my surgery time; three p.m. I pick up my phone just to make the screen light go on so I can check the time. 11:11. Jesus fuckin Christ. Less than four hours. While the phone is in my hand I imagine what Lenny is up to right now. He's probably knocking on Alan Keating's door. What the fuck is he going to ask Keating? How can he get any more information out of him that the police didn't get in their investigations? I know it's an impossible ask. But I can't lie here, with death's door opening up to me, and not do all I can to find Betsy.

My head is melting. I'm torn between relaxing ahead of these surgeries and doing all I can for my daughter. Fuck! I allow a massive sigh to rasp itself up from the pit of my lungs and all the way through my open mouth.

Elaine reaches her hand and places it on top of mine. Then she smiles at me; not a purse of the lips this time, an upturn of the lips.

'It's why I keep asking you if there's anybody who can come up to visit you, Gordon. Company will help you relax. Are you sure you don't want me to ring your ex wife for you?'

'I thought you want me to relax,' I say, offering her a smile of my own.

'No other friends I can call?'

I shake my head.

'What about the friend who you've been on the phone to and who was up earlier... can he come back to you? Keep you company?'

I blow from my lips, making a bit of a motorboat sound, and then shake my head.

'He's out doing a job for me; don't worry, it's all being taken care of.'

Elaine looks at me the way a teacher looks at a cheeky student; her face stern, trying to hide the hint of a smile that's threatening to force its way through.

'Surely you have other friends who can be here for you. Who was best man at your wedding?'

'Guus Meyer,' I say.

'Well let's call Guus. I'm sure he would—'

'We haven't spoken in years,' I tell her. 'We blurred the lines of business and friendship. It's true what they say; don't mix business with pleasure.'

'I'm sure given the circumstances...' Elaine says, but I shrug my shoulders at her, allow another tear to drop from my eye. My head is spinning. I don't know how to feel; how I'm supposed to react to the news I've been given this morning. And I'm torn; I don't know who my main concern should be right now; me or Betsy. Maybe she's been my concern for way too long. Probably why my heart's fucked.

Elaine stands up, fixes my sheet so it's nice and snug under both of my arms. I stare into her face as she's doing it. I like her freckles. She's not unlike Michelle. They don't necessarily look alike, but there's a similar energy they both give off. I mean the Michelle I knew when we first met, not the bitchy Michelle who exists now. As I'm staring at Elaine I figure she must be the same age Michelle was when I first met her.

'How old are you?'

'Twenty-six.'

Yep. That's the age Michelle was when I sat beside her on a bus one day coming home from town. I'm pretty sure I fell in love with her before we both got off that bus half-an-hour later. I never thought, not for one millisecond back then, that I would ever hate her. But I do. She fucked me over. I feel another tear drop from my eye. Elaine notices, reaches for the tissues on my bedside cabinet.

'Thank you.'

I breathe in heavily, try to soak the surreality of the morning up my nose and deep into my lungs. Who do I love more? Me or Betsy? It has to be Betsy. Of course it's Betsy. It's always been Betsy. Fuck relaxing. Fuck my heart rate. I reach for my phone; tap into my call history and hover my finger over Lenny's number. I need to know where he is; what he's doing.

'Y'know… if you don't have anyone to come up to see you, how about I sit here with you for a while? We can watch some TV together… just relax?'

I haven't had anybody offer anything quite like that to me in years. Company.

'That'd be lovely,' I say, placing the phone back down onto my lap.

I can't make up my fucking mind.

FIFTEEN YEARS AGO

Betsy

SOMETIMES IT IS REALLY HOT IN MY ROOM. SOMETIMES IT IS really cold. It has been cold for a lot of days now. Every morning I wake up I feel the cold. I stay in my bed, under my blankets all day, most days. Once I have my books – and Bozy – that is okay. I read my books to Bozy all the time. He likes them as much as I do. His favourite is *Pirates in Pyjamas*. My favourite is *The Enormous Crocodile*.

I have thirty-three books. Eight of them are by a man called Roald Dahl. I would like to be a writer like him one day. I am going to write a book called *Bozy's Adventures*. I have asked Dod to bring me some paper to write a book on but he hasn't brought it to me. He keeps forgetting. But he is kind. Sometimes. He brings me lots of different books. I love books. I am thinking about going over to get *The Enormous Crocodile* to read it again but I don't want to get out of the bed. It's too cold. Then the door opens and Dod walks down the steps. I know if he is going to be good Dod or angry Dod from how he comes down the steps. I think he is good Dod today. He is walking properly. He is not falling against the walls.

'Everything okay, Betsy?'

'It's cold, Dod.'

He makes a noise but I don't know if he said anything. I don't know if I should say something back. Sometimes he gets angry if I don't talk back to him. But I don't think he wants me to talk back to him this time. He is just looking around my room. He rubs his hands together.

'I'll get you another blanket or maybe a duvet if I can find the time to buy one.'

'What is a duvet?'

'It's just a heavier blanket for your bed.'

He is definitely being good Dod today. I see him put his arms around himself and shake a little bit. That's what I do when I'm cold too.

'Come in.'

I open up the blankets on the bed. He looks at me. Then walks over and gets into my bed. I put the blankets over him and high up to his chin. He laughs a little bit. I really like it when Dod laughs. He doesn't laugh many times.

'Would you like to read me a story?'

He looks at me and then he nods his head. That means yes.

I reach under the blankets and pull out the first book I can feel.

'This one.'

It is a Peppa Pig book called *Daddy Pig's Big Chair*. I used to like it but I think I am a big girl now and don't need to read Peppa Pig books anymore. But it is okay. Because reading is fun all the time. And if Dod is reading, then it is even more fun.

'Daddy Pig's Big Chair.' Dod laughs again when he opens the book.

Before he starts to read I say something. I only say it because Dod is happy and I like it when Dod is happy.

'My Daddy had a big chair too. I miss my Mummy and my Daddy sometimes.'

He closes the book and then gets out of the blankets and off the bed. Oh no. I think he is angry Dod now.

'What have I fucking told you, Betsy? They're gone. They're not your parents anymore.'

He throws *Daddy Pig's Big Chair* against the wall and it makes a big noise.

I go under my blankets. Dod has never said that before. He never said they're not my parents anymore. Why is he saying this?

'You fucking mention Mummy and Daddy again and I'll hurt you, you little bitch. Do you hear me? Do you fucking hear me?'

I can't see him. My face is under the blankets. But he takes the blankets off the bed. His face is really red. This is bad. When his face is red he is really, really angry Dod. I am frightened. Frightened and cold. I am shaking so much.

Dod lifts me up. He holds me in the air. He is shouting but I can't hear what he is saying. He throws me against the wall. I land on top of *Daddy Pig's Big Chair*. My back and bum hurt. Really, really hurt. I don't want to cry but I can not stop it. I start to cry really loud. Dod picks me up again.

'Shut the fuck up crying, Betsy, or I swear to God I'll fucking kill you.'

I stop crying. Well, I stop making crying noises. But tears are still falling down my face. I wipe them away and then he throws me again. But this time it doesn't hurt. He throws me on the bed. Then he bends down. He takes my hands away from my face and looks at me.

'Are you okay, Betsy?'

I shake my head. And then rub my hands against my back. 'Show me.'

He turns me around and pulls up my top. It's really sore.

Then he runs up the steps. I want to cry again but I don't. I hold up Bozy and give him a hug. That makes the pain go away a little bit.

Dod runs back down the steps. He has a bag with him. He turns me around and then lifts my top again. He puts the bag on my back and it is really cold. Really, really cold. It makes me laugh. Then Dod laughs.

'I'm so sorry, Betsy.'

He lies me down in the bed and then gets into the bed too. He puts the blankets over the two of us.

'Betsy. I have something to tell you. Do you know what heaven is? Has heaven come up in any of your books?'

I shake my head.

'Heaven is a place you go after you die. When people stop being alive they die.'

'And then they go to heaven?'

'Yes. And that's where your Mummy and Daddy are, Betsy. They are in heaven.'

I turn my head to look at Dod. I'm shaking again. Even though I'm under the blankets.

'My Mummy and Daddy are not living anymore?'

Dod kisses me on the nose.

'You're so clever, Betsy. Yes – your Mummy and Daddy are not living anymore.'

11:10

Lenny

Lenny's bottom lip hangs out, his eyes wide. He assumed Keating would intimidatingly tower over him. But here he was, standing two feet from Ireland's most notorious gangster; Keating's nose at Lenny's nose's height. And Lenny's only five foot seven.

Keating's infamy has painted him as a bigger presence than he actually is. In fact, Keating – in the flesh – reminds Lenny of his late uncle Arthur. And Arthur was the most gentle of souls Lenny had ever known. Keating doesn't look like a gangster at all; not with the cute little side parting in his thinning hair and his bulbous purpling nose. He's wearing a pale blue shirt with grey trousers that are pulled up way too high over the waist; above his belly button. Ol' uncle Arthur used to do the exact same thing. Most men in the later years of life do; they lose their hips and their trousers don't have much to cling on to, so the roundest part of the gut has to do.

'I'm eh...' Lenny hesitates, his eyes blinking. 'I'm Lenny Moon. Private Investigator.'

Keating's eyebrows arch, then he breaks out a little smile.

Or is it a grin? Lenny's unsure. He's watched a lot of gangster movies over the years; is a big fan of Guy Ritchie flicks and knows gangsters mostly smiled when they were being menacing. Yet Keating didn't look menacing. He just looked like good ol' uncle Arthur. Harmless.

Keating doesn't speak. He just keeps the grin on his face; inviting Lenny to continue talking. The rain's falling heavily now, but Keating's certainly not offering Lenny the chance to stand inside his doorway.

'I'm investigating the disappearance of Betsy Blake.'

Keating laughs. Then stares at Lenny, still not saying anything; still waiting to learn why this weird looking fella with the kiddish Sherpa hat and God-awful yellow jacket has had the audacity to ring this doorbell.

Lenny jumps backwards as the roaring barks of Keating's dogs echo from behind their owner. They both sound as if they're eager to get outside, eager to confront Lenny on their owner's behalf. Lenny glances down, sees one of them through Keating's legs; foam dripping from its mouth.

Keating stays still; doesn't even blink at the sound of the barking. He just stares straight ahead, eyeballing Lenny and welcoming him to keep talking.

'I eh... have been hired by Gordon Blake to eh... to see if... are they Rottweilers?'

Keating nods his head, squats down to his hunkers, grabs each dog by the collar.

'This is Bernie,' he says, speaking for the first time. 'And this one here, this is Barbara.'

Being held by their owner hasn't calmed Bernie and Barbara down; they're still barking, still foaming at the mouth.

Lenny holds the tips of his fingers to Keating's car as he stands back, anticipating he may have to leap upon it should one of the Rottweilers break free from their owner's grasp.

'Get your fuckin' hand off my car,' Keating snaps, standing back up.

Lenny swipes his hand away, places it inside the pocket of his puffer jacket and then stands still, as if he's frozen. Keating yells 'release' and the dogs shut up barking, swivel and go back down the hallway.

Lenny gulps, then almost mouths a 'thank you' to Keating, such is his relief.

Keating steps outside, the heavy rain not a bother to him.

'Betsy Blake... you were saying...'

Lenny gulps again, then holds a blink closed for a few seconds, taking the time to remind himself that he should grow some balls, man the fuck up, be an investigator.

'Gordon Blake is dying. Could be dead by the evening. He's in Tallaght Hospital right now. He's hired me as his last chance to find out what happened to his daughter.'

'Shit. Poor ol' Gordy. What's wrong with him?' Keating says, looking genuinely concerned.

'Heart problems. He has to have emergency surgery this afternoon at three o'clock. Doctors are only giving him a fifty per cent chance of making it through.'

Keating bites his bottom lip, shakes his head.

'He's only young. Must be twenty years younger than me... What's he – fifty?'

'I'm not entirely sure of Gordon's age, Alan. But—'

'The poor fucker.'

Keating seems ashen-faced by the news Lenny has just shared with him, even though he hasn't worked with Gordon Blake for seventeen years – not since Betsy went missing.

'As an associate of Gordon's at the time of Betsy's disappearance, I wouldn't mind asking you some questions, Alan.'

Keating looks behind him, stares at his door as if that was

going to remind him of what happened when Betsy Blake disappeared.

'Gis a sec,' he says, before pushing at the door and walking back inside.

Lenny's eyes flick from left to right, his pulse quickening. He holds his blink closed again, reminding himself that he is an investigator; that there is no need for him to be intimidated; that he's only doing his job. But he's finding it difficult to convince himself. He leaps when a high-pitch beep sounds behind him; the lights of Keating's Merc flashing on, then off.

'Get in,' Keating says, walking back out the door and banging it shut behind him.

Lenny turns, stares down the row of houses, contemplating whether or not he needs this job, whether or not it's all worth it. He blinks repeatedly again, for so long that Keating is already inside the car before he has re-adjusted his eyes. Then he grabs at the handle of the passenger door and pulls it wide open. As soon as he gets in, he removes his hat. He stares at it, realises immediately what Keating must have been thinking when he saw him; that he looks like a kid with this blue and black chequered tartan piece of shit atop his head. It has the same pattern of an eighties' Christmas jumper. It's okay for going incognito to spy on unsuspecting insurance claimants, but not ideal for confronting the country's biggest criminals.

'I don't deal with pigs,' Keating says, taking Lenny's gaze away from his hat.

It takes a couple of seconds for Lenny to realise what Keating's saying.

'Oh no; I'm not a cop. I'm—'

'You're investigating, aren't you? You're questioning me over the disappearance of a little girl, right?' Keating sniffs sharply in through his nose three times. 'Well that means I smell bacon.'

'Alan – I'm not investigating you. I'm just… it's just… you were a close associate of Gordon Blake at the time of Betsy's disappearance and I'd just like to ask you if you were aware of anything out of the ordinary that was happening in or around the Blake family in 2002. Anything at all. Lenny has asked me to beg you – it's his last chance.' Lenny says all of this so quickly that his intimidation is blatantly obvious.

'Lenny Moon, that your name, yeah?'

Lenny nods.

'Well, Lenny Moon. Let me finish this investigation for you in the next two seconds, huh? Betsy Blake is dead. She was hit by a car and whoever hit her with the car disposed of her body.'

Lenny coughs into his hand. Clears his throat. He doesn't want to sound intimidated, doesn't want his voice to crack.

'Gordon Blake doesn't believe the findings of the Gardaí. He's certain somebody kidnapped his daughter,' he says, slowing down his pace.

'Lemme guess… he thinks Barry Ward kidnapped his daughter on my orders?'

Lenny coughs again. Then blinks; not one long blink, repeated blinks, as if he's readjusting his eyes to a bright light. He'd love nothing more than to chew on the rubber case of his mobile phone right now, but is already aware he has come across as inexperienced to Alan Keating in the four minutes they've been talking.

'This isn't news to me,' Keating says before Lenny has a chance to reply. 'Sure that's what he told the cops in 2002. And sure poor ol' Gordy has even been hanging around outside Barry's house over the years; as if one day Barry's gonna walk out holding his daughter's hand. He's a brave man, doing that to Barry. But Barry doesn't mind. Neither of us do. We feel sorry for Gordy.' Keating uses his hands as he talks; it's another reminder to Lenny of ol' uncle Arthur. But he shakes his head of his thoughts, tunes backs into Keating's words. 'Listen, Lenny Moon; there are two truths you need to face up to. One; Betsy Blake is dead. And two; Gordon Blake is as deluded as a flat-earther. He went mad. Listen, it's understandable,' Keating says, shifting in his seat to face Lenny. 'I've two daughters. If one of them was killed and I never got answers, I'd go fuckin mental meself.'

Lenny shifts in his seat too, mirroring exactly what Keating had done moments prior, but not to talk, just to listen.

'I liked Gordon Blake. As I said, I feel sorry for him. Always have. In fact, I sent my lads out to help look for Betsy. We put sounders out, came back with nothing. I tried to help Gordy. My heart has always gone out to him and his wife. It's the only reason I'm sitting here talking to you now. Otherwise, any fuckin pig knocks on my door, I don't hold the dogs back, ye get me?'

Lenny nods. Then he blinks again, repeatedly, until he finds – somewhere deep within his blinking – an ounce of courage.

'It's just Gordon insists you threatened him just before Betsy went miss... he said you guys fell out.'

Keating laughs. Again, Lenny isn't sure if it's a sinister laugh or whether or not he actually found what was said funny.

'What did he say exactly?' Keating grunts as the rain falls heavier on the car.

Lenny allows a silent exhale to seep through his nose.

'Nothing much. Just that you were pushing him to do things with the money he was handling for you. And when he refused, you held him up against a wall; told him he shouldn't be fucking with you.'

Keating laughs again.

'That's not how I threaten people, Lenny Moon,' Keating says, the laughter disappearing from his face abruptly. 'That's just how I deal with people who work for me. I just wanted to get as much out of Gordy as I could. And I did. He was great for me. Y'know... I actually haven't had somebody cook my books quite like him ever since I lost him.'

Lenny nods at Keating, then forces his lips into a sterile smile.

'Thank you for your time, Alan. I eh...'

'Ah don't go. Is that it? You come knockin' on my door telling me ol' Gordy Blake is on death's door and desperately wants to find out what happened to his daughter before he dies and now... and now, what, you're just leaving me?'

Keating stretches his finger towards his door, clicks a button. Lenny instantly feels panicked at the sound of all car doors locking simultaneously. He reels back in the passenger seat, holding his hands up as if he's being robbed at gunpoint; the strings of the Sherpa hat he's holding dangling over his face.

'Alan, I don't know anything more than you do at this—'

'What did Gordy Blake say about me; tell me!' Keating says, the creases on his forehead wedging deeper, the tone of his voice demanding. It's striking to Lenny just how instantaneously ol' uncle Arthur can turn into Scarface and vice versa.

Lenny's breaths grow sharp, not just with fright, but with uncertainty. He doesn't know what to tell Keating, doesn't know how he's going to get himself out of this situation.

'I only spoke to Gordon for five minutes. He rushed me out of his ward... told me to get on with the investigation. To do what I could in the few hours he has left. He gave me a thousand quid up front, told me if I found anything new –

anything he hadn't heard before – that he'd leave me his house in his will.'

Keating relaxes his brow, but his eyes still burn through Lenny.

'His house?' He clenches his jaw as he says it. Then continues. 'He musta said more than that. Why are you here? He obviously told you to pay me a visit.'

'He... he... gave me a list. A list of people he suspected might've had something to do with Betsy's disappearance.'

Keating sits back in his chair, rests both his hands on the steering wheel, then laughs to himself. Lenny sits upright too, just to stare through the windscreen at the image of the houses blurred by the rain. He's well aware of Keating in his peripheral vision, anticipating any movement. Then it comes. Movement. Keating holds his hand out, palm up. Lenny gulps, then reaches inside his jacket pocket and takes out the note. Keating eyeballs Lenny as he places the paper atop his palm and then, almost in slow motion, he holds it up in front of him and begins to read; his laugh growing louder as each second passes.

He crumples the note up and throws it back at Lenny.

'I've been called worse,' says Keating. Then he turns his key in the ignition and rolls the car out of his driveway and down the street past Lenny's little Micra.

'Where we going?' Lenny asks, not bothering to hide the fear in his voice.

'Do you believe everything I said to you, Lenny Moon?'

Lenny nods his head. 'Yes, yes, Alan – everything. I believe you. I don't think you had anything to do with Betsy Blake's disappearance.'

'Good. Then you can scratch me off the list.' Keating drives under the archway, back out of his estate and turns left at the roundabout. 'So open up your note again there, Lenny Moon.'

Lenny picks the note up from his lap, uncrumples the paper and then stares back at Keating.

'Who's the next name on the list?'

'Eh… Barry. Barry Ward.'

Keating turns to Lenny, winks.

'Good – let's go have a word with him then, shall we?'

11:30

Gordon

I KNOW DAYTIME TV SO WELL THAT I CAN CALL THE BEATS.

I always know which items are going to sell for a profit on this show. Dickinson records his little voice overs after the scenes are shot, so there's always little clues in there as to whether or not the antique will do well when it comes to auction. I knew that little ornament would sell for more than the thirty-eight quid they bought it for because Dickinson suggested it was a bargain when they got it. It's so fuckin predictable. Had it not have ended up with such a heavy profit, Dickinson's voice over would have been a lot more negative.

'Told ya,' I say to Elaine. She smiles up at me.

'That you did! You must know your antiques, huh?'

'Nope. I just know my tele,' I say.

I look at her as she returns her gaze to the screen; even the way she's sitting reminds me of Michelle.

I am certain I fell in love with Michelle during that first bus ride, but it took her a lot longer to love me. I'm pretty sure she ended up falling for me only after she got wind of how much money I had. I've often felt she fell in love with the idea of being married to a rich business man, not the businessman himself. But we had good times, did me and Michelle. We travelled the world together. I was only too delighted to bring her to places she had only ever wished to go to before she met me. The first six years were dream-like really. It's difficult to explain what it's like being in love; I've often measured it as being the opposite of being depressed. Depression is difficult to explain, it's just a sour feeling, a negativity that resides in both the bottom of your gut and in the centre of your mind. Being in love is the total opposite in every way. I know. I've felt both.

We got married in St Michael's Church in Inchicore in 1994; reception in the K Club, overlooking the eighteenth green. We were both high as a kite; had no idea what bizarre fates lay in front of us. It took us almost four years to get pregnant. My balls were the problem, we found out. I had become a little infatuated with the laptop I had bought, holding it too close to my balls as I was working. When I resisted using the laptop for its exact purpose – typing on the lap – my little swimmers woke the fuck up. Michelle held a white stick with a blue cross on it in front of me one Saturday morning and we celebrated as if Ireland had won the World Cup. Over the next few months we both felt as if all of our stresses and strains had packed up and fucked off thanks to the little bump. We'd no idea that bump would one day deliver the biggest nightmare any parent could ever possibly fathom.

'Okay… that's it,' Elaine says as the shite end title music to Dickinson's Real Deal begins. 'I gotta go do some work. Just press this if you need me.'

'Elaine,' I say, unsure of what I'm going to say next.

She turns, purses her lips at me, then smiles again when she realises exactly what I called her for – no reason.

'Stay relaxed,' she says. Then she leaves.

I push the butt of both my palms as far as I can into my eye sockets and twist them. Then I let out a yawn that sounds more like a deep sigh than anything. Maybe it was a sigh. I pick up the TV remote, begin switching through the channels; skipping by *This Morning* because Holly Willoughby's not on it, skipping by an old episode of *The Ellen Show*, skipping by *Morning Ireland* and by *Jeremy Kyle*. I stall at Sky News just to read the scroll banner. As soon as I see the word 'Brexit' I click on, only to be met by white noise. That's it. Six fucking channels. What a load of me bollocks. I grasp the remote control firmer and swing my arm back, but rather than throw it across the room like I want to, I just let it drop onto my bed.

I twist my body, grab my mobile phone from the bedside cabinet and deliberately don't even look at my call log button.

I scroll into the Sky Sports app instead, try to catch up with any football news. But there's fuck all new on there. Nothing's been added since I looked at it just before Douglas and his team came in to give me a harsh reality check over an hour or so ago. Then I click into the WGT Golf app, decide I'll have a game. It might pass some time. It's the only game I've ever played on a mobile phone. It can get quite addictive. I play it on the loo mostly. A shite these days isn't enjoyable for me unless I'm putting for birdies at the same time. The load icon appears, scrolling from twenty per cent to thirty per cent to forty per cent to... Betsy. Betsy.

Fuck it. I tap out, straight into my call log. I've gotta get onto Lenny; find out what he's up to. I can't be playing bleedin' golf games when I've only a few hours left to live. I tap at his number, hold the phone to my ear.

'Heya, Gordy,' comes a voice. I sit up straight in my bed, instantly know it's not Lenny on the other end of the line. Only one person's ever called me Gordy.

11:30

Lenny

LENNY CONTINUES TO STARE STRAIGHT AHEAD; NO PART OF HIS body – except for his eyeballs – have even twitched over the course of the twenty-minute drive. He's just sat upright the whole time and listened to Keating sing along to Frank Sinatra's greatest hits. The gangster crooned to *My Way, Got You Under My Skin, Come Fly With Me, Witchcraft* and was at the crescendo of *Lady is a Tramp* when he began backing the car into a parallel parking position outside a row of terraced houses.

Lenny was actually impressed by Keating's vocal, but stayed mute all the way, not even nodding in compliment for fear of disrupting him. He was practically scared stiff, though the score was keeping his heart rate quite consistent. It is, after all, almost impossible to be scared while a big band are providing the backdrop. But he now understood for certain that Keating's smiles weren't smiles at all; they were gangster grins. The man is a living parody of a Hollywood gangster. A sociopath.

As Keating takes the keys out of the ignition, ending his duet session, Lenny turns his head for the first time.

'That's Barry's house there, number thirteen,' Keating says. He then gets out of the car, waits for Lenny on the footpath, still oblivious to the rain. Lenny thinks about putting his hat back on his head, but instead crumples it up and stuffs it inside his jacket pocket, making it look as if he has one of those bulbous hernias bursting from his gut.

'This'll be fun,' Keating says, holding the gate open for Lenny to walk through.

'Thanks, Alan,' Lenny says. He was unsure what tone to talk to Keating in; wondered was thanking him for holding the gate open even applicable conversation to have with a gangster. Keating hadn't explained anything on the drive over and Lenny was still wondering why they had both made the journey; whether Keating was genuinely trying to help him with his investigation or whether he was just taking the piss and trying to intimidate him. He took his mobile phone from his pocket, just to check the time as they waited on Barry to open his door after Keating repeatedly rapped his knuckles against the window panes on it. 11:37. He's wasting time here; is certain Keating and Barry have fuck all to do with Betsy Blake's disappearance. Poor Gordon's time is ticking away; no impact is going to be made on his final wish; not today.

'Whatsup, boss!' Barry says holding his hand for Keating to grab. They greet like gangsters do, a grasp of hands that helps them lean in for a half-a-hug.

'Who this?'

'Barry, meet Lenny Moon. Lenny Moon's a PI.'

Barry looks Lenny up and down, then stares at Keating, his eyes squinting, his mouth almost forming a smile.

'A PI? Ye don't look like a PI. Ye look like the fuckin' shit member of a shit boy band.'

Keating laughs as he enters Barry's hallway. 'You rolling?'

'I'm awake amn't I?' says Barry.

Barry swings his hand, welcoming Lenny inside his home, the whiff of cannabis in the hallway alone enough to get anybody stoned. They all enter the square living-room, Barry making his way straight to a glass decanter in the far corner. He picks it up, shows it to his guests.

'Jesus no, too early for me,' says Keating.

Barry stares at Lenny, awaits his response.

'Eh… too early for me, too,' he says.

Barry and Keating take a seat on the dated furniture, leaving Lenny standing. He stares around the room, takes in the impressive artwork on the walls. They look so out of place in the tiny gaff; probably just as valuable as the gaff itself.

'Sit down, PI,' says Barry. Lenny does as he's told, plonks himself on the couch next to Keating. He becomes aware of his left knee bouncing up and down, so places his hand over it, holds it in place.

'Wait till ye hear this,' Keating says, turning to Lenny. 'Go on… tell Barry why you're here.'

Lenny takes in a breath, then blinks rapidly.

'I'm investigating the Betsy Blake disappearance on behalf of her father Gordon Blake. He—'

Lenny is interrupted by Barry's laughter. Then it stops abruptly, almost as if he was half-way through his laugh when a sniper aimed a dart into his neck.

'Well, you've come to the right place, PI. She's under the stairs.'

Lenny swivels his head to peek out the sitting-room at the door leading under the bannisters and is then met with an even bigger laugh. This time Keating joins in; bringing Lenny back to school, back to the days he used to be picked on for being the oddest boy in the classroom. But back then it was only harmless insecure teenagers picking on him – not Ireland's most notorious gangster and his psycho sidekick.

'Ye know what?' Lenny says, standing up. 'I have decided to stand down from this job. I will be notifying Gordon Blake of my resignation and – gentlemen – I am so sorry to have disturbed your mornings.'

'Sit down, Lenny Moon,' Keating orders. Lenny does as he's told, his eyes blinking. 'Barry – are you just gonna let that J sit in the ashtray or are you gonna offer your guest a welcome puff?'

Barry bends down to his glass ashtray, picks up the joint he had started to smoke when the knocks came at the door. He holds it in front of him, ignites the flame on a lighter with his other hand, then holds the flame to the joint until it catches. Lenny squints. He had smoked weed before, back when he was studying for a pointless certificate in media at college, but had never seen this technique for lighting a joint before, didn't think it was possible to light one without inhaling.

'No thank you,' he says when Barry holds the joint towards him. 'Too early for me.'

Barry laughs again.

'I understand it being too early for whiskey, but no such clock exists for this shit.'

Lenny turns to look at Keating beside him, hoping ol' uncle Arthur would appear; pat him on the back, tell him to get home if he wants to. But Keating holds Lenny's gaze, again staying mute, allowing Lenny to do the talking. Lenny reaches out, takes the joint, assumes being on friendly terms with these two is probably his quickest route to getting the fuck out of here.

He inhales slowly, making sure the smoke isn't too harsh on his throat. The last thing he needs right now is these two laughing at him for coughing up a storm.

'Gordy Blake's dying,' Keating speaks up as Lenny exhales. 'Lenny Moon here has told me he may only have a few hours left to live. Has to have a massive heart operation later today that he might not wake from. He's hired Lenny as his one last shot at finding little Betsy. And… guess who he came to investigate first?'

Barry arches his right eyebrow, breaks out a tiny smile and then shakes his head.

'Poor Gordy. I'll miss him. Y'know,' he says, turning to Lenny, 'he's hung out a few times on this street, stalking me. Haven't seen him in a long, long time… but Jesus yeah, I'll miss the poor fucker. We've always felt sorry for him, haven't we, boss?'

Keating nods his head then pinches the joint out of Lenny's hand as Barry continues.

'I did my best to look for that little girl. Even held a lot of fuckers heads under water trying to get answers. Nobody knows anything. She wasn't taken, wasn't kidnapped. She died, didn't she? Hit by a car.'

Lenny clears his throat, his attempt at ridding his mouth of the stale taste of tobacco. It's been so long since he's inhaled smoke, inhaled weed. Can already feel his head spin a little.

'I believe so yeah… Gardaí closed the case in absentia.'

'Are you talking fuckin Latin now, PI?'

'Without a body,' Keating says while exhaling a huge cloud of smoke. 'They closed the case and announced her dead without finding a body.'

'Well they're hardly gonna find her body if she's living under my stairs, are they?' Barry says.

Keating coughs out a laugh.

'I'm just… I'm just trying to carry out Gordon's last wish; trying to give the investigation one last roll of the dice,' Lenny says. 'That's all. I'm just doing what I was hired to do.'

Keating leans forward in his chair, passes the joint to Barry.

'Here, show Barry the note.'

Lenny rolls his eyes sideways – almost in slow motion – to stare at Keating. Then he reaches inside his pocket, flattens out the crumpled paper and holds it between his fingers, stretching it towards Barry. Barry takes it, squints at it. Laughs. Takes a drag of the joint. Laughs again.

'Freak he calls me?' he says, 'That's rich coming from that nut job. Listen, PI… it's no surprise Gordy thinks me and Keating are top of this list; he's hung onto that theory for… I don't know how many years it's been.'

'Seventeen,' says Keating.

'Is it that long? Fuck! Listen, PI; Gordy Blake's a nut job. He goes around believing his daughter's still alive, when it's been proven she died. His daughter disappearing didn't just break his heart, it broke his head too. The man's sick. We had nothing to do with his daughter's death. Pigs initially thought it was Gordy himself, then when they cleared him, they came straight to us. Gordy told them he'd been working with us. But the cops knew we didn't have anything to do with it. What the fuck would we want with a bleedin' four-year-old girl? That's twelve years below the age I like.' Barry laughs, then takes another quick drag of his joint before passing it to Lenny.

'If you wanna get honest answers for Gordy Blake before he dies; go to the cops, get them to give you the proof that Betsy is dead… Tell him and make him believe it. Because if he wants closure, he has to believe the truth.'

Lenny smiles a thank you, hands the joint towards Keating without taking another drag and then stands back up.

'Gentlemen, thank you very much for your time.'

'Where d'ye think you're going?'

'To eh… the cops, as you said. I wanna get confirmation of what really happened, to stop messing around following up the false leads on that note.' Lenny takes his hat out of his pocket, then holds a hand out towards Barry. Barry remains sitting, hands still flat on the arms of the chair.

'Who the fuck is the Jake Dewey fella on the note?'

'I eh… I know only what's on that note,' Lenny says, blinking. 'Gordon was keen for me to get out and interview all three men named on there and kinda just rushed me out of the hospital, telling me to get on with it, that time was ticking.'

'It's Michelle Blake's new husband isn't it?' Keating says.

Lenny nods his head. 'I assume so, judging by what's written there.'

'You're not a very good private investigator, are ye, kid?… Here.' Keating says, handing Lenny the joint back. 'Take a couple of drags, calm yourself down.'

Lenny pinches the joint, looks at both men and then sits back down.

'How did you become a PI?' Barry asks.

'Had to leave the force.'

'Ah… so you were a pig. Knew I could smell it on ye.'

Lenny looks at Keating, then back at Barry. He feels like he isn't in his own head; can't quite fathom the reality he's finding himself in: about to open up to The Boss and his main henchman about his ambitions for a career in serving out justice.

'I didn't last long as a cop. Was looking to go down the detective route… made good progress in my first eighteen months but eh… then… then… We have twins, me and my wife. She suffered with post-natal depression from the day they were born. It's been…' Lenny stops, swallows back the emotion that threatened to run to the back of his eyes. 'It's been a testing five years for us. She tried to commit suicide a couple of times. So I quit as a cop; decided to start my own PI business so that I could be close by at all times, case she needs me. I rent a little work space five minutes from where we live. It's tiny. Quarter the size of this room.'

Barry moves his eyes to look at Keating.

'So you've been a PI how long?'

'Almost six years.'

'How come I've never seen you sniffing round us before today then?'

Lenny sucks in a tiny inhale of the joint, passes it to Barry. He's starting to feel slightly relaxed; feels as if sharing his truth about Sally has endeared him to the gangsters. He doesn't feel as intimidated.

'I only really work for bloody insurance companies. I'm not an investigator really… I'm eh… I don't know what you'd call it. I find out if people claiming from insurance companies are telling lies or not. Today's the first day I've ever been asked to investigate a criminal case.'

Lenny's phone buzzes. He slides it out of his jacket pocket, stares at the screen.

'That's him ringing now. Gordon Blake.'

Keating takes the phone from Lenny's hand, stabs his finger at the answer button.

'Heya, Gordy,' he says.

There's a silence on the other end of the line. Barry, Lenny and Keating all inch their ears closer to the phone.

'Alan Keating!' Gordon says.

'Long time no speak, Gordy. Y'know… I still wish you were running my books. I've never quite replaced you; isn't that right, Barry. Don't I say that often?'

'He does, Gordy,' Barry says.

'Jesus Christ. Lenny must be a good investigator after all. He found both of you in the same room, huh?' Gordon says.

'Don't get carried away with compliments for Lenny. He didn't orchestrate this – I did,' Keating replies.

A gulp can be heard coming down the line, followed by a distant beeping sound.

'So, it's true is it, Gordy. You're in hospital, fifty-fifty chance of ending the day alive?'

'Let Lenny go,' Gordon says.' He's an innocent man. Is only carrying out what I paid him to do.'

'You just worry about yourself, Gordy, yeah? We'll look after Lenny for ya.'

Lenny double takes; stares at Keating, then at Barry, then back to Keating, his eyes blinking as he does so. He can't read what's going on.

There's a long silence, Keating stretches the phone outward a bit; insisting he's not going to talk next. Lenny cops it; Keating had been playing this game with him since he met him; staying silent. He waits on information, he doesn't offer information.

'Look, lads... I just asked Lenny to put my mind at rest before I die,' Gordon says. 'The only people I'd fallen out with around the time of Betsy's disappearance was you guys. It's all I've had to go on all these years... Just you two and that fuckin smug asshole my wife shacked up with. I just want to cross you off my list once and for all.'

'What do you think we did, Gordy; kept Betsy chained up in Barry's gaff all these years?'

The line falls silent again.

'Tell ye what,' Lenny pipes up. 'We're in Barry's house now. I know you've hung outside here over the years. Would it eh... would you be willing for me to cross this theory off your list for good? What if I was to just call out Betsy's name while I'm here – so you will know with absolute certainty before you go for your surgeries that these guys had nothing to do with this? That she's certainly not shacked up in Barry's home.'

Barry snarls up at Lenny, his confusion made obvious by

the deep vertical line that has just formed above the bridge of his nose. Then he looks at Keating wondering how the fuck he should react to this. Keating doesn't move, doesn't say a word. Lenny realises what he's just said is quite risky. He hadn't thought it was as he was saying it. He was genuinely thinking of the best way he could move on, get the fuck out of the situation he was finding himself in. Perhaps it was the weed talking for him.

'I don't really know whether or not Alan and Barry had anything to do with this, but yeah… yeah… anything to get something off my mind. If you can confirm for me that Betsy isn't in that house, I guess that's something.'

Lenny's heart begins to rise again. Not out of fear – out of excitement. Gordon told him earlier that if he got an answer for him that Gordon hadn't got before, he'd leave him his house in his will. Or maybe he's just getting carried away, getting high. He looks at Barry, then at Keating. Keating shrugs his shoulders.

'Just because we feel a real sympathy for you,' Keating says. 'So you can put this theory to bed.' Keating licks his lips, looks agonisingly at Barry. Barry's been unusually silent; probably caught off guard.

'Ye might as well start here,' Keating says, brushing past Lenny and into the hallway. He twists at the knob on the door under the stairs, pulls it open. Lenny walks towards it, stares into the darkness, then at Keating.

FOURTEEN YEARS AGO

Betsy

DOD DROPS FOUR NEW BOOKS ON MY BED. I CRAWL OUT FROM under my sheets and give him a hug. I wrap my arms around the top of his legs. Squeeze him tight. Then I pick up the books and smell them. It's the first thing I do every time he gets me a new book. My favourite smell in the whole world is books.

The first of my new books that I look at is called *The Letter for the King*. It says on the back that it is 'suitable for eight-year-olds'. I'm only seven but I know I can read it. I'm so good at reading. That makes me lucky. Because I am good at my favourite thing to do. I look at the other books. *A Series of Unfortunate Events*. That looks good. *The Wind and the Willows* and then… yes! – another Roald Dahl Book. *Matilda*. I turn around and squeeze Dod's legs again.

'Thank you.'

He doesn't say anything. Just smiles. He has been smiling so many times when he comes to see me these days. I haven't seen angry Dod in a long time.

'Ah for fuck sake.'

I stand still when I hear him say that. I wonder what I did wrong. Then I turn around slowly.

'Not you. Not you, Betsy. Just this... fuckin...'

He likes to say the word fuck or fucking a lot but I don't really know what they mean. They're never in any of my books. I guess it just means Dod is angry. I turn around. He is looking into my basin. Into where I wash and pee. And poo.

'You're filling this a lot lately.'

He lifts it up. It looks heavy. Heavier than the other times he has had to lift it up before. Then he walks up the steps.

When I first came to this room I had to pee and poo on the floor. Then Dod brought me a box to go toilet in. Then he brought the basin. I think that was two years ago now. Yeah – when I was about five, I think. I've been living here for about three years. A little bit more. Sometimes I wish I lived in a place like the one Charlie Bucket from one of my favourite books lives in. It says in the book that he is poor and his family don't have many things. But I think he has everything anybody would ever need. He has his Mummy and Daddy. And he has his granddads and grandmothers. I only had grandmothers in the outside world. I think both my granddads were dead. They must be in heaven now with my Mummy and Daddy. I hope they are having fun. Sometimes I wish I could go to heaven to be with them. But I have to wait until I die. I don't know how long that will be.

'Betsy.'

I look up. Up the steps.

'Betsy.'

Dod is calling me from the top of the steps. He has never done this before. I can't really see him because the light behind him is too bright. He is like a shadow. Then he takes one step down and I notice his hand. It is waving me to come up the steps. I take one step forward. Then I stop. I'm afraid. Dod gets really angry when I go near the steps. I don't want him to be angry. Even if he is calling me. I don't know what to do. I turn around. I grab Bozy.

'C'mon, Betsy. Come up. It's okay.'

I squeeze Bozy and then walk onto the first step. I look up and wait for Dod to shout at me. But he doesn't. He is just waiting for me at the top. Then I walk onto the second step. Then the third. And fourth. Dod is still quiet. I close my eyes. That way, he won't get angry if I see anything. I don't think I'm allowed to see what's up the steps. I walk up the rest of them. All thirteen. I know there are thirteen. I count them every day.

Dod puts his hands on my shoulders when I reach the top.

'It's okay, Betsy. Open your eyes.'

I do. I open them wide. But it's too bright. It hurts my eyes a bit. It smells different up here. In my room it is mostly the smell of poo. Except for when I smell my books. Then the poo smell goes away for a few seconds. But up here smells like… I don't know. Different. Nice.

Dod keeps his hands on my shoulders and walks me down a room that has a brown wood floor. It's nice. It looks a lot nicer than my stone floor. More flat. Then he makes me turn around. I still can't see much. The light is too bright.

'This is my downstairs toilet.'

I blink my eyes until I can see more clear. Then I see white walls with a big white bowl. It makes me think of my Mummy and Daddy's house. We had a big white bowl like that too.

'You can do your pee and poo in here.'

Dod opens a lid on the big white bowl and I look into it. There is a little bit of water in it.

'What do you mean?'

'If you need to poo or pee just knock on the door and I will let you come here to do it.'

I look up at Dod. I am a little bit scared.

'Am I okay to walk up the steps and knock on the door?'

Dod laughs a little bit.

'Yeah.'

'And you won't get angry. Won't turn into angry Dod?'

Dod laughs again. This time louder.

'You're becoming a big girl now. I can't be carrying that basin up and down the steps all the time. You can pee and poo in this, and see here...' He points at another white bowl. It's like the first one. Just a bit smaller and a bit higher up. 'You can wash yourself some mornings in this one.' He turns the shiny bit on top and water comes out. I think of my old house again. Mummy and Daddy's house. I think they had the same bowl too.

I smile a big smile. But I am also a bit scared. I'm afraid of being up the steps and inside the light rooms. I turn around and look at Dod. He is smiling too. I notice another bright room behind him. It has a big blue chair in it. I wish I had a chair like that in my room.

'No looking in there.'

Dod says that a bit angry. But then he smiles again. I don't know what to do. So I just squeeze Dod's legs.

'You're welcome.'

He bends down towards me so that his nose is close to my nose. There's always a bad smell when his face is close to me.

'But there's one condition. Anytime you're up here, you need to be really quiet okay?'

I nod my head.

'And I mean really fucking quiet. If you ever raise your voice or make any noise up here at all, I won't just hurt you. I will kill you.'

11:55

Lenny

LENNY FEELS A TSUNAMI OF RELIEF WASH THROUGH HIM AS THE hall door closes and he finds himself outside. Never before has rain felt so good. Keating and Barry almost folded over with laughter as soon as Lenny called out Betsy's name. Then the light switched on under the stairs. He was staring into a space a human could barely stand up in, let alone be held captive in.

He thought Barry was going to throw up, so heavy was his convulsion of laughter. He looked at both of them, then headed for the door.

He removes his phone from his pocket as he paces down Barry's tiny garden path and then begins to jog down Carrow Road. He fidgets with his phone, is keen to ring Gordon back, ask him if getting into Barry's home and concluding with absolute certainty that Betsy isn't there constitutes triggering the gentlemen's agreement they made earlier.

But he also knows Gordon heard the men laughing, that it was all a joke and he isn't quite sure how he's going to take it. Maybe it won't constitute enough to activate the will.

He turns around to walk backwards, such is the force of the wind driving down the canal. When he reaches the junction that the old Black Horse pub used to sit on he squints into the distance, into the greyness of the day in hope of seeing a taxi light approach.

It doesn't take long; just five minutes, though those five minutes felt a lot longer than five minutes to Lenny. He's soaked by the time the taxi pulls up alongside him; his hat weighing heavy on his head. On numerous occasions during his short jog he had wished the phone call from Gloria Proudfoot at Excel Insurance had come before his phone call from Gordon Blake – that way he'd be most likely snug and warm in some gym taking sneaky pictures with his dated film camera instead of feeling like a drowned rat in the back of a taxi going in search of somebody he knew he couldn't possibly find. But that house, that big old house on South Circular Road won't leave his mind. What if Gordon Blake is telling the truth; what if he genuinely left it in his will to Lenny, Sally and the twins? Soaked to the bone or not, chasing a lost cause or not, Lenny had to admit to himself that this was one hell of an interesting morning.

'Fuck the warmth of a gym,' he mutters to himself in the back of the taxi. As the driver is turning on to the Naas Road, Lenny's phone vibrates in his jacket pocket. He knows who it is; it's midday.

'Hey, sweetie,' he says.

'I know you rang me since our last call, but I still thought I should ring you at twelve.'

'Of course.'

Lenny had made a pact with Sally that she would ring at ten a.m., midday and then again at two p.m. every day just so Lenny could rest assured that the day was going well for his wife. The story he'd shared with Keating and Barry was true. Every word of it. Sally is suicidal. Has suffered with high levels of depression ever since the twins were born. In fact, she'd shown signs of depression even in pregnancy; her levels of anxiety rising so much she had to be kept in hospital on occasions. Lenny assumed post natal depression was inevitable for Sally, yet he never quite knew how awful it would be. He found her one morning standing atop their toilet seat trying to put her neck in a noose she had tied using the belt of her woollen bathrobe. The twins were only eight weeks old then. On his first day back in work – three months later – he got a phone call from Sally who told him he had to get home quick before she started to slice at her wrists with a Stanley knife. She was sitting in a corner of their sitting room with the blade in her hand when he arrived home, the twins both crying upstairs. There were no cuts on her skin, but Lenny has never been entirely convinced of what would have happened had he not been fortunate enough to have his phone in his possession when she rang that day. As a police officer, he was supposed to have it turned off.

His station chief offered him six months leave after Sally's second suicide attempt, but Lenny knew it wasn't enough; that he could never return to a job in which he had no control over his time, over his phone. It was a shame; Lenny had always wanted to be a Garda, had ambitions to be a detective from quite a young age. Sally hasn't made any suicide attempt since, but her moods have still not evened out or even become consistent day-to-day. Every morning he wakes up, he doesn't know how Sally is going to be feeling.

'Any more work today?' Sally asks. She sounds okay, monotone but alert.

Lenny pauses; the hesitation even obvious to the taxi man.

'Leonard,' Sally says re-prompting her husband.

'Sorry, love, phone is playing up a bit. Eh... yeah. I've to go to some gym in Coolock now; usual stuff. Got to take a photo of a girl who—'

'Think you'll be home to go meet the teacher today?' Sally interrupts, clearly not interested in the answer to the initial question she'd asked. This wasn't unusual. Their phone calls weren't about anything, merely routine.

'Yeah... yeah,' Lenny says, his eyes blinking. It was unusual he'd blink when speaking to his wife. But that's because it was also unusual he would lie to her. He didn't want to tell her about the Betsy Blake case, didn't want to raise her anxiousness levels in any way. 'Yeah – I'll be there if you can get a three o'clock meeting.'

'Good. I'll make an appointment so,' Sally says.

Lenny thanks her and after the phone call ends he bites at the cover of his phone, disappointed with himself. He knows there's a chance he won't make that meeting; hates that he might let not only his wife down, but his sons too. Particularly Jared. He's having an awful time of it at school. Not only is he being bullied, but he's being drowned in the politics of the education system. The school don't know what to do with him; so low is his comprehension. Lenny's only concerned about the bullying, not bothered about the latter. He genuinely feels institutional education is vastly overrated. Though he is keen to stay on top of things if only for Sally's sake. If she's worried, then Lenny is worried too. He lets out a little sigh. The meeting he just agreed to attend is supposed to take place straight after the kids leave school at three p.m., exactly when his case with Gordon Blake is due for conclusion too.

Lenny shakes his head as the taxi man pulls into Peyton estates, ridding his mind of the worry.

'If you can pull over at the orange car there please...'

Lenny almost tuts as he hands the taxi man a twenty euro

note. He hates spending money, unless it's on something that would cheer either his wife or the twins up.

He runs the five yards to his car door, wrestles with the lock and then jumps in. It was pointless trying to be quick; he really couldn't get any wetter than he already is.

He starts the engine, begins to pull out of Peyton estate when he hears an unusual sound. His car slogs, even though he's pressing hard on the accelerator. He squints at himself in the rear-view mirror, then his eyes widen. He begins to slap at the steering wheel; the penny finally dropping. He doesn't stop slapping, not until the palms of his hands sting unbearably.

Then he gets out of his car and looks up and down the driver's side, walks to the other side of the car and does the same thing. He clenches both fists, tilts his head back – eyes open, mouth open – and lets the rain shower down on his face.

'Fuck sake!' he roars into the sky.

12:10

Gordon

I FINISH WRITING UP THE LETTER AND WILL; TUCK THE FLAP OF the envelope inside itself and then push it under my pillow. I want Lenny to know I'm deadly serious; that I will leave him my house if he can somehow get me some answers today. I may have come across like a right twat having him call out Betsy's name in Barry Ward's gaff, but I don't mind looking like a twat. I'd do anything to find some answers. Her disappearance plagues me every day; her loss from my life eats at me. But it's the guilt that makes the most impact. It resides in both my stomach and my head, and it won't go away. It was my fault she went missing. It was on my watch.

I wasn't a lazy dad; I was just like any other dad – unfocused. Mothers are great at paying their children every nuance of attention. But dads? Fuck no. We're easily distracted. I was busy working. Guus had managed to bring in two massive clients to our company just before Betsy went missing; they were million euro deals. I was finalising one at home while I was supposed to be looking after my daughter. I think she got bored, walked away from me, walked away from our home. One of the main reasons I feel guilt is because I'm genuinely not sure how long she was gone before I realised she was missing. May have been just ten minutes, could've been two hours. I was too consumed with work.

I went into shock when I realised she was gone; ran into the streets shouting her name. I stopped people, asked if they'd seen a four-year-old with mousy brown hair. Nobody'd seen anything. I thought I was going mad. I remember running back into the house and checking everywhere for her; under the beds, in the closets, the washing machine. I even checked the fuckin microwave. I don't know why. I think I was beginning to lose it. I rang the police before I rang Michelle; knew it'd be a much easier call to make.

'My child's gone missing,' I said matter-of-factly down the line. I know I said it matter-of-factly because it was played back to me about eight times when I was being questioned by Detective De Brun a few days later. I was their first suspect; they assumed I had something to do with her disappearance. By that stage I was convinced it was Keating who'd taken my girl. I told the police about my dealings with him; spilt the beans. But they were still convinced I knew something. I didn't. I hadn't one fucking clue what happened to Betsy. I still don't. I still don't have one iota of an idea what happened to her that day, or what has happened to her any day since. But I know she's alive. I know deep down in my gut she's out there somewhere. If only the cops had acted sooner, instead of wasting time questioning me, I'm pretty certain they could've found her. But now – just over seventeen years later – there's probably no chance whatsoever that I'll ever see her pretty little face again. I can't give up though. I've told anyone who's ever listened to me over those years that I will fight until my dying day to find Betsy. Well, today may well be my dying day, and I ain't stopping. I guess I just have to put all of my hope in little Lenny Moon. Not that I've given him much to go on; same old leads I've looked into hundreds of times – all of them producing sweet fuck all over the years. But fair play to him, he got into Barry's house within an hour or so of starting his investigation. That's some going. It took me four years to get inside that gaff.

'That time again, Gordon,' Elaine says, opening up the door to my ward. I twist my head on the pillow, crease my mouth into a slight smile.

'You look more relaxed anyway,' she says.

I just maintain the smile, pull my T-shirt over my head again and wait for her to attach the blue tabs to my chest.

'The theatre will definitely be ready for three p.m., Gordon. Everything's running on time. Dr Johnson and Mr Broadstein are due to land at one p.m. and should arrive here at the hospital around two-ish. The surgery that's going on in the theatre right now is expected to be finished in a couple more hours. Half an hour clean up and prep after that, then we'll get you down there.'

I'm listening to what Elaine is saying, but I don't react, except for nodding my head out of politeness.

'Okay... heart rate is still high,' she says,' but it's come down a good bit. Keep that head back on your pillow and just relax, Gordon. It's your best chance of beating this.'

I just nod again.

'You okay... You've gone very quiet on me?'

I look up at her, meeting her eyes for the first time since she re-entered the ward.

'Just letting it all sink in,' I say. 'Y'know what's upsetting me the most?'

She doesn't finish wrapping the rubber tube around her hand, instead she puts it aside, squints at me, then perches on the bed.

'Ever hear of Betsy Blake?' I ask her.

She squints again. The name didn't immediately register with her.

'Girl that went missing seventeen years ago, was taken outside her home?'

'Oh yeah,' Elaine says. 'South Circular Road. I was too young to remember at the time, but I've heard about it since.'

'My daughter,' I say. Her mouth opens a little, then she places her hand on top of mine again.

'Oh I'm so sorry, Gordon.'

'It's okay, Elaine... you didn't take her.' I sit more upright in the bed again. 'It's just, the thought of dying without ever finding out what happened to her is... It's...' I pinch my thumb and forefinger into the corner of my eye sockets.

'Gordon... we'll get you through this,' Elaine says, rubbing her fingers across the top of my hand. 'I thought... I thought...' she hesitates. 'I thought they concluded Betsy's investigation... wasn't she supposed to have been found to have been knocked down... they found a car or something with her DNA in?'

'That was all baloney,' I say, removing my fingers from my eyes. 'That was the cops trying to close off a case many years later because it was costing them too much money, costing them too much time. They've always been embarrassed by the fact they never found out who took Betsy... So they made that shit up.'

Elaine's brow creases.

'Are you serious?' she asks.

'Dead serious.' Then I breathe out a long, drawn out sigh. I haven't opened up about Betsy in years.

'I had no idea,' Elaine says, still rubbing at my hand. 'Listen. I have to go downstairs to Mr Douglas' office for a consultation about your surgeries. I'll be half-an-hour, forty minutes at most. When I'm back, I'll pop in to you. You can tell me what you want... we can keep quiet... we can watch more TV; whatever it is you would like to do.'

She's so lovely. Very genuine. Very natural. I wonder if Betsy would have grown up to be just as impressive.

'She'd be only five years younger than you are now, y'know?'

'Really?' Elaine says as she scribbles a note on the clipboard. 'I'm so sorry for your loss, Gordon. I don't know what to say. Y'know I thought about you and your whole family a number of times over the years... I guess most people have. Everybody's hearts went out to you.'

I smile my eyes at her and then wave my hand.

'Go on, go to your meeting and... yes please, drop in when you're done. I'd love the company.'

She takes a step towards me, rubs at my hand again, and then pinches each of the tabs off my chest.

'You just relax for the next half-an-hour, Gordon. Put the back of your head on that pillow and close those eyes.'

As soon as the door's closed, I do exactly as Elaine suggested. Closing my eyes relieves some of the throbbing in my temples. I breathe in and out really slowly, allow the whole mess my life has turned into to float away from my mind. Rather than thinking about my surgeries and rather than thinking about Betsy, I reminisce... I go back over my life. I remember when I was the age Betsy was when she went missing; my first day at school was fun, adventurous. I remember the holidays my mam and dad used to take me on to Blackpool; the donkey rides on the beach, the rollercoasters on Pleasure Beach, the pinging sounds of the arcades. I remember my first girlfriend; Linda Tillesly – she was so pretty. I was thirteen when we shared our first kiss; round the back of Goldenbridge School. Neither me nor Linda had a clue what we were doing, we both just went with it until it felt right. I allow myself my first genuine heartfelt smile of the day; then the ward door opens, taking me out of my daydream.

'Jaysus, Gordy; ye certainly look as if yer dyin' anyway.'

I open my eyes, notice the waistband of his trousers pulled up over his belly button and then mouth the word 'bollocks' to myself.

FOURTEEN YEARS AGO

Betsy

'Do you think I should do it, Bozy?'

I always make up what Bozy says to me and say it back to myself in a silly voice, but this time I can't think of what he would say. I'm scared. My hands are shaking. A bit like when Jim Hawkins is hiding in the boat in *Treasure Island*. That's a book Dod bought me a few months ago. I've read it three times now. It's really good. Probably my new favourite.

I stare up the steps. Maybe I shouldn't do it. It could hurt. A lot. My breathing gets bigger. And quicker. Then I take one big, big breath in and hold it. I look at Bozy. Then I let the breath out.

'Fuck it, Bozy. I'm going to do it.'

I walk up the steps. Slowly. Really, really slowly. I stop at the top, then look at Bozy again. But he still doesn't know what to say to me. I give him a big squeeze and a kiss. 'I love you, Bozy. You have been my best friend.'

Then I place him down on the top step and close my hand tight. I knock at the door. Sometimes I have to knock a few times. Sometimes Dod doesn't answer at all. He might not answer now. He has been angry Dod for a long time. He's always shouting. He hasn't smiled for ages. Sometimes I wonder what makes him sad. Maybe he is sad for the same reason I get sad. Maybe he doesn't have a mummy and a daddy either. Maybe they're in heaven too.

No answer. Not yet. I close my hand. Knock again. Then I hear him. His footsteps getting close.

'Need to do a poo.' I say it from behind the door. I hear him make that breath sound that he makes when he is being angry Dod. This is probably the wrong time to do this. But I am doing it because he always seems to be angry Dod these days. He hasn't let me out to wash in a long, long time. Hasn't bought me any books in lots of weeks. Maybe months. He just comes into my room two times a day and leaves some food and water. Sometimes he doesn't say anything. Then he leaves. The only other times I see him is when I need to do a pee or a poo.

He unlocks the door and doesn't say anything. He just pulls it open and I put my hands up to my eyes stop the bright light from hurting them. I always do this. He sometimes says something like 'hurry up' or 'don't be long' but he says nothing today. I walk down the wooden floor and then turn in to the toilet room and close the door behind me. The door has a small lock on it. Dod told me to never go near it. But I do. I slide it really slowly so that he can't hear it. When I turn around a tear drops from my eye. I wipe it with my hand even though there is toilet paper in front of me. I sit up on top of the toilet with the lid shut. I remember what Dod said to me the very first time I was ever in this room. I keep hearing him saying it. Like I'm hearing it in my head.

If you make any noise up here at all, I won't just hurt you. I will kill you.

I know what 'kill you' means. It means I will be dead.

I hold in another big breath and then I just do it. I scream. Really loud. Really, really loud. I don't stop. I stand up on top of the toilet seat and just scream. I hear Dod at the door, banging away at it. But I don't stop screaming.

'Shut the fuck up. Betsy, I swear to you I'm gonna fuckin rip you to pieces when I get in there.'

I stop. Rip me to pieces? Probably he's not going to kill me. I want to die. I want to go to heaven. I want to see Mummy and Daddy. Probably he's just going to hurt me. I sit back down. My body begins to shake. My legs shake. My arms shake. I am so scared. The door is banging. Really loud. So is my chest. Dod isn't saying anything. He is just banging on the door. I think it is with his foot. Then there's a big hole in the door. Dod puts his face in the hole. I can see his eyes and his nose.

'I'm gonna fuckin hurt you, Betsy.'

Then his arm comes through the hole and his hand goes to the lock and he slides it back.

When the door opens, he stands there. His face is all red. His hands are closed tight.

'You little fuckin bitch. You better hope nobody heard all that.'

Then he grabs me.

12:15

Lenny

'ANSWER YOUR FUCKING PHONE!' LENNY SCREAMS INTO HIS mobile. The taxi man eyeballs him in the rear-view mirror. Lenny notices; holds his hand up in apology.

'Excuse my language. Some bastards just slashed all four tyres of my car.'

'Jaysus, yer jokin',' says the taxi man. 'Why'd anyone do that?'

Lenny sighs.

'Long story.'

The taxi man opens his mouth to ask more questions, but manages to bite his tongue. Instead, he just stares at Lenny through the mirror, noticing the passenger's irritation pour from every nuance of his body language; the constant blinking, the scratching at the back of his neck, the sharp breathing. He wants to advise him to call the cops but is beginning to think Lenny might be caught up in something he doesn't want to get involved in, so he remains mute. He doesn't have far to drive, another few minutes and he'll be dropping this drenched passenger off at the entrance to Tallaght Hospital.

Lenny presses buttons on his phone again, brings it to his ear. He can sense the tone ringing in sync with the throbbing in his head.

Still no answer.

He doesn't overreact this time. He just brings the butt of his phone back to his mouth and begins to chew.

'Fuckin Jesus bleedin Christ,' he mumbles to himself.

The taxi man flicks his eyes back up to the rear-view mirror, doesn't say anything.

Lenny fumbles with his phone again. He doesn't like sending text messages – they take him too long to type out – but he feels he's been left with no choice. His phone is so dated that he has to punch a couple of times at each number to produce even one letter of text. After a couple of minutes he's done.

Answer your phone. Please.

He wanted to add an exclamation mark after 'please' but didn't know how to. He's also wary of Gordon's delicate situation and doesn't feel as if it's fair to vent his frustrations at him specifically.

'Ye want the A&E or will I drop you at the main reception?'

Lenny looks up, realises they're already inside the hospital grounds.

'Main reception.'

Lenny stares at the meter. That's another twelve euro spent. He hands over a tenner and a fiver; waits for his change.

The rain has tempered somewhat, it's just lightly spitting now, but Lenny is still kicking up puddles as he races across the zebra crossing. He allows his breathing to slow down once he's inside and then rolls his eyes back into his head. He's trying to think through how he should play this with

Gordon. Should he go in all guns blazing, demanding that he is paid his expenses so far? Should he be angry at Gordon for getting him in this mess in the first place? Or should he forget his misfortune, start talking about his fortunes instead? After all, Lenny found out for definite that Betsy wasn't in Barry Ward's house. Surely that was enough for them to trigger their agreement; that Gordon's home would be left to Lenny in his will should he not make it through his surgeries. By the time he's reached St Bernard's Ward, his mind is made up. He needs to be fair to Gordon, fair but firm.

'Sir,' a female voice calls out, just as Lenny reaches a hand to push at Gordon's door.

He spins around to be met by the pretty nurse – the same pretty nurse who showed him to Gordon's room earlier this morning.

He smiles at her, waiting on her to explain why she called out to him.

'Are you visiting Mr Blake again?'

Lenny nods his head, then mutters a 'huh-huh'.

'Would you mind if I gave you a small note?'

Lenny squints, takes a step towards the young woman.

'It's just – as you likely know – Mr Blake's situation is very delicate. He would largely benefit from relaxing ahead of his surgeries. Any... any sort of rise in heart rate this morning could prove fatal to him later.'

'I'm not here to cause Gordon any stress,' Lenny says. 'Just here to support him.'

Elaine smiles.

'Good... it's just that—' Elaine stops talking; Lenny has already turned away from her, is entering Gordon's ward. Gordon is sitting up in the bed, almost as if he had anticipated Lenny's arrival.

'Gordon, Jesus Christ, I know you're not having the best

day of it yourself, but those fuckin savages just slashed every tyre in my car. I've had to get a taxi here to see you.'

Gordon holds a finger to his lips.

'Who?' he then asks, raising his voice.

'Fuckin' Keating and that Barry Ward fella.'

Gordon stares at Lenny, can see the confusion stretching across his brow.

'Well, at least I think it was them. Can't have been anyone else surely. Listen...' Lenny says, then pauses as he whips off his hat and puffer jacket before sitting back down on the blue plastic chair. 'You're gonna have to pay me some expenses. I've already paid out thirty-two quid on taxis and... Gordon, I just don't have the money to be splashing out left, right and centre. Unless...' Lenny pauses again, stares up at Gordon, his eyes tense. 'Unless... you said if I found out something brand new for you today that you would leave me your house in your will.'

Gordon nods his forehead forward once.

'Well... I confirmed for you that your Betsy isn't in Barry Ward's home. He isn't holding her captive.'

'That's not really new to me,' Gordon says as he reaches for a book on his bedside cabinet. Then he clicks at a pen and continues talking as he scribbles on a blank page.

'Keating and Ward are just two gangsters who happened to be in my life when Betsy went missing, so it was always obvious that they would be suspects. After all, I didn't hang around or know anybody capable of crimes... but they're not so bad, Keating and Ward. Not really. I never really believed they had taken my Betsy.' Gordon continues to scribble away as he talks. Lenny pivots his head, so he can try to make out what Gordon is writing.

Keating's hiding in my toilet cubicle.

Lenny turns back, stares at the bathroom door.

'Keating may be interested in controlling street affairs and drug distribution in Dublin but he's harmless really when it comes to hurting people. I don't think he's capable of hurting a four-year-old girl. I really don't...'

I was getting your calls and your text messages, but didn't want to answer while he was here. I knew Betsy wasn't in Barry's because I've been in Barry's house before. I broke in. A couple of times. Went looking for any trace of Betsy, but there was none.

'...I just wanted you to rule them out once and for all. Given what you've told me, that they welcomed you into Barry's home to help you with the investigation, I am content that they haven't had anything to do with Betsy's disappearance.'

Lenny keeps twisting his head from Gordon's scribbles, to the door handle of the toilet cubicle. He's not even listening to a word Gordon is saying, he knows he doesn't have to; that Gordon is just talking for the sake of appeasing a listening Keating.

'...What else was I supposed to do, just lie here and die? I hired you to...'

If you clear Jake Dewey, I will leave you the house. I promise.

'...look again at the suspicious people who were around me, around my family at the time of Betsy's disappearance. I'm sorry you have had to pay out some expenses but I can't afford to pay you any more. I don't really have much more money.'

Gordon underlines – with emphasis – the last line he wrote. Then he looks up at Lenny, meets his eyes and winks.

'I promise,' he whispers really softly.

Lenny's eyes almost water. He genuinely believes Gordon. As Lenny is imagining his twins running around a much bigger home, Gordon twists in the bed and removes an envelope from under his pillow.

'I think it's probably best if we call an end to the job, Lenny, but I am very grateful for your time. I need to relax ahead of my surgeries and the nurse is getting all antsy because my heart rate's been high since I hired you...'

As Gordon continues to talk, he removes a letter from the envelope, pivots it so that Lenny can read it.

This is the will and testament of Gordon James Blake.

I hereby wish to leave the home, addressed 166 South Circular Road, Inchicore, Dublin 8, Ireland to Leonard Moon.

Signature 1
Signature 2
Signature 3

Lenny eyeballs Gordon again, then blinks rapidly.

'My signature plus two witnesses,' Gordon whispers. 'I promise that I will have two nurses sign this here today and then I'm gonna leave this will there.' He nods at his bedside cabinet.

Lenny stands up, places his hand on top of Gordon's and then gives an affirmative nod.

'I am so sorry I couldn't do much more for you, Mr Blake. I'll get going back to my office. I wish you all the very best with your surgeries this afternoon. I'll be thinking of you.'

Then he bends down close to Gordon's ear.

'Jake Dewey's address?' he whispers.

'I'll text it to you,' Gordon whispers back.

'Goodbye, Mr Blake.'

Lenny never could act. He can't even lie. And you have to be able to lie convincingly to be an actor.

Although Gordon seemed to cringe a little at Lenny's acting attempts, they both feel as if they did a good enough job. Lenny picks up his yellow jacket and hat, then strolls out of the ward and heads straight towards the lift. After the lift doors close, Lenny produces a little dance – the type of dance a fourteen-year-old girl would do if the boy she'd had a crush on for months text her to ask her out on a date. He believes Gordon, genuinely believes that if he can eliminate Jake Dewey from having any involvement in the Betsy Blake disappearance then he truly will be left a million euro house.

'Who else is he gonna leave it to?' he says to himself in the mirror of the lift after finishing his dance. When the lift doors ping open, he heads straight to the shop next to reception.

'It says ATM on the window?' he says to the young girl behind the counter.

She doesn't answer verbally, she just points. Lenny paces down the back of the shop, takes his debit card from his wallet and places it in the machine. He then taps in his pin number and selects 'View Balance'.

€1,166.

The grand Gordon transferred into his account this morning would keep the Moon's heads above water this month; but in a more pressing way, it would allow Lenny to take taxis for the rest of the day, would help him get to Jake Dewey's home, help him eliminate him from Betsy's disappearance and – ultimately – help Lenny come into possession of a million euro gaff.

Lenny removes the three twenty euro notes at the same

time his phone pings. He checks the screen. A text message from Gordon Blake's number.

Jake's address: 49 Woodville Road, Terenure, D 6.

Lenny smiles to himself. Then tucks the notes and his phone inside his jeans pocket and heads straight towards the rain.

FOURTEEN YEARS AGO

Betsy

I ROLL BACK OVER IN MY BED. ONTO THE OTHER SIDE. I'M trying to make my back feel better. But nothing is working. I stare at the floor. The pages of my books are all ripped. Every time I look at it, it makes my belly sore. It means every part of me is sore. My head, my face, my belly, my back, my legs.

I see the cover of my book *Fantastic Mr Fox*. It's silver. Shiny bright silver. I can see my face in the cover. I saw it for the first time a few months ago. It was scary a bit. But now I like seeing my face in the cover. I'm pretty. I think. I have brown hair and brown eyes. And a little nose. A really small nose. I crawl really slowly out of the bed and try to grab at the book but it's too far away. So I crawl a bit more. My back is really hurting me doing the crawling. But I get the book and then crawl back to the bed. I pull the sheets across me again. Then I look at the book cover. I twist it until I can see my face. I don't look pretty anymore. My whole face is red. There is a really dark red ball at the side of my eye. I cry again. But even crying is making my back hurt.

I shouldn't have done that. I shouldn't have screamed. I was silly. I look at Bozy lying on my pillow. I am so glad Dod didn't rip him up. Just the books. But I'm still really sad. Really, really sad. Sad like the first night I came to this room when I was only four years old. I know Dod is angry Dod and has been angry Dod for a long time. But I think I have been angry and bad too. Bad Betsy. Dod told me to be quiet when I am up the steps. I should do what he says all the time.

Then I hear the door opening. I throw the sheets over my head.

'No. No. No. Not again.' I say it really quietly. So just me and Bozy can hear.

'Betsy.'

Dod says my name nicely. Like he's not angry Dod anymore.

I take the sheet down from my face a little bit and see him standing by my bed. His face isn't as red anymore. His hands aren't closed as if he is going to hit me again.

'Why did you do that, sweetheart?'

He only calls me sweetheart when he is being good Dod. Maybe he is good Dod again. Good Dod hasn't been here in a long time.

'Why did I scream?'

Dod nods his head. I look at Bozy and then back at Dod. I don't know if I should tell him the real truth. But maybe I should be telling the truth all the time. Maybe I won't get hurt if I tell the truth all the time. I wipe my eyes and then look up at Dod.

'I wanted to go to heaven.'

Dod's eyes get bigger. I think he is going to hit me again. But he just sits down. He puts his back against my wall and then puts his hands on his face. I think he is crying. I look at Bozy. Then back at Dod. Dod's shoulders are going up and down. I take my sheets away and put one foot out of the bed. Then I put the other foot out of bed even though it really hurts my back. I take one step to be beside Dod and then put my arms around his shoulders to stop them going up and down. It's like a hug. He *is* crying. I can hear him now. His cry is getting louder.

'Don't be sad, Dod.'

He grabs me. Puts his arms around me and we hug really tight. Really, really tight and for a long time. The hugging is hurting my back a lot. But I feel a bit happier. I am less scared.

'I am sorry.'

Dod takes his arms away from around me and then he wipes his face with his two hands. He looks at me. There are more tears in his eyes. But they are not coming out.

'No. I'm sorry.'

He grabs me for another hug. Another really tight hug. It hurts. But I don't say anything. I just hug him back.

'I will never, never do anything like that to you again.' He says it really quietly into my ear. 'I love you.'

'I love you, Dod.'

I think I do. I read about love in my books. You love people who are your family and your friends and your wife and your husband. I don't think Dod is any of those things to me. But I must love him. Because him and Bozy are the only people I know. Bozy is not even a person. But I definitely know I love Bozy.

'I'm gonna buy all those books again. And more new ones. I promise.' Dod is on his knees now. Staring at my face. 'And you just need to promise that you will never do anything like that again. The neighbours could have heard you. It's very dangerous.'

I've been really bad Betsy. Screaming was very dangerous. Very stupid.

'I promise. I won't make any noises again, Dod.'

He blows out through his mouth. His lips shake as he does it. It makes a silly noise. Like a fart.

'Look at your eye.' He rubs his thumb against my face. Up and down slowly.

'Where hurts you the most?'

I turn away from him. Then I pick up the back of my T-shirt as far as I can. He helps by pulling it up a bit more. Then he sucks in a really big breath through his teeth.

12:35

Gordon

'You can come out now, Keating.'

The door handle of the toilet cubicle clicks and his fat belly makes its way back to the ward first, followed by the rest of him; his sleazy fuckin grin stretched wide across his face. He wears that grin when he feels he needs to. He was wearing it the very first day I met him.

Our business was doing well. Guus and I had grown it into something really special; turning over a couple a million a year. It didn't start out that way. When I first began as a freelance accountant, I was only really interested in making enough money to get a roof over my head. After I'd left University, I started to work for a big accountancy firm – Fullams. Three years later I realised for certain that working for somebody else wasn't for me. So, using just eight loyal clients, I set up on my own. After a couple of years of continued growth, I decided I needed a partner. Guus was the first person I'd thought of, in fact I'd thought of him as a business partner long before I even realised I actually needed a business partner. We'd worked together at Fullams, sparked up not only a great friendship but a perfect working relationship too. His strengths paper over my weaknesses and my strengths paper over his. With my attention to detail on the numbers combined with Guus's ability to sell our vision to new clients, we were the perfect cocktail. And we thrived. The zeros in our business accounts stretched month on month as soon as we partnered up. But of course, I got greedy. When Alan Keating arranged a meeting with me one Friday afternoon about twenty years ago, I was fascinated by his plan. He was turning over a few mill a year – and we'd get ten per cent if we were willing to cook his books for him. It felt like a no-brainer at the time; easy money. But I was being cocky; I was being a fuckin idiot. Had I not seen the dollar signs in front of my eyeballs and accepted Keating's proposal that day I'm pretty certain that not only would I still be running my business, but I'd also still have my daughter, still have my wife. Still have my life. This fucker grinning in front of me right now ruined me.

'So you've called off little Lenny Moon, yeah?'

I just nod, still unsure how or even why I'm letting this prick talk to me again.

He opened the door to my ward about twenty minutes ago, began to tell me that he was the one person who could fulfil my dying wish. Then we heard Elaine outside talking to Lenny. Keating said I shouldn't mention that he's here, to just get rid of Lenny and that he'd oversee the investigation for me. He hid in the toilet cubicle. I didn't know what to do, what to say. I still don't.

'As I was saying, Gordy, I did my own investigation at the time; it didn't pull up anything. But let me have another dig around for you today. Who d'ye think's more likely to get you answers in what could be your final few hours: Alan Keating or little Lenny Moon? He's not even an investigator, he's a fucking insurance pussy. He rats out people who are making scam insurance claims. He has no chance of finding answers for you about Betsy.'

I nod my head, melt my face into a soft look. I felt, for years, that this cunt was responsible for Betsy's disappearance, yet I've never been able to join up all the dots.

'I know you've always suspected me and Barry, but – trust me, Gordy – we had nothin' to do with Betsy goin' missin'. And I know you know that deep down. You've always known it.'

I shift in my bed a little. It's funny that he thinks I'd trust him to find answers for me. I wouldn't trust him with a bucket of water if my balls were on fire. I suck in a breath through my nostrils, but remain silent. I just tilt my head to look at him, wait for him to talk.

'I'll get on to the cops; I have a few of them in my pocket. I'll get all of the information they have on the investigation into Betsy's disappearance and I'll act on it for you, how about that?'

I shift again in the bed. I really don't want to give this prick the satisfaction of my forgiveness. But what else can I do? I may be dead in a few hours time. The more people out there looking for my Betsy, the better, even if I do get a huge sense that he's bullshitting. I know Keating definitely has some cops on his payroll, but not high-ranking detectives; not cops who'll give him classified information about a seventeen-year-old case.

'But sure the cops think she's dead,' I say, finally speaking up.

'You know as well as I do that that was just a theory because they couldn't close off the investigation, right?'

He looks up at me with puppy dog eyes, as if him going all coy will bridge my forgiveness. He can do that, can Alan Keating; transform from looking like Ireland's most notorious gangster into looking like a cute old granddad. He has the most persuasive forms of seduction; the fucker can get anybody on his side. It's why I was intrigued by his business proposition twenty years ago. But I don't trust the fucker. I wonder what he's after. Alan Keating doesn't do anything unless there's something in it for himself.

'Why would you do this for me… after all the years I've insisted you had something to do with Betsy's disappearance?' I ask him.

'I've always felt sorry for you, Gordy. For you and Michelle. I helped at the time, had my men look for Betsy. And I would've offered to help a lot more over the years only you went really cold on me. You made some outrageous claims to the cops about our dealings; almost got me into a lot of trouble.'

I shift again in the bed. I can't get comfortable, not with this gurning prick in my room. But he's right. I did rat him out; revealed all about his money funnels to Ray De Brun. I'm still not quite sure why it didn't go much further. Keating covers his tracks too well, I guess. The small businesses he had set up under different names to filter his money through saved his bacon. That and the fact that I refused to become a witness for the state. I didn't care about Keating's money laundering then; the only thing that consumed my mind was finding Betsy.

'Yeah… well I'm sorry about that, Keating, but y'know, I still don't know who took Betsy and you were the only person at the time who had a problem with me… So I went on auto pilot, told the cops everything. I'd have done anything to find my daughter… still would.'

He places his hand on mine, much like Elaine did about half an hour ago.

'I understand why you told the cops everything and I understand why you initially suspected me and Barry. But c'mon… still suspecting us today and having your little PI hang around our homes is crazy, Gordy. You need to believe me; I had nothing to do with Betsy going missing. I'm not that kinda gangster. You know that.'

He sits back down, his puppy dog eyes still on show. I don't get why he's being so nice to me. The fucker has always had intrigue pouring out of him.

'Listen, our slate is clean. Let me help you investigate. What've you got to lose?'

I stare up at the stained ceiling of the ward, my mind racing in a million different directions.

'You don't do anything for nothing,' I say.

His silence makes me turn to face him again. Then he shakes his head, removing the puppy-dog eyes; transforming from the cute old granddad back into the grinning gangster.

'Just put the same offer you made to Lenny Moon on the table for me.'

I laugh. Should've known.

'Ah, so you got out of Lenny just what I was offering him. You want my house.'

'It's a grand oul house,' Keating says. He sucks his teeth as he says it too.

Then he takes a step towards me again. He doesn't place his hand on top of mine this time. Instead he reaches for the pen on the bedside cabinet and then holds it towards me.

'Rewrite your will, make me the benefactor of that house.'

FOURTEEN YEARS AGO

Betsy

'It's nice that, isn't it?'

I don't answer by talking. My mouth is too full. So I just rub my belly and smile at Dod. He smiles back at me.

'I've more up in the kitchen. Think I'll have one myself later.'

Dod's sitting on the edge of my bed while I sit on my new chair. I love it. It's all squishy and comfortable to sit in. I do a lot of my reading in this now, not in my bed like I used to. Though my bed is more comfortable than it's ever been. Dod bought me loads of new things – a chair, a bed, shelves for all my books, lots of new books including loads of my favourites that he ripped up during that really angry night, magazines, colouring books, wallpaper. I forgot what wallpaper even was. When Dod put it up in my room I remembered I had some back in my Mummy and Daddy's house. I had pink wallpaper then with my name Betsy written across it in white.

I tried not to feel bad when I thought about my old bedroom back at Mummy and Daddy's house because Dod was being so nice to me and trying to make my bedroom all nice and fresh. The wallpaper he put up in here is yellow. Bright yellow. Yellow isn't my favourite colour, but I still like it. Even though Dod has put loads of new things in my room, the room looks bigger. I have sixty-one books now. Amazing. My new favourite books are called *Chronicles of Narnia*. It's seven different books all in a little box that Dod bought me.

He has been really nice ever since the angry night. I think that when I said I wanted to go to heaven that Dod felt really sad. That's why he made my room more bright and beautiful and why he bought me loads of things. He buys me new things every day now. Today I got an ice cream. I'd never heard of an ice cream before, but it is delicious. It said on the wrapper that it was called Orange Split. I lick at the little stick, taking all of the cream off and then breathe. I think I ate all the ice cream without breathing.

'Jaysus, ye milled all that.'

'Milled?'

'Yeah… like you ate it really fast, really quickly.'

'Oh.'

I grab at my notebook and pen and write down the word 'milled' and then beside it write 'to eat something really fast'.

I do this all the time if I am reading and don't know a word. I'll try to work it out for myself and if I can't I'll ask Dod when he pays me a visit. I love learning new words.

'Can you get me another notebook, Dod, please?'

'Ye running out of room on that one already?'

I flick through my notebook.

'Not yet… but I want this one to be for new words but in a new notebook I would like to write my own story.'

'A story? What's your story going to be about?'

I look up at my ceiling. Even though the stone walls are now covered with wallpaper and my stone floor is mostly covered with an orange rug, the ceiling is still stone. It's still cold.

'I might write it about you.'

'Bout me?'

'Yes. I think I might call it Dod's Adventures.' He smiles a little bit at me. 'It would be about what you do when you are not in my room. What you do when you are up there.'

I just point up the steps, I don't look up them. Dod hasn't been angry Dod in ages – not since the really angry night – but I still don't want to make him turn into angry Dod, so I don't look up the steps.

Dod laughs a little bit.

'And what do you think I get up to up there?'

I stare up at the cold ceiling again. I don't want to mention my Mummy and Daddy because I know that is how good Dod can turn into angry Dod.

'Eh… I remember from before I came here that there was a thing called television. I used to watch a show called *Thomas the Tank Engine*. It was about trains. I think you probably watch television when you are not here with me.'

I close my eyes a bit because I'm not sure if talking about what happened before I came here will turn him into angry Dod. He moves off the bed and comes near me. He gets down on his knees right beside me.

'And what do you think I watch on the television?'

I can smell his breath. It's the same all the time. It smells warm. Every time I smell it, it reminds me of the day he stole me away from Daddy.

I open my eyes and look at him. He is smiling. That is good.

'Do you watch *Thomas the Tank Engine?*'

He laughs. Then he shakes his head.

'I eh… don't know. How many things are on television?'

'Too many things.'

I laugh this time.

'I don't know, Betsy… I watch the news.'

'The news?'

'Yeah – it's a television programme where somebody reads out what happened around the world every day.'

'Wow.'

That sounds really good. Really, really good. I would love to watch the news. But I don't say anything else to Dod. I can't ask if I can go up there anymore. He's afraid I will scream again even though I never would. My back hurt for so many weeks after that last time. I still don't think my back is as good as it used to be. I read in a book once that somebody broke their bones. I think I might have broke a bone in my back. But Dod doesn't let me see doctors or let doctors see me. Dod doesn't let me see anyone. See anything.

'You were on the news lots of times.'

I look at Dod.

'Me?'

'Yeah – lots of times. For lots of years.'

Dod stands up, puts his hand on my head and messes my hair like he does sometimes. Then he walks back up the steps.

'I'm gonna go get me one of those Orange Splits.'

I turn around and watch as he goes up the steps and closes the door. Then I get out of my chair and crawl under my bed sheets to find my best friend.

'Did you hear that, Bozy. We were on the television lots of times.'

12:40

Lenny

LENNY ASKED THE TAXI MAN TO TURN THE RADIO OFF AS soon as he got in the back seat. He needed all the headspace he has to think through his morning and is a typical man when it comes to multitasking; if Lenny needs to think, he needs to do so in silence. Right now, the only thing playing in his head is the vision of the will Gordon showed him when he was back at the hospital twenty minutes ago.

He stares at his phone.

'I'm buyin' a fuckin good phone from that grand,' he mumbles, before eyeballing the rear-view mirror to see if the taxi man heard him.

'Sorry?' the taxi man says.

'Ah nothing. Just this piece of shit phone. I need one of those with some internet on it. All it's good for is making and taking calls.'

Lenny blinks rapidly, then his eyes widen. He clicks into his call history, sees the name 'home' and taps at it.

'Hello.'

'Sweetie, I need you to do me another favour,' he says.

'Go on.' There was no sigh this time. Sally must be having a really good day.

'Can you eh… can you check on Google what the requirement is for a will in Ireland?'

'A will?'

'Yeah – as in a will somebody leaves behind when they die.'

The line goes silent for a few seconds.

'You planning on dying on me, Lenny?'

There's a small hint of humour in Sally's response; on any other day hearing his wife crack a tiny joke would overjoy Lenny, but he's too distracted today.

'Course not. Just a client of mine was asking and my phone is a piece of shit. I can't get the information I need.'

'Okay… lemme see,' Sally says. Lenny can hear her tap away at the keyboard of their home computer. He eyeballs the rear-view mirror again, wonders what the poor taxi man must be thinking.

'Jaysus, I'm just getting pictures of men called Will,' Sally says.

Lenny fake laughs awkwardly, then rolls his eyes.

'Ye know what, Sally, I have to get myself a good smart phone, I get caught out too many times when I need to find certain information.'

Lenny winces a little as he says this, his shoulders slumping in anticipation of his wife's moan. But she doesn't say anything at all, almost as if she didn't hear what he'd just said.

'Ah… hold on a second,' she says. 'Got it… ye ready?'

'Uh-huh.'

'For your will to be valid in Ireland it needs to be handwritten and signed by you yourself, plus two witnesses.'

'Okay… and?'

'And that's it… that's all it says.'

'Really?'

'Well... it says that the witnesses must witness you signing it and that's it.'

Lenny blows out his lips, allows himself a little smile. Gordon was right. The will he has written up in hospital would be valid.

He slows his breathing, doesn't want to get over-excited, certainly not on the phone; he doesn't want to disclose anything to Sally. Not yet anyway. If she got carried away by the hope of getting that house, she would crash hard if it didn't come to fruition. And if she crashes hard, the unthinkable could happen. Lenny's tried to rid their home of items Sally could use to kill herself, but it's impossible for a home not to have knifes, not to have belts.

'Okay, sweetie, thank you so much.'

'That it?'

'Yep, that'll do for now. I'm so sorry I've had to bother you a couple of times today to do things for me.'

'I don't mind,' Sally says. 'I like hearing your voice. But Lenny...'

'Yeah?'

'Y'are in your shite getting one of those expensive smart phones. We just don't have the money.'

Lenny rolls his eyes again, then blinks them rapidly.

'Okay, sweetie,' he says. 'I love you. Speak soon.'

Lenny brings his cheap phone to his mouth after he has hung up, begins to gnaw on the edge of the rubber case again.

'Fuckin hell,' he mumbles. 'A bleedin' massive gaff for a few hours work.'

He tries to stem his excitement by wondering if he's being played. Maybe this is all just one huge hoax. But he knows it's not. It can't be.

'Y'know... that's right. I only did my will there at the

beginning of this year,' says the taxi man. 'I turned sixty-six in February – felt it was about time I finally put it all down on paper. I just went into a solicitor, wrote it all down and had him and his assistant sign it.'

'It's that easy?'

'Yep… was surprised how easy it was meself. It doesn't even have to be signed by a solicitor… anyone can do it.'

Lenny's nose stiffens; his attempt at holding back the smile that's threatening to spread across his face. Then he throws his head back to rest on the top of the seat and allows himself the daydream of living in a much bigger home. He wonders if a bigger place would take Sally out of her depression; perhaps being cooped up in their tiny terraced house in Springfield plays its part in dampening her mood. Or maybe he could sell the house, pocket the million so he doesn't have to work. He lets the smile spread across his face and it remains that way until the satnav calls out to him; informing him he has arrived at his destination.

He sits upright, takes in the house they have pulled up outside. A bright yellow door, hanging baskets of flowers either side of it, the latest BMW 3 Series in the driveway. Michelle must've married well the second time round.

'Nine euro, mate,' the taxi man says.

Lenny continues to stare at the big house as he hands a ten euro note over the shoulder of the driver. As usual, he waits for the change before getting out of the car and strolling up the driveway.

He hasn't yet decided how he's going to approach this. The will occupied way too much of his thinking on the way over here. But the will is redundant should Lenny not get any original information out of Jake Dewey. He already assumes Jake has had nothing to do with Betsy's disappearance, much like he felt that Keating and Barry didn't have anything to do with it either. But maybe if he can get confirmation of that, it might be enough for Gordon to trigger their agreement.

As the taxi man pulls away, Lenny bides himself some thinking time by checking out the BMW. Maybe he could afford a car like this if he sells the million euro gaff. He nods, impressed by the cream leather interior. Just as he places both of his palms either side of his face to get closer to the driver's window, a voice calls out.

'Excuse me,' she says.

Lenny, startled, places both of his hands towards the woman in apology. He instantly recognises her. Whereas Gordon looked different to the man who appeared at press conferences and in newspapers following Betsy's disappearance, Michelle has barely changed. There are a few more lines round her eyes, but there's no mistaking who she is.

'I'm so sorry,' he says. 'But I'm looking to speak to Jake Dewey.'

'And did you think you were gonna find him in the car?'

Lenny shakes his head and smiles.

'Sorry – I'm just a big fan. Thinking of buying one for myself actually. Does Jake enjoy driving it yeah?'

'Jake's never driven it. That's my car.'

Lenny's mouth makes an 'O' shape, then he slightly gurns with embarrassment.

'It's Michelle, isn't it? Michelle Blake?'

Michelle's stare turns inquisitive.

'Dewey. I haven't been called Blake for fifteen years.'

'I'm so sorry… of course. Dewey. Mrs Dewey.'

'Ye know, I've been talking to you for one whole minute and you've apologised to me three times already… whaddya want?'

'I'm sorry eh…' Lenny scratches at his forehead, blinks

rapidly. 'I need to speak with Jake as a matter of urgency. Would it be okay if I came inside?'

Michelle tilts her chin into her neck, then opens her eyes wide.

'Lookin' like that?'

Lenny stares down at himself, realises he looks like a drenched rat.

'I got caught in the rain and...' he shrugs his shoulders.

'Well, Jake's not in; he's away in Belfast working.'

Lenny squelches up his mouth, wants to swear; feels as if the possibility of him earning a million euro gaff may have just evaporated.

'Who'll I tell him was looking for him?' Michelle asks.

Lenny pauses, looks back down the garden path, then at Michelle again.

'I'm Lenny Moon – Private Investigator.'

Michelle takes three steps closer to him, folds her arms.

'Oh yeah – what are ye investigating? How to piss people off by staring into their cars?'

Lenny huffs out a small laugh, rubs his hands together back and forth as he blinks his eyes.

'I'm eh... I'm eh...'

'Go on, spit it out,' Michelle says, now resting both of her hands on her hips.

'I'm investigating the disappearance of your daughter.'

12:55

Gordon

HE STANDS UP TO WATCH OVER ME AS I SCRIBBLE ON ANOTHER torn page from my novel.

This is the will and testament of Gordon James Blake.

His big belly inches closer to me, almost resting on the edge of my bed. I feel nervous writing this, as if I'm back at school doing an exam. Don't know why I'm nervous; I stopped being intimidated by this asshole years ago.

I hereby wish to leave the home, addressed 166 South Circular Road, Inchicore, Dublin 8, Ireland to Alan Keating.

I draw three lines to fit the necessary signatures and then smile up at him.

'Good man, Gordy. I promise I will get you some information on Betsy's disappearance. Something that will give you peace of mind going into your surgeries.'

He scratches at his nose as he says this, a sure sign he's

lying. Then he removes his coat from the back of the chair he'd been sitting on and throws it on.

'So you'll just leave that there,' he says, pointing at my bedside cabinet, 'and if I do find you something original you'll activate that will, yeah?'

I nod my head.

'Sure thing, Keating.'

He takes a step closer to me again, his face turning back into the kind old granddad he can inhabit any time he wants to.

'I'm really sorry about everything that's happened to you, Gordy. Not just Betsy, but this... this situation you find yourself in today. You were always a good man; you haven't deserved any of the shite you've been served in life.'

I offer him another of my fake smiles and then mouth the word 'thanks'.

'I'll be back with you before three... and I'll have something. I promise I'll do my very best. And if I do have something for you, I'll look after that house, Gordy. I'll treasure it.'

He winks, strolls away from me and out of the ward. Before he's three steps down the corridor I pick up the will I had just written for him and rip it into tiny pieces, then toss it on the floor.

It was weird talking to that cunt again. I've blamed him for all that's gone wrong in my life. But I'm as certain as I've ever been that he had nothing to do with Betsy's disappearance. Though just because I can rule him and Barry out, it doesn't make me feel any better.

Not only did I lose Betsy in 2002, I lost my wife as well. I knew even before Betsy disappeared that I was losing Michelle anyway. I was aware she was having an affair. I didn't catch her or anything, I could just tell. Not only had we stopped having sex, but we'd stopped communicating with each other. She was beginning to 'work late' at the bank and basically showed me every sign I needed to see that she was fucking somebody behind my back. I didn't know who it was until months after Betsy went missing. Michelle had the audacity to stamp on my heart when my heart was already broken. She said she was falling out of love with me anyway, but the fact that I looked after Betsy so carelessly – to the extent that she went missing on my watch – ensured she didn't just no longer love me, but hated me.

That's what she said to me three months after Betsy went missing. She screamed it at me in the most explicit of terms. 'I fucking hate you, Gordon... properly hate you. I'll never forgive you for this.'

It's still never been made clear to me, because she never looked me in the eye and suggested such a thing, but I think deep inside me that she felt as if I had something to do with Betsy's disappearance initially, especially around the time the cops were questioning me. But she did stick up for me in some respects; she told the police I had always cared for Betsy, even if I was never likely to be named 'father of the year'. But soon after I was cleared as a suspect, Michelle broke the news that she was leaving.

I found out about a month later that she was seeing this Jake Dewey bloke. I needed to find out about him; wondered from very early on if he had something to do with Betsy going missing. Perhaps he snatched her so that me and Michelle would split up. I haven't found anything on the fucker, aside from the fact that he's a smug cunt. But I still haven't ruled him out, probably because I've got nothing else to go on. If Lenny can give me something... anything today that clears Dewey, then I will genuinely leave him my house. I've got no one else to leave it to.

'Hey,' she says, offering me a big smile.

'Hey yourself.' She sidles towards me, takes a seat. 'How did your meeting go?'

'All good. We have everything in place to be set up. You're going to be in great hands with Mr Douglas – he's the best heart surgeon in Ireland. Once you do your part – staying relaxed – we're very hopeful we can get you through all this.'

It's either the tone of her voice or the delivery of what she says that reminds me of a young Michelle. I'm not quite sure what it is. I just know that I feel comfortable in Elaine's company.

'So... eh...' she says, 'would you like to continue what we were talking about... or d'you want to talk about something else or just watch tele... whaddya think?'

She crosses her legs, gets as comfortable as anyone possibly can in those horrible plastic chairs.

'Sorry?' I say, scratching at my head. 'What was it we were talking about?'

'Betsy. You just informed me Betsy Blake was your daughter before I had to go.'

'Oh... I could talk about Betsy all day, every day.'

Elaine smiles again, but it's not a happy smile, more sorrowful than anything.

'Are you sure you want to talk about her today... if... y'know... if you're supposed to be staying calm, keeping relaxed?'

I sigh a little, scoot down in the bed a bit and let the back of my head sink into the pillow. So much has happened this morning that I can't get my head straight. I remember talking to Elaine now, just before she headed out for her meeting. She knew of Betsy, was totally shocked when I told her she was my daughter. I stare up at the stains on the ceiling.

'She was only four years old... would be twenty-one now,' I find myself saying. I hadn't even decided in my own head that I was going to continue talking about my daughter. 'I was supposed to be looking after her while Michelle – my wife at the time – went shopping for the afternoon. It's all my fault. All my fault.' I pinch my forefinger and thumb into my eyes. I feel Elaine reach out a hand and rest it on my knee. 'It wasn't the first time... I once left Betsy alone in the kitchen and didn't she split her head open, falling off a chair and onto the tiles. I loved her, still love every inch of her, but I wasn't a great dad. I was too easily distracted.'

'Gordon,' Elaine says, now standing up. 'You don't have to... not if you don't want to. We can talk this all through tomorrow if you want... after you recover from your surgeries.'

I take my fingers away from my eyes, open them. She's staring down at me, that sorrowful smile still etched on her pretty face.

'Why don't we turn on the tele, watch some crappy daytime TV, huh?' she says. 'It'll help you relax.'

I sit back up, dry my eyes by sweeping the palm of my hand across my face, then smile back at Elaine.

'Anything but *Loose Women*,' I say.

Elaine laughs as she reaches for the remote control. After a few clicks of a button, she stops on an old episode of *Top Gear*.

'I like this,' she says, 'my dad got me into cars.'

I look over at her, wonder how much more perfect her dad was to her than I was to Betsy. I bet Elaine's dad never left her alone while he was working, I bet he never left her alone in the kitchen to split her head open.

'Perfect,' I say.

I try to get as comfortable as I can in my bed, then watch Jeremy Clarkson make a tit of himself by interviewing an A-list celebrity. The guy's such a buffoon. Though the buffoon seems to be having a positive effect on me. It's either him or

Elaine's company. She's right, watching tele does allow me to escape from my own head. Suddenly I'm matching Elaine's little giggles. Never in my life did I think I'd ever laugh at something Jeremy fucking Clarkson said.

'That you?' Elaine says turning to me.

'Huh?'

'The buzzing.'

I look down to my lap. My phone's alight. I pick it up, the number ringing unfamiliar, then press at the green button.

'Hello.'

'Is this Gordon Blake?'

'Yes… who's this?'

'Gordon, I just heard your terrible news, it's me – Ray De Brun.'

ELEVEN YEARS AGO

Betsy

'DOUBLE FIGURES, HUH?'

Dod pushes his shoulder against mine as he says that and smiles at me.

I never thought of it like that. Double figures.

I suck in a big breath and then let it out as hard as I can. I miss just one of the candles. But Dod blows it out for me, then looks up at me and laughs. I laugh too. I love when it's my birthday.

Dod didn't just bring a cake down the steps with him, he brought three presents too. I really hope they're all books – every one of them. But I know one present looks too small to be a book.

'Go on then.'

I reach for the rectangular present first, rip the paper off it and bring it close to my eyes. It's a box-set of books: called Harry Potter. Six of them. Brilliant. I think I read the name Harry Potter in one of my magazines before. Didn't know who it was. But I will soon. I hug Dod really tight. Really, really tight.

'Supposed to be the best books ever written.'

'Really?'

'So they say.'

I stare at him. He looks just as excited and as happy as I am. I don't know why. It's my birthday, not his.

'Has Harry Potter been on the television as much as I have?'

Now he looks confused. He turns his head and stares at me as if he doesn't know what I'm saying.

'Remember you told me I was on the television a lot?' I say.

He still looks confused.

'You said that to me a few years ago. That I was on television lots of times.'

'Did I?'

It makes me sad that he's forgotten. It's one thing I will never forget. It has actually made me happy ever since Dod told me I was on television and now he's just forgotten all about it. I really like Dod. He buys me lots of things and makes my room really beautiful and bright. But sometimes he hurts my insides a little bit. I don't think he means it. Not in the way he used to hurt my outsides; like the time he dragged me down the steps by my hair because I screamed in the upsteps toilet, or the time he threw me against the wall. But my insides seem to hurt when he has forgotten something he's said to me or the way he doesn't let me talk about the memories I had before I came to this room. I wish he would let me talk about my memories because it helps me remember Mummy and Daddy and my old house. The memories seem to be getting smaller and smaller. That's why I talk to Bozy about them when I can. I talk to Bozy about my Mummy's smile and about playing football with my Daddy.

'Go on... open this.'

I take the present from him and rip the paper really

quickly. It's not more books. It's a box with a really bright yellow coloured blob on it.

'What is it?'

'It's a lava lamp.'

'A lava lamp?'

'Yeah – you can put it in the corner here.' He points over to the corner near the steps. 'It'll help brighten that area up and look...' He opens the box, takes out the lamp. 'The colours all change and go in different directions.'

Dod looks more happy about this lamp than I am.

'Ye don't like it huh?'

'I do. I do. Thank you, Dod.' I wrap my hands around him again for another hug.

'You wished it was more books, didn't you?'

I lean off him. I don't want to hurt his insides, but I remember that I should always tell the truth to Dod.

'I love books the most.'

He doesn't get angry. He hasn't been angry Dod for years now. I think angry Dod is gone forever. I hope he is.

'Well, I think you'll like this present more than books.'

He picks up the small present and hands it to me. I shake it and wonder if I can get any clues from how it sounds. But it doesn't make any noise. Not really.

Then I open it quickly. It's weird; black with loads of buttons on it.

'What is it?'

Dod smiles. It's a big smile.

'Come with me.'

I follow him up the steps. Even though he hasn't been angry Dod for years I still feel frightened when I'm up the steps with him, just in case I make a noise or something. When we are at the top he walks into the room I am not allowed to look into. I just wait outside and close my eyes.

'C'mon.'

'What?'

'Come in.'

I open my eyes.

'Come into that room?'

'Yep.'

I feel really frightened now. But I walk in only because Dod asked me to. It's beautiful. It has three really big brown chairs in it. One with room for three people and the other two have room for one person. There is carpet. I haven't seen carpet since Mummy and Daddy's house. And there are big white curtains. I feel like I'm going to cry. I'm not sure if I'm excited or frightened. Dod kneels down beside me, holds up my hand that's gripping the strange present I just opened.

'Here... press this red button at the top.'

I do press it and then the big black box in front of me shines a big light... it's a television. Dod's television. I see the first person I have seen that isn't Dod in six years. She is beautiful. All smiley with blonde hair. Tears come out of both of my eyes.

'Told you you'd love it.'

Dod grabs me and holds me really tight to him.

'One hour every day I'm going to let you watch television with me. You're a big girl now. Happy birthday, Betsy.'

13:00

Lenny

MICHELLE HOLDS HER HAND OUT TO TRY TO STEADY HER balance before giving in and slumping down into an armchair. Lenny has never met the woman before but he already knows that she's more pale in the face than she is on any normal day. She fidgets with her fingers, then begins to pull her wedding ring on and off rapidly.

Lenny remains quiet, was oblivious to how Michelle would react to such news. His assumption led him to believe she hated her ex husband, that she really didn't give two shits about him. Certainly not to the extent that all of the blood would drain from her face.

'When you say fifty per cent, what do you mean exactly?' she says, staring at nothing.

Lenny shifts his balance from his left foot to his right foot.

'I don't know the ins and outs specifically, but eh...' he says. Michelle stares up at him, awaits an answer to the question she posed, 'his surgeries are so complicated that there is a major risk of him not waking up.'

'I can't believe it. I probably should believe it. He's not even capable of looking after himself... but I... I...'

Lenny sits down without being invited to do so on the couch across from Michelle. She doesn't react, continues to stare into space.

Lenny squelches his mouth with unease. He genuinely didn't give himself time to think this through.

'Which hospital is he in?'

'Tallaght,' Lenny says.

'I can't... I mean... I can't get up to see him. I've got to wait for the twins to come home from school.'

'Twins?' Lenny asks.

Michelle stares at him. Then looks towards a family portrait in a glass frame that's sitting on the mantelpiece.

'I'm sorry,' she says, her eyes refocusing, almost as if she has been turned back on after being on standby for the past two minutes. 'You're a PI did you say... did Gordon send you to tell me this news? That why you're here?'

Lenny blinks. Sometimes his blinking sorts his mind out for him, bides him vital seconds to think things through. But he's stumped. He only came here with one goal: securing Gordon's big house by eliminating Jake Dewey as a suspect. But he didn't realise the full complications of his call to this home.

'Michelle, your ex husband didn't want to spend what could be his last few hours lying in a bed and doing nothing. He wanted to spend that time at least trying to find out what happened to Betsy.'

Lenny watches as the blood returns to Michelle's face; her cheeks turning from faded pink to a roaring red. Her jaw swings. Then she holds her eyes closed, takes a big sigh and sucks a long, slow breath in through the gaps in her teeth. Lenny can sense she is doing her best to refrain from saying exactly what she wants to say. Michelle then places her hands on her knees, stands up and walks to the doorway of the sitting room. She swings it open, takes one step aside.

'Thank you, Mr Moon, you can leave now,' she says.

Lenny stands up, wringing his Sherpa hat through his hands. His mood has changed from excited to gloom over the past few minutes. If Jake Dewey is up in Belfast on business; the chances of Lenny ruling him out as Betsy's abductor are limited. The million euro house is locking its doors on him.

'Michelle – listen; I don't believe at all that he had anything to do with it. But can you give me something concrete that Jake was not involved in Betsy's disappearance?'

Michelle's face stiffens; her nose, her chin, her lips. She reaches a hand towards her sitting room door again and ensures it's as wide open as it can be.

'Out!'

Lenny shuffles his feet towards her, pauses to say something when he's as close to Michelle as he can possibly be.'

'Mich—'

'Out!' she shouts without even opening her mouth. It roars from the back of her throat.

Lenny feels bad. He didn't want to upset Michelle; she'd been through enough in life. His trainers squelch down her hallway, towards the hall door. He fumbles with the latch before opening it. Then he stalls in the door frame, looks back.

'I'm so sorry for upsetting you, Michelle,' he says. He steps out and pulls the door closed behind him.

He covers his face with his hat on her doorstep.

'Fuckety fuck!' he says into it as he strolls down the garden path, kicking up rain spray as he does so. Then comes to rest against a lamppost outside the next-door neighbour's drive. He looks up to the clouds to feel the sprinkles of rain fall on his face. It's only light rain, but the greyness of the clouds suggests it won't be light for long.

He breathes in his thoughts. All he has to do is to close Jake Dewey off as a suspect, then the house is his. But how can he do that? How can he get closure for Gordon?

He removes the phone from his jacket pocket, begins to nibble on the rubber case once again. Instead of thinking about the Blake family, he thinks about his own. He's barely noticed Sally is in great form today; when he imagines her, she's normally mute, downbeat. He wonders what she's up to now; probably carrying another heavy basket of clothes towards the washing machine, getting down on her knees and sighing as she carries out another boring, routine daily task. Then he imagines Jared and Jacob; the two of them sitting in class wondering what the fuck their teacher is rambling on about. He blinks rapidly into the rain, then turns on his heels.

'Fuck this,' he says to no one. 'If you're gonna be a good PI, be a good fucking PI.'

He paces up Michelle's drive again, doesn't even take a split second to look at her beautiful car this time. He heads straight for the door, his finger stretching for the doorbell.

Michelle's eyes look heavy when she answers; as if she's been twisting the palms of her hands firmly into them. Lenny doesn't give her time to snap at him.

'Michelle, I'm just trying to carry out Gordon's dying wish. He's been living with so much guilt for so many years and—'

Michelle shoots a laugh out her mouth.

'Guilt? Gordon doesn't even know what the word means.'

Lenny tilts his head back to look up at the dark clouds

again, then pivots his chin back down to stare into Michelle's eyes.

'If I could step in for just five minutes... I can explain everything to you.'

Michelle pushes the door open wider, giving Lenny the space to pass her. He walks up her wooden-floored hallway again and this time enters the living room without even being invited to. The first time he walked into this room – not more than ten minutes ago – he was struck by the size of it; the richness of it. But this time, all he's drawn to is the tiny family portrait encased in a glass frame atop the mantelpiece.

'Got twins myself. Boys – Jared and Jacob. We tried for four years, couldn't get pregnant. Had to spend almost fourteen grand on IVF before we finally got a positive result.'

He looks back at Michelle, offers a sterile smile. But she doesn't react. She's mute, her arms folded under her breasts.

'We thought it would be the start of a great life when they were born; a life we've always wanted. But it's been traumatic. My wife's had post-natal depression; has tried to kill herself twice.'

This makes Michelle squint a little. She unfolds her arms, allows them to hang by her side.

'We're taking it each day as it comes. I used to be a cop, y'see. I always wanted to be a detective; but the circumstances meant... I just... I had to be close to my wife at all times, couldn't risk not being on call for her if she needed me. That's why I opened up my own private investigating business.'

Michelle stiffens her mouth, nods.

'I'm just trying to do my job here, Michelle, much like Jake is in Belfast today. We're just trying to provide for our... for our twins, for our wives, right?'

Michelle plonks herself on the sofa. Lenny's not sure if

she's listening to the words he's saying now, wonders if she's still in shock with the news he gave to her earlier.

'Your ex-husband needs to go into his surgeries with a clear mind. He just asked me to rid his mind of all of the evil thoughts he's had over the years. Of course he doesn't believe Jake had anything to do with Betsy's disappearance.' Michelle's head stays still, but her eyes look up, her tongue swirling in her mouth. 'In the same way that Gordon felt Alan Keating and Barry Ward didn't have anything to do with Betsy's disappearance, but he asked me to talk to them this morning, just to clear his mind of any small doubt.'

'You spoke with Alan Keating today?' Michelle asks, her face contorting.

Lenny sniffles his nose, then nods his head.

'He was very helpful... Gave me—'

'Alan Keating is a fucking scumbag. Of course he didn't have anything to do with Betsy's death, but that doesn't stop him being a scumbag.'

Lenny pauses, tilts his head and then walks tentatively towards Michelle and sits beside her on the sofa.

'Betsy's death?'

Michelle turns her head, stares at his face from about ten inches away.

'Oh for fuck sake, I can't deal with this right now. Please. Please.' She holds her hands to her face, her fingers gripping at the top of her crown. Her shoulders shake, a sobbing sound purring from somewhere deep within her.

Lenny winces in his seat. He holds out a hand to place around Michelle's shoulders, then pauses, unsure whether to follow through or not with his embrace, his arm remaining stretched and hovering behind Michelle's head. He holds his eyes firmly shut, wondering what to do next. The buzzing inside his jacket pocket makes his mind up for him.

He relents, takes his arm back and then fumbles inside his

pocket and removes his phone. A strange number. Michelle continues to cry, continues to break down right beside him, but Lenny – unsure how to react – stands up, presses the answer button and holds the phone to his ear.

'Hello,' he whispers.

'Lenny Moon?'

'Yeah.'

'I'm Detective Ray De Brun; Gordon Blake has asked me to call you.'

'Oh.'

'Listen, I don't have a lot of time; large pike are prime for catching this time of year, so I'm gonna clear the case you're working on in the next five seconds. Betsy Blake is dead. Was killed when she was hit by a car on the day she was reported missing. Was put into the boot of that car and driven away. Body's never been found, but she wasn't kidnapped, wasn't taken by some psychopath, isn't trapped in somebody's basement. She's gone, Lenny – dead. Has been for seventeen years.' Lenny stands in silence. Doesn't know how to respond to De Brun's bluntness. 'Listen, I feel really sorry for Gordon Blake; I always have done. That's why I told him I'd take two minutes out of my day to ring you... so, I've rung you and, well... that's that.'

'No wait... Hold on, De Brun,' Lenny says, sounding desperate, panicky.

Michelle removes her hands from her soaked face and an in almost slow-motion rises from the sofa.

'Is that Ray fucking De Brun?' she asks, both of her fists clenched.

Lenny inches the phone from his ear, nods his head once.

'Arghhh!' Michelle roars. She takes two large strides towards her mantelpiece, holds out her arms and with one large sweep, she cleans the marble top of all that was sitting on it; the candle sticks, the glass picture frame, the glass clock. They all come crashing down on to the designer floorboards, smashing into an array of shards; the noise echoing through the room.

'What the hell's going on?' De Brun squeaks down the line. 'Lenny... Lenny...'

13:15

Gordon

'Gordon, what is going on?' Elaine asks with genuine concern in her eyes. I place the phone back down on my lap, then swallow hard as I realise, inside my head, that there's no way I can lie my way out of this.

'That was Ray De Brun,' I say, nodding towards my phone. 'He was the lead detective in Betsy's case. I rang him this morning after you and the whole surgical team came in to give me my news. I just didn't want to… I didn't want to…'

I try to not sob, but I can't stop my shoulders from jittering. Elaine holds a hand towards my left bicep, rubs at it gently. I look up at her. Her body language is screaming sympathy, but the look on her face is in total contrast; she looks stern, disappointed. She doesn't say anything, just continues to gently rub at the top of my arm as she waits on me to finish what I'd started to say.

'I don't want to die without knowing the truth. My worst nightmare is coming true.'

As soon as I say that my shoulders do more than jitter; they shake uncontrollably. The tears jump from my eyes, from my nose too. I cover my face with my hand, then feel one of Elaine's hands at the back of my head. What a fucking mess I am. Surely there can't be anything more pathetic than this.

'Oh, Gordon,' she says. 'We'll do our best to get you through this, to make sure you still have an opportunity to find out what happened to Betsy once you recover from your surgeries.'

I'd love to answer her back, tell her that there's just as much chance of me dying on the operating table as there is of me recovering fully, but I can't... the crying has totally consumed me, rendered me speechless.

'I understand the news we gave you this morning is a massive shock... and I also understand that your mind would have gone straight to Betsy and to the fact that you haven't had the answers to questions that must have eaten at you for years. But... but your best chance of getting answers is by living longer. I'm sorry to say, but it's highly unlikely you'll get answers in the next couple of hours anyway, is it?'

I suck up my tears as soon as she's finished. It's not as if I haven't been thinking along those lines all morning, but hearing somebody else say it really highlights how deluded I've been. I feel lost inside my own mind, trapped in a bizarre swirl of confusion. I've been confused and heartbroken for the past seventeen years, but I don't recall being this discombobulated since the time Betsy actually went missing. I guess hearing you may only have a few hours left to live will do that to a man.

I've been a mess in different ways ever since Betsy went missing, but that first ten or twelve months was a total headfuck. I was so pissed off with De Brun once he relieved Keating and Barry Ward of any involvement in the case. I was convinced at the time that they had something to do with it; but then my suspicions turned to Jake Dewey, probably out of sheer jealousy and heartbreak. The cops wouldn't entertain my opinion; so I took it upon myself to look into him. I began to stalk the fucker. Two months later I was told I had to stay away from him for twenty years; that he'd filed a restraining order, using one hell of a lawyer to pull it off. I couldn't cope; decided to fuck off on a break around Europe to get away from it all. The cops cleared me, said I could go. I took the car on a ferry to the UK and then to France, drove all through central Europe; Belgium, Holland, Germany, then back around through Austria and Northern Italy before coming home. I was away for seven weeks in total, and there were times on that trip that I felt I'd sorted my head out. But when I arrived home, my mind became more discombobulated than ever before. I was a changed man, but not for the better.

I know I'll never get over Betsy's disappearance, not until I have answers. But I really don't know how to get them. Don't know what the fuck I'm doing. I could curse De Brun forever for closing the case with his made-up theory that Betsy died; it means nobody is out there looking for my daughter. Except of course little Lenny Moon this morning. That's so fucking pathetic. I know I'm going to die today, I can feel it deep in the pit of my stomach, and with that, I know I'll never find out what happened to Betsy.

My shoulders begin to shake again, my hands going directly back up towards my face in an effort to stem more tears from falling. But Elaine grabs at my wrists.

'Gordon, let's get you out of this room for a few minutes, huh? Will we go for a little walk, try to get you into a more positive mind-set?' I shake my head. I can't, I can't face real life. Not now. 'Because, Gordon, I have to say, that if things continue the way they are, I'm going to have to inform Mr Douglas that you're not mentally fit enough to go through with the surgeries and... and... well, if you don't have surgery on that heart as soon as possible, Gordon, well, we both know an unrecoverable heart attack is inevitable.'

I look up at her, blinking the wet away from my eyes.

'I either get into a positive mind-set and give myself a chance of living… or I die?'

Elaine nods her head slowly.

'It's what we've been saying all morning. It's your only chance.'

I throw my legs over the side of the bed.

'Okay, take me for a walk. Let's try and calm my mind down.'

Elaine gathers my sneakers at the foot of the bed and I slip my feet into them. I look a right state, but why am I even bothering to give a fuck about what I look like? Just as Elaine holds my right arm to lead me out of the ward, my phone buzzes. I reach back towards the bed for it, but Elaine snatches at it before me.

'Ah, ah,' she says. She holds down the standby button, then scrolls across the screen to turn the phone completely off. 'The investigation is over for you for today. I'll turn your phone back on for you in the morning when you recover and you can take it from there. How about that?'

I don't say anything. I just watch Elaine place my phone in the drawer of the bedside cabinet and then allow her to link my right arm and lead me out of the ward.

TEN YEARS AGO

Betsy

THE SIMPSONS IS MY FAVOURITE. IT ALWAYS SEEMS TO BE ON when Dod lets me up the steps to watch television at six o'clock. It's funny. Bart is funny, Homer is funny. But watching television isn't better than reading a book. No way. It is nice to be up the steps and out of my room for an hour every day though. It's different.

We normally watch *The Simpsons* and then a show called *The Weakest Link*. A woman asks loads of questions but I never know the answers. Dod knows some of them some of the time. I think he is clever. He reads lots of things, but not books. Just normally loads of pages with loads of words and numbers on them. I'm not sure what they are.

I always feel a bit sad when I have to go back down the steps but today it has gone past seven o'clock and Dod hasn't told me to go down yet. He is in the room next to me. I can hear him with plates and stuff. It's the first time he has ever left me alone in this room. I click at the buttons of the remote control to see if there are any other cartoons on but I can't find any.

'Betsy.'

'Yes.'

'Come in to me here.'

I walk out of the television room and then stop at the door of the kitchen where Dod is.

'Come on – you can come in.'

I step inside. I've never been in the kitchen before. It is all white. The table in the middle is white, all the little doors around the walls are white, the walls are white.

The smell is delicious. It makes me lick my lips.

'I'm cooking a stir fry.'

Dod tilts the pan he is holding towards me and I see loads of different colours in it. I think they're all different types of peppers; red, green and yellow ones. I take a step forward and breathe in the smell again. The closer you are to it, the nicer it is.

'I've decided I'm going to teach you how to cook with me after we watch television every evening. How about that?'

I don't answer him by talking. I just throw my arms around him and squeeze him tight. Really, really tight. Like I do when he buys me books. I'm really happy. It means I get to spend more time out of my room and up the steps with Dod. I'm becoming a big girl now. I squeeze him even tighter.

'Whoa, whoa; careful, I'm holding the pan.'

'Thank you, Dod.'

I smile a big huge smile.

'Okay, sit up here.'

Dod puts down the pan then grabs me and sits me up on the counter where all the food is.

'I really trust you now.'

I smile again.

'I think you are getting old enough to be able to do things around the house, so you don't have to spend too much time down in your basement, what do you think about that?'

I feel really excited. My belly has that fuzzy feeling it can get sometimes when things are good.

'What would you like me to do?'

'Well, has cooking come up in any of your books?'

I nod my head.

'Sometimes. Some books talk about making breakfasts and dinners but I don't know how to do it. It doesn't say how to cook in the books, just that dinners are cooked. That's all... I think.'

Dod laughs a little at what I'm trying to say. I feel a bit embarrassed.

'Well, see these books here?'

Dod reaches past me and to four really big books. They're huge. Really thick. There must be a million words in them.

'Well, I know you like reading, so maybe you can read some of these and they'll teach you how to cook.'

I take the first book off him. It says *Gordon Ramsay: Easy* on it. I flick through it then nod my head.

'I can read this. Thank you, Dod.'

'Great. Soon you'll be like my little housewife.'

I look at Dod and am not sure whether to laugh or not. I'm not sure if he was making a joke. Then he leans towards me and kisses me on the lips. That's weird. He hasn't done that before.

'I think you're old enough to be a little housewife now,' he says.

13:20

Lenny

LENNY GRASPS MICHELLE BY BOTH WRISTS. HE WANTS TO stare into her eyes, but can't really make out her face, not with her hair strewn over it.

'Michelle, it's okay. It's okay.'

He helps her to an upright position and walks her to the sofa where she sits. She parts her hair from her face and then covers it with her hands.

'Michelle, we are only looking after Gordon's last wish,' Lenny says. 'I didn't mean to bring back so many horrible memories for you, I'm sorry.'

Michelle blows out a sigh, then wipes her hand across her nose, sniffing as she does so.

'It's not you I'm angry with. It's bloody Gordon. I haven't heard from him for years... and now this... *this*.' She stretches her arms outwards as if she's preaching at a ceremony.

'Just gimme one sec,' Lenny says before spinning on his heels and making his way to his mobile phone he'd left resting on the arm of the chair.

'Ray...' he says.

'What the hell is going on there, Lenny?'

'I'm eh... I'm with Betsy's mother Michelle right now; she's obviously and rightly upset by all of this. Can I please ring you back in ten minutes? I'd love to talk to you.'

There's an obvious and awkward hesitation on the other end of the line.

'Okay – but don't leave it longer than ten minutes. I'm all set to go back out onto the lake.'

Lenny thanks Ray, hangs up and then moves slowly towards Michelle again. She's removed her hands, is now staring into space, oblivious to the mess of broken glass on the floor.

'Michelle, can I make you a cup of tea or get you a water or anything?'

Lenny's question is met with silence.

'Michelle... Michelle.' He inches closer to her. Then her eyes refocus and her head snaps to face Lenny.

'So he's probably gonna die today huh?'

Lenny stiffens his nose, then nods.

'It's not definite, he still has a fighting chance, but...' Lenny plonks himself on the sofa next to Michelle and holds out his hands as if he's finishing his sentence through body language.

'I feel sorry for him, but this... bringing all this shit to my door again. Lenny – it's not fair. I've never done anything wrong in my life. And I've just lost my job as well. Why does he always—'

'He just wants closure before his operations,' Lenny says, interrupting Michelle in an effort to stop her from flying into a rage again.

She turns her soaked face towards him.

'We got closure twelve years ago. Betsy's gone. She's dead.'

Lenny swallows hard, then taps his hands against his knees, unsure what way to continue the conversation with the devastated woman next to him. Even when Lenny had dreamt of investigating real crimes, he never quite concocted a case in his head that would involve such complicated conversation. When he was training to be a policeman, his tutors touched upon the communications required with family members of deceased persons, but nothing could have prepared him for this. He subtly presses at a button on his phone so he can see the time on his screen. 13:24. He only has an hour and a half to ensure Gordon activates the will. Lenny clenches his teeth, then speaks up.

'Are you absolutely certain in your heart that Betsy is deceased?' he asks.

Michelle turns her head slowly to face him again.

'You're as bloody deluded as he is. Aren't you supposed to be an investigator? Some investigator you are. It's on record… go, go on, ring De Brun back, he'll tell ye. Then you can give up the ghost. You can go back to Gordon and tell him his dying wish is not achievable. That Betsy is gone. And it's all his fucking fault for never being mature enough to be responsible for somebody else.'

Lenny cringes a little inside. He knows he fucked up. It wasn't his place to ruin poor Michelle's day. The woman had been through enough over the years. Last thing she needed was him dragging all of her miserableness back into her home. He reaches out to her, places the palm of his hand on her shoulder.

'Get your hands off me,' she snaps. Then she stands, her arm stretched towards her door. 'Get out of my house. Out you go. And don't come back this time.'

'But Michelle—'

'Out!' she screams, so loudly that Lenny immediately takes a step back.

He places his phone back in his pocket, picks up his hat and heads for the door without saying another word. He'd like to offer Michelle more apologies but feels every time he opens his mouth to her he says the wrong thing.

When he gets outside the rain is falling harder than it has at any point so far today. He wonders if he should call a taxi or Ray De Brun first. As he's thinking it through, he strolls down Michelle's drive, plonking his hat atop his head, then comes to rest against the lamppost outside the neighbour's house – much like he had done fifteen minutes ago. It's a bit like Groundhog Day – one of Lenny's favourite movies – only Lenny's mind was swirling too much for him to entertain such a notion.

'You're a fucking idiot, Lenny,' he says to himself as he bumps the side of his head against the lamppost. Then he holds the phone to his ear and awaits an answer.

'Yep.'

'Ray, it's Lenny Moon. Thanks for taking my call. So sorry to disturb your day, but as you know, Gordon Blake is in a very bad state, may well be dead in the next couple of hours—'

'Lenny – let me stop you there so we can end this conversation quickly and get back to our day. As I said, Betsy Blake is dead. If Gordon wants finality or closure or whatever it is he's looking for; that's closure right there. She's gone. She was killed the night she was reported missing... there's no investigating needed anymore. Case is closed.'

Lenny sucks cold air through his nostrils. He knows this information is likely true, given that not only Betsy's mother, but the lead detective in the case has confirmed it for him in the past ten minutes. But he's also aware that going back to Gordon with this information most likely won't be good enough reason for him to activate the will. Lenny needs something, something Gordon hasn't heard before.

'Is there anything... anything about the case that Gordon and Michelle won't have known?' Lenny asks, almost cringing as he does so; his eyes shutting, his neck hunching under his raised shoulders.

'What do you mean?'

'I just want to find out as much information about the investigation as possible.'

A snort of laughter comes down the line.

'Lenny… Please.'

'I'm sorry, it's just…' Lenny doesn't know what to say.

'What happened with Michelle; is she okay?' De Brun asks.

'Yeah – she just got upset at me dragging back up her past. I'm an idiot. I should've handled it more sensitively. Gordon sent me to her house. He says Jake Dewey might've had something to do with Betsy's disappearance.'

'Well… I've mishandled things many times as a detective when it comes to dealing with families, so you have my sympathy. As does Michelle… and Gordon. They've always had my sympathy. But listen, Jake Dewey had absolutely nothing to do with Betsy's death.'

'What about Alan Keating and Barry Ward?'

'Lenny, you sound like Gordon. Listen to me, it wasn't Jake Dewey, wasn't Keating or Ward, it wasn't Gordon Blake himself and it wasn't… Look, Betsy is dead.'

'Hold on – it wasn't who… who was the other suspect you were gonna name there?'

'Lenny, Betsy is dead. We found a car many years later that had her DNA in it. And that DNA pointed to her dying. We believe the driver of that car that night hit Betsy when she ran out onto the road and, rather than face the music, he scooped her up, put her in the boot and dumped or hid her body somewhere… She's gone, Lenny. Betsy died. She's not being held captive anywhere. Case is closed.'

'But who was the other suspect you were about to name there? Please.'

'Listen, all suspects were cleared, okay... cleared because they didn't have anything to do with Betsy. Lenny, I gotta go. I can't give you specific details of any suspects and you know it, or you should know it.'

Lenny slouches against the lamppost, breathes out a cloud of a sigh, then holds his hands together as if in prayer, the phone sandwiched between them.

'I am begging you, Ray. Just for something. I'm a poor guy... I have nothing, my family has nothing. Gordon Blake promised me some riches if I could find anything out today. If I don't find anything—'

'Don't believe anything Gordon Blake tells you, Lenny. I'm sorry... goodbye.'

Lenny kicks at the lamppost when he hears the dead tone whistle through his phone. Then he stares back at Michelle's house and pictures the poor woman inside balled up on her sofa crying. It makes him kick the lamppost again. This time harder.

'She's dead. Course she's dead! What was I even thinking?'

Lenny opens his hand, stares at his phone and then begins to dial for a taxi. He's half way through punching in the number when the phone begins to vibrate.

'Hello.'

'Lenny; listen,' says De Brun. 'This is only because you pleaded... I can't give you any inside info from our side, but if you want to know what happened in the Betsy Blake investigation off the record, then perhaps you should speak to Frank Keville. D'ye know who he is?'

'Frank Keville? The journalist fella who's in a wheelchair?'

'Yep – he covered the case for years, knows it inside out. Perhaps he'd be willing to share information with you that I can't.'

TEN YEARS AGO

Betsy

MAKING CURRY IS MY FAVOURITE. ME AND DOD BOTH REALLY like Chicken Madras. I cut up the chicken breasts so they are really small, like little Lego blocks, and then I cut some onions and green peppers. After I fry them in the pan for six minutes, I add the sauce. I love the smell of the sauce. I am so happy Dod lets me cook. I have learned so much from the Gordon Ramsay books. Me and Dod have curries every Tuesday and Thursday. On Monday, I cook a stir-fry and Dod cooks the other days. He doesn't let me up the steps to eat every day, but I come up most days.

It depends on how he is feeling. He's not always happy, but he is definitely never angry Dod anymore. He doesn't hurt me. He doesn't pick me up and throw me around. He hasn't done that for years. I feel happy when I am around him. Not scared like I used to be. The only weird thing now is that he keeps kissing me on the lips, not on the cheek like he used to. It doesn't taste nice.

'How long?' Dod asks. He is on the sofa watching the television.

I check the time on the top of the oven.

'Two minutes,' I say.

He says something else. I can't really hear him that well. The curry is sizzling too loudly. I step down off my little step that Dod set up for me in the kitchen and then go see what he was saying. I walk into the television room.

'I couldn't hear you. What did you say, Dod?'

'I said hurry up, I'm bleedin' starving.'

I feel sad. Dod is not good Dod today. I walk a little closer to him.

'Are you okay, Dod?'

He stares at me. He has that angry look in his eye. I hate it when he has that look.

'Are you a fuckin doctor now?'

I shake my head. I don't know what to say. He is still looking at me. Then I hear a loud beep sound.

'Ye little shit,' Dod says. He runs by me and into the kitchen.

'Look, you fuckin idiot.' He shows me the pan. The food has gone a little bit black. It's not much. But Dod is angry. He presses a button that turns the beep off and then throws the pan against the wall.

'Clean that shit up and start the dinner again.'

He walks out of the kitchen. I think if I was younger I would cry. But now that I am eleven and nearly a grownup I don't cry. I just get down on my hands and knees and begin to clean up. I like to think about story ideas when I am doing things I don't like.

I have a story idea about a girl who becomes a magician and goes to a magic school. It's a bit like Harry Potter but I want it to be different. Except anytime I sit down to write I get confused. My writing is not good and it takes me ages to write even one sentence. I wish I had have gone to school like the characters in my books do. If I did, I bet I could write much better and much quicker. Reading books has taught me a lot about words and I can talk really well. But when it comes to writing words, it takes me ages to spell them out. It has taken me nearly three months to write two pages of my story. The Harry Potter books have two-hundred and fifty pages in them. It will take me years to write a book that size. But there isn't really anything else for me to do when I'm in my basement. So maybe I will finish my book one day. I think it's going to be called *Magical Mabel*. That's the name of the girl: Mabel. She is seven years old in it, has red hair and loads of freckles. Then she gets kidnapped and taken to a big school with lots of other children who have the same magic powers as she has. But she doesn't like the school and wants to escape. Sometimes I think I would like to escape from here. But I can't. If Dod caught me he would really hurt me. I don't want to be hurt again. My back still gets sore from the last time. And that was years ago.

'Here, let me help you,' Dod says. He gets down on his hands and knees too and helps me put the dinner back into the pan. Then he brings the pan to the bin and tips the food into it. 'I'm sorry for being so... so snappy,' he says. 'I'm just not feeling well.'

'Did you call a doctor?'

'I was at the doctors last week.'

'Oh, that's where you went that time you locked me in the room?' I ask.

He nods his head.

'Yeah, the doctor says I need to take some tablets and get some rest. But none of that seems to be working. I'm sorry I shouted at you and threw the pan against the wall. I'm gonna order us some take-away instead. You like pizza?'

'Pizza?' I never heard of it.

Dod laughs.

'C'mon, come in and watch television with me. You can stay up here late tonight.'

We walk into the television room and I go to sit in the chair I sit on all the time.

'Nah, Betsy. Come over here with me.'

Dod lifts the blanket he is lying under and I get in it with him. He throws his arm around me and hugs me as we both look at the television.

'This is nice, huh?' he says. I just nod my head. But I don't think it's nice. I would be more comfortable sitting on the chair I like. On my own. Then Dod kisses the back of my neck. Yuck.

13:25

Gordon

WALKING THE CORRIDORS OF A HOSPITAL IS HARDLY A RECIPE for relaxation. Every ward door that's open offers me a view to another grey-skinned person lying in a bed, much like I had been minutes ago. Still, Elaine – god love her – is doing her very best to soothe me. She keeps talking about football, has assumed that because I said I like the sport that I know as much about it as she does. She's been rabbiting on for the past couple of minutes, ranting about how much her beloved Manchester United have damaged their reputation ever since Sir Alex Ferguson retired. The amount of statistics she has thrown at me in the past three minutes is, I'm sure, quite impressive. But it all sounds like gobbledygook to me.

She stops talking, then turns to face me.

'You're not really that big a fan of football are you?'

It didn't take her long to realise that. I laugh, my first laugh of the day, then shake my head.

'Certainly not as much as you are. No, I mean – I might watch the odd game if it's on tele, but no... maybe I exaggerated a bit. I'm not that big a football fan.'

She giggles.

'Okay – then what do you like, what can we talk about that will help you relax?'

I shrug both shoulders.

'Don't know really.'

'What hobbies have you got? What do you do when you're not working?'

'I don't work. Not anymore. Got paid off by the company I founded less than a year after Betsy went missing. I understood why. I couldn't focus. But it was tough. Y'know... I lost my daughter, my wife and my business all in the space of ten months.'

Elaine does that pursed lips thing again, then reaches her left arm around my shoulders as we continue to walk.

'I'm so sorry, Gordon.'

She doesn't know what else to say other than apologise for something that isn't even remotely close to her fault. I wrap my arm around the small of her back and suddenly we are strolling as if we're a happily married couple. I know it feels a little awkward for both of us, but I'm gonna take the slight intimacy while I can get it. After a few seconds, she relents, takes her arm from around me so that we're just linking arms again.

'So what do you do with your spare time?' she asks.

I don't have an answer. Not really.

'I watch some TV and I eh... obsess about Betsy. Y'know... talking about Betsy is probably the only thing that would relax me.'

Elaine makes a slight pop sound with her mouth, then stops walking.

'Okay, well... tell me all about Betsy.'

I raise my eyebrows, then let out a steady breath as we stand facing each other in the middle of a corridor.

'She was the cutest little thing, y'know. Brown hair, a

splash of freckles across her face. She had the smallest little nose too. Tiny it was.'

I already feel my shoulders relax.

'I bet you doted on her, huh?' Elaine says.

'Yeah,' I reply smiling. But my smile is disingenuous. I was a shit dad. And I know it. I was just too obsessed with work at the time to care for the little person who was turning our house upside down. Ironically, back then Betsy was second in my thoughts. Now I can't stop obsessing about her. 'I'd give anything to go back in time.'

Elaine takes a step closer to me, then places a curled knuckle under my chin and lifts my head slightly.

'You're supposed to be relaxing now, okay? Not evoking feelings of guilt. You shouldn't feel guilt anyway. You are not the one who took her.'

That's the first time anyone has agreed with me in years; that Betsy was taken... abducted.

'Y'know the police don't believe somebody took her. They think somebody knocked her down, killed her, then hid her body. All seems a bit convenient to me, that. It took them seven years to come up with that theory.'

Elaine stares into my eyes, intensely.

'Gordon—'

'It's fine. I'm relaxed talking about her. Honestly.'

'Okay,' Elaine says, relenting. She links my arm again and we continue on our mission to walk up and down every corridor of floor three.

'Y'know they all think I'm mad when I say she was taken. But I'm not mad, Elaine. I'm not crazy. I just have a feeling deep in the pit of my stomach that somebody took her and that she's still out there... out there somewhere. I just hope wherever she is, she's happy; that she's being taken care of.'

Elaine seems to have fallen silent, is either happy to just listen, or perhaps she agrees with the rest of them. That my theory is the one that's wrong. I place my hand across her, stop her from walking and then stare into her eyes.

'You don't think I'm mad, do you, Elaine?'

She squints a smile at me, the tiny lines on the edge of her eyes creasing.

'I think you're being a great dad. You're not giving up on your daughter. I know that if I was Betsy, I'd hope I had a dad like you who would never give up trying to find me.'

I step into Elaine, give her a hug and breathe in her hair. It feels so good to have somebody who'll listen to me.

'That's why I have a private investigator looking for her now,' I whisper into her ear. 'I just couldn't lie there on that bed after being told I may only have five hours left to live and not do anything.'

Elaine nods her head slowly on my shoulder. I know from a personal point of view she agrees with me, but I also know she's conflicted; from a professional point of view she thinks I'm doing the worst thing I could possibly do given my situation. I hold her off me a little, so that we are facing each other.

'Don't answer this question as a nurse,' I say. 'Answer it as the beautiful human being you are, okay?'

She nods her head, then squints her eyes at me again.

'I'm doing the right thing amn't I?'

Elaine glances down at her feet, then back up at my face.

'If I was your best friend, not your nurse, I would be giving you this advice, Gordon. Your best chance of finding out what happened to your daughter is by staying alive and giving yourself more time to look for her. Surviving the surgeries is everything to you right now. It's all you've got. I'm sorry to say this, because I know it's not the answer you want to hear, but... relaxing right now, not obsessing over finding Betsy, is genuinely the best thing for you to do.'

I look up to the ceiling. Then rub my thumb firmly across

my forehead, as if I'm erasing what I've just heard from my memory.

'It's just the detective who looked after the case is currently talking with the private investigator I hired this morning. What if… what if somehow—'

'Gordon,' Elaine says, just like a school teacher would say to a student who's rambling on too much about nothing. 'It's been seventeen years. The fact of the matter is, Betsy is not going to be found in the next hour or two. I mean, what more can I say? You have to agree with me on that.'

I look back down at her, stare at her entire face.

'I do agree – of course I do. It's just… if I do die today… I wanna give it my all until my last breath. Like you said, if you were Betsy, you wouldn't want your dad to stop looking for you, would you?'

I can spot a moistness form in her eyes. I'm not the only one close to tears. She removes her old-school pocket watch from the top of her scrubs and sucks at her own lips.

'You're going for make or break surgery in the next hour and a half. I'm going to be straight and honest with you. You're not going to get any information in the next ninety minutes that you couldn't find in the past seventeen years. I'm sorry if that's a hard truth for you to take; but I owe it you to be totally honest.'

I thumb the tear that has just fallen out of her eye away from her cheek, then grab her close. The two of us sob in unison in the middle of the corridor; her sobbing with pity for me, me sobbing because I'm being pitied. Again. Surely there can't be anything more pathetic than strangers pitying you a couple of hours after they've just met you for the first time? But everyone pities me. I am the living, breathing definition of a loser. I literally lost everything I ever had.

13:25

Lenny

'INDEPENDENT HOUSE, HOW CAN I HELP YOU?'

'I need to talk with Frank Keville please?'

'Frank Keville – and which newspaper does he write for?'

'Ah... I don't know, doesn't he write for them all? Surely you know Frank Keville, the guy in the wheelchair, does all the crime stuff?'

'Hold on one moment, Sir.'

Lenny tenses his jaw, his eyes focused and controlled by his deep thoughts. He can't even feel the rain anymore; the weather a concern deep beneath him now. He continues to walk towards the main Terenure Road where he told the taxi company he would be waiting.

'I'm afraid Mr Keville is busy right now; is there anybody else you can speak to?'

Lenny takes the phone away from his mouth and exhales a disappointed grunt.

'I need to speak to Keville urgently. It's an emergency. Can you ask him to ring this number as soon as he can? My name is Lenny Moon; I'm a private investigator and I need to talk to him about a story he spent years working on.'

Lenny listens in as the receptionist mumbles back his name and number, then politely says goodbye before hanging up.

A small ball of excitement has resurrected itself within him. He knows quite well that he's not going to solve the case of Betsy Blake's disappearance, but that's not his task. All he has to do is bring something different to the table, then Gordon Blake will sign off on the will.

Lenny bites his bottom lip as his selfishness calls out to him. It's becoming more and more apparent to him that he may be an hour away from hoping a man dies; a man that has already given him a thousand euro. A man who's had an awful life. Poor Gordon Blake.

But Lenny can't allow sentiment to get in the way; there's fuck all he can do about Gordon's chances of surviving the surgeries. All Lenny has to focus on is the task in hand: speak to Frank Keville, find out who the other suspect was that Ray De Brun had alluded to. Gordon mustn't be aware there was another suspect. Otherwise he would have named him in the note earlier. If Lenny finds out who the other suspect is, then that's brand new information. That should be enough.

Lenny picks up his phone, dials Gordon's number and waits. But the tone is dead. He tries again. Same result. He's gurning and tutting to himself when he hears a car horn. A maroon-coloured taxi has just pulled up outside the Centra and is awaiting his fare.

Lenny opens the back door, slides into the seat.

'Thanks. Independent House, ye know it? On Talbot Street?'

'That's where all the newspapers are, mate?'

'That's the one.'

Lenny chews on the butt of his mobile phone as the taxi man pulls away. He's cursing, under his breath. The fact that Sally has always dismissed his need for a smart phone is grating on him now more than ever and it's always grated on him in some way.

Lenny looks up, realises the taxi man's smart phone – resting in the small cradle on the dashboard – is not currently in use.

'Guess you don't need the satnav to get to Talbot Street, huh?' he says.

The taxi man looks in the rear-view mirror, offers a polite laugh.

'Course not,' he says.

Lenny grinds his teeth together, blinks rapidly.

'Any chance I could take a look at your phone. I don't need to call anyone, but I need to check something online. My phone's a piece of shit and... look, you can add an extra fiver to the journey fare.'

The taxi man sniffs.

'Make it an extra tenner and I'll give it you, but I'm locking the doors.'

'Perfect,' Lenny says, shifting in the back seat. He reaches forward, takes the phone from the taxi man.

He immediately presses at the internet browser and then hesitates, biting his lip.

He types the words 'Betsy Blake Dead' into the search bar. The first option that pops up is an article from the *Irish Independent*. Lenny speed reads it, finds out little information than he had already been given. Ray De Brun closed the case in 2009 after a Toyota Corolla that had been used in multiple robberies over the years had been found with Betsy's DNA inside it. Lenny shakes his head, realises it was ridiculously farfetched to conclude that the cops made all this up just to close the case. It has to be true. Betsy must be dead. He continues his internet search, desperate to find out why the owner of the car hadn't been charged or even arrested over the findings, but the report was void of these details. He swipes out of that story, into the next one. Ironically, it was written by the man he was hoping to meet in the next few minutes: Frank Keville.

This article included more detail. It suggested the car wasn't specifically registered to anyone on the date Betsy was supposedly killed, and that it had been swapped between many different arms of criminal gangs over the years. It had once been owned by a woman called Sandra Wilson who had reported it stolen in 2000, but since then it was off the grid until the cops found it abandoned almost eight years later. It was suspected of being involved in a post office heist and when the cops carried out tests on it they – rather surprisingly – answered the question a whole nation had been asking for years: whatever happened to Betsy Blake?

'Fuckin hell,' Lenny mutters to himself.

The taxi man twists in his chair.

'Y'okay, mate?'

'Sorry – yeah. Just having one of those days.'

Lenny tilts his head down, gets back into the information on the taxi man's phone. He decides to Google 'Frank Keville'.

Like most people in the country, he's aware of what Keville looks like. Aside from writing the news, Keville had also become the news. He often appears on TV chat shows and has a picture by-line in the newspaper that's ridiculously oversized. It's Keville's professional mission to rid the streets of gangland crime. And he's good at his job; so good in fact that a gangland member tried to assassinate him. Lenny was aware – as was most of the country – that it was most likely Alan Keating who ordered the failed hit on him – but trying to prove that was an impossibility.

Lenny smirks to himself at the craziness of the underworld he has somehow found himself entangled in today; mucking around with The Boss and now Ireland's best crime reporter all in the space of a couple of hours. He's still smirking when the taxi man spins around to him again.

'Can't get fully down Talbot Street, mate; I'll leave ya here. Independent House is that one there on the left-hand side, can ye see it? The one with the glass shelter outside it.'

Lenny looks up, can just about see the building the taxi man is pointing at through the greyness of the rain, then hands the phone back to the driver.

'You're a legend,' Lenny says, tapping him on the shoulder.

'Well that's eighteen euro for the ride, plus the tenner you owe me for using the phone.'

Lenny fumbles in his pocket, takes out a few of the notes he had withdrawn from the ATM at the hospital, separates a twenty and a ten and then hands them over to the taxi man.

'Here, take thirty – and cheers for lending me your phone. It's been very helpful.'

The taxi man unlocks the doors and Lenny pops out, then runs towards the building with the glass shelter. He's not running to get out of the rain – Lenny's already drenched to the bone. He's running because he's in such a hurry. He's aware, because he looked at the taxi's dashboard before he got out, that it's just gone half one. Time isn't on his side. Gordon Blake will be going under the knife in less than an hour and half.

Lenny tries to push at the door at the entrance to Independent House but is stopped in his tracks, his face almost squashing up against the glass. He then waves at the security man inside and, after being eyeballed, the security man reaches for a button under his desk and presses at it to release the door.

'Thanks,' Lenny says, as he scoops the drenched hat off his head and steps inside the marble reception area. 'I need to speak with Frank Keville as a matter of urgency.'

'Ah – you were the man on the phone to me about fifteen minutes ago, huh?'

'Yep, that's me,' Lenny says, almost dancing due to his lack of patience. 'I'm in a real hurry and need to speak with Keville straight away.'

The security man picks up a large black phone receiver and then dials three buttons.

Lenny stares around the reception area, notices the list of newspaper brands encased in glass frames on the wall. Six national newspapers are all produced from this one building in the heart of Dublin's city centre.

'Sorry, no answer from his phone,' the security man says, placing the receiver back down.

Lenny takes a moment to stare at the nametag on the security man's navy jumper.

'Gerry... please, I need to speak with him as a matter of urgency. I don't have time to waste.'

Gerry stands up, showing not only his height, but his weight; his belly hanging over the waist of his trousers as if it's eager to touch the floor. Then he shrugs his shoulders and places a red lollipop in his mouth.

'Sorry – there's not much else I can do if he's not answering his phone,' he mumbles, before popping the lollipop out of his mouth. 'Would you like to take a seat over there?'

Lenny glances over his shoulder at the green sofa in the corner of the reception area, next to a glass table adorned by a helping of the day's national newspapers.

'Please keep trying his number,' Lenny says after sighing. Then he solemnly walks towards the sofa, wringing the hat through his hands with impatience. He sits, observes Gerry picking up the phone receiver, holding it to his ear, then placing it back down again. He watches as staff come in and then out of the elevator. When one stands at reception, blocking his view of Gerry, Lenny walks slowly to the elevator and waits on the doors to slide open. When they do, he steps inside, stares at all of the buttons and shrugs his head before deciding to start by pressing number one. But even after pressing the button the doors remain open, the lift not interested in taking him anywhere.

'Fuck sake,' he mumbles to himself.

'Sorry?' a woman asks, entering the lift.

'Oh – was just talking to myself. One of those days,' Lenny replies.

The woman laughs, then lifts her security pass to a reader above the number pad on the elevator and presses at the number three. The lift doors close at the same time Lenny's eyes close. He mumbles a quiet thank you under his breath and when the doors open he steps out with the woman.

'I'm sorry,' he says, offering his gentlest smile. 'I might have got off on the wrong floor. I'm looking for Frank Keville. I have a meeting scheduled with him and I'm running a tad late.'

'No,' says the woman. 'You didn't get off on the wrong floor. His desk is through that door, on the left side.'

Lenny bows as a thank you, turns on his heels, then presses at the door release and walks through to be met by a young woman sitting behind a large mahogany desk.

'I'm looking to speak to Frank Keville,' he says. The young woman smiles back at him, then stands up and tries to peer over the top of a tall fake plant by the side of her desk.

'He should be just behind that,' she says, pointing her pen.

Lenny thanks her, walks around the plant to find an empty desk. He lets out a dissatisfied sigh and then rings his wet hat in his hands again, his knuckles turning white with frustration.

'Can't catch a fucking break,' he snarls to himself. He then peers down the length of the newsroom, takes it all in. He'd never been in a newsroom before, often wondered what one looked like. It's just like any other office; though the walls aren't painted a neutral bland colour like most offices are, they're bright red – the colour of the branding of almost every tabloid newspaper in the country. Then he spots what he's looking for: wheels. They're parked up in amongst a group of people who seem deep in conversation. As he moves closer he makes out the familiar profile of Keville.

'Frank, Frank,' Lenny calls out. Everybody in the office turns to face him. 'I need to speak to you urgently.'

Keville scowls up at the man approaching in an awful-looking yellow puffer jacket.

'Sorry, but we're in a very important meet—'

'I have a story for you,' Lenny shouts out, interrupting Keville. 'Remember Gordon Blake – Betsy Blake's father? He's dying. May well be dead by this evening. I've lots to tell you.'

NINE YEARS AGO

Betsy

I'M STRUGGLING TO READ. NO. I'M NOT STRUGGLING TO READ. I'm struggling to find books as good as the Harry Potter books. I've read all six of them three times since I got them. That was about nine months ago now. They are brilliant. But no other book has been as good since. I wish I could write like JK Rowling. He is so clever. I wonder how long it took him to write all of those books. I'd love to meet him. I have a million questions I would like to ask.

I'd like to meet anybody. Me and Dod are great now. He is never really angry Dod anymore. We watch TV together. We cook together sometimes. We always eat together. And he never shouts at me. Not anymore. But I would just like to meet another person. To have another friend. I wish I had a friend like Hermione. That would be cool. So many of the characters in the books I read go to a school. But none of the schools seem to be any better than Hogwarts. Sometimes when I am in bed and before I fall asleep I imagine I am in Hogwarts. I think I'd be really good at Quidditch. Sometimes I try to play it. I use Bozy as the Quaffle, and my bin as the basket. Bozy doesn't mind. It's fun. But it would be great to have somebody to play it with.

When I am upstairs watching TV, sometimes I see people walking by the house. They just look like shadows from where I sit, but my heart always gets a little faster when somebody does walk by. Sometimes I make up who they are in my head. As if they're characters from a book.

I keep trying to write a book. But I'm not really good at it. I keep getting words wrong. I can read. But I can't really write good. That makes me sad. Hopefully one day my writing will get good enough to write a big book. If I went to a school, I bet I could learn to write much better.

I close *The Golden Compass* and leave it on my bed. It's a good book. It's just not Harry. Then I let out a big breath. I always seem to do that when I'm bored. I take a few steps towards the end of the steps and wait. And wait. I know Dod will open the door soon and call me up to watch TV with him. I never know what time it is. I don't have a watch. Or a clock. But I always know when he is going to open the door. I think it is because I know the sounds of him upstairs so well.

I am not waiting too long when I hear the key in the door. And when it opens the light shines down the steps and I walk up towards it.

'Hey, Dod,' I say.

'Hey, Betsy.'

We both walk into the TV room. He doesn't stare at me all the time now. I think he trusts me more. I get up into the big sofa and then Dod comes and sits beside me. He looks at me then gives me a big kiss on the lips. I don't really like it. But he seems to do it every day now.

'Here,' he says. He gives me the remote control.

I press at the buttons until *The Simpsons* comes on. It's so funny. The only thing better than watching *The Simpsons* is reading a book. Even a bad book is better than anything on the TV. I think my favourite thing about *The Simpsons* is that it makes Dod laugh. I like to hear him laughing. It makes me feel good. It makes me feel safe.

As soon as it starts I know I've already seen this one before. It's the one where Mr Bergstrom becomes Lisa's favourite teacher in school.

I look at Dod and watch him smile. He laughs again. And again.

'What's with you?' he says. He looks at me.

'What do you mean?'

'Why aren't you laughing?'

'Oh.'

'I eh... I'm just thinking instead of watching,' I say.

'Thinking about what?'

I wiggle my feet. Maybe I shouldn't say it to him. He might turn into angry Dod.

'Thinking about what, Betsy?' he says. He sounds nice. He's not angry. I don't think so anyway. Maybe I can say what I want to say.

'Thinking about what it would be like if I went to school.'

I look away from him as I say it because I don't want to see if his eyes go that funny way they go when he is turning into angry Dod.

'Children hate school,' he says. 'I hated school when I was your age.' I look up at him and then blink. 'I love you, Betsy. But it's not right for you to go to school. Not all children go. You are one of the luckiest ones. You get to spend all of your time at home... with your books. And with me and with Bozy.'

He puts his arm around me and hugs me in close.

We just continue to watch *The Simpsons*. None of us talking anymore. None of us laughing anymore.

'I love you too,' I say after ages. 'And I love Bozy. And all of my books. But it would be just nice to see other people.'

I hold my eyes closed after I say it. I know that that's bad. I know that saying that will turn Dod into angry Dod. But he doesn't do anything. He doesn't even say anything. He just keeps watching *The Simpsons*. And so do I.

Lisa hates it when Mr Bergstrom leaves the school. She thought he was a great teacher. It actually makes me sad a little bit. Even though I know everything works out well in the end.

I turn my eyes a little bit and try to look at Dod. I think that maybe a tear is falling down his cheek. I turn my head fully and stare at him. It *is* a tear.

'What's wrong, Dod?'

He wipes the tear and then smiles a big wide smile.

'Nothing. Nothing,' he says.

I don't believe him. He can't be crying because Mr Bergstrom left the school. Dod's already watched this one with me. He knows everything works out well in the end. I wonder why he's crying. I snuggle my head into him. He wraps his hand around me and holds me while we watch the end of *The Simpsons*.

When it's over, Dod stands up.

'Come here with me,' he says. He holds his hand out for me and I grab it. We walk towards the edge of the stairs. Not the steps that go down to my room. But the stairs that lead up to the room Dod says he sleeps in. I've never been up there before. But Dod takes a step up while he is holding my hand. So I do the same. And then we go up the next one, up the next one and all the next ones until we are at the top of the house. It looks magical up here. The walls are like a purple colour.

Dod opens a door and then turns back to me.

'You have to get down on your hands and knees okay?'

I smile a little but only because I think I'm a bit afraid. I'm not sure what is happening. I get down on my hands and knees, like a dog, and then follow Dod into the room. I can't see much. Just a really big bed. A much bigger bed than mine. Dod walks around it and then stops. I look up. He has stopped near a really big window.

He holds his finger to his mouth. It means I should try and be as quiet as I can be.

'You ready?' he says.

I look at him funny because I don't know what he means, but then I just nod my head.

'Okay, put your hands here and pull yourself up a bit.'

I do. And then I see it. A magical place. Just like in one of my books. There are lots of houses. Some with blue doors, some with green. One has a black door. One has a red one. There're lots of cars parked outside the houses. All different colours too. I rest my head against the window and then my breathing makes it go all funny. Dod laughs and then wipes it all away. And then I see one. A person. She is beautiful. She has long brown hair and a red coat on. And a really pretty face. Very pretty. More prettier than mine.

I look up at Dod. I know my eyes are bigger than normal because I can feel it. He rubs at my hair, then bends down and kisses me on the top of my head.

'I'm so sorry, Betsy. I can't let you go outside because… well… because I love you so much. I can't lose you.'

13:40

Gordon

I'VE OPENED AND SHUT THE BEDSIDE CABINET DRAWER THREE times since Elaine left me alone. On each occasion that I've done that I've hovered my hand over my phone, then pulled it away. I hugged her before she left me, promised her I would just lie back and relax.

I really like Elaine, but I can't allow my smittinness to control me. Lenny's out there – somewhere – trying to find Betsy. Surely I should turn my phone back on, see what he's up to. I let out a frustrated sigh. My mind keeps changing. I can't get a fucking grip on my thoughts. I can't get them in order.

I pull at the drawer again, and this time I grab at the phone without pausing for thought. I take it into my chest, hold down the standby button and wait for the screen to blink on. Then the ward door swings open.

'Gordon,' Mr Douglas calls out like a teacher. He's got one eyebrow slightly raised as he strides towards me. It's only when I hear tiny footsteps behind him that I notice Elaine has followed him in.

'I stressed to you this morning the importance of keeping your mind positive and your bloods even, isn't that correct?'

I just nod my head once, stare up at him in anticipation of being barked at. I can't believe Elaine ratted me out. Especially after I'd totally opened up to her on our little walk.

'You may shrug at me, Gordon, but the truth is you haven't been adhering to that advice have you?'

Douglas scowls at me. It's almost laughable how serious he is taking all this; as if it's his life at stake.

I don't say anything. I just switch my glance from Douglas's scowl to Elaine's guilty eyes. She can barely look at me.

'Well if you don't want to talk, I will,' Douglas says as he plants his hands onto his hips. 'It has been brought to my attention that you have had quite the morning. Look at this,' he says, turning his clipboard to face me. He jabs his fat finger at a line of digits. 'Your heart rate has gone from 122 this morning at eight a.m., to 152 at ten a.m., back down to 130 at just gone eleven a.m. And when Elaine last checked your heart fifteen minutes ago you were back up to 155. I can *not* stress to you how dangerous it is for us to operate with your heart rate fluctuating.'

I take the clipboard from him, squint at it as if I can comprehend in any way what I'm staring at.

'Gordon, the risk of you forming blood clots during the procedure is enormously high. Even in the 120s these procedures are a big risk, but the 150 range makes your chances of survival minimal at best.'

I shake my head slowly, still nothing coming from my mouth. I need to speak up. Need to justify myself.

'I eh... I'm sure Elaine has told you. I have a fear of dying without ever knowing what happened to my daughter and I just wanted to—'

'I understand your situation,' Douglas interrupts. 'But what is most important is that you understand everything we have advised you. Your best chance of finding out what happened to your daughter is to survive these procedures. Then you can live your life thereafter, in any way you please.'

I look down at the foot of my bed, feeling like a teenage kid being told off.

'Gordon, I'm not sure we can continue with these procedures,' Douglas says, his voice shifting to a more direct tone.

My head shoots up to stare at him.

'But then I'll just die.'

Douglas arches his eyebrow again, then offers me a tilt of his head. The cheeky fucker. I swirl my jaw towards him.

'How the fuck does that make sense? If I'm going to die anyway, isn't it best that you at least give me the opportunity of surviving the surgeries?'

'Gordon, if you don't mind curtailing your language,' Douglas says as he takes his clipboard from my hands. 'There's something you don't get.' He looks back at Elaine, then returns his gaze to me. 'As a surgical team we are measured on our abilities to oversee successful procedures. The last thing a surgeon wants is his patient dying under the knife. My – our,' he says returning to Elaine before looking back at me, 'our reputation is at stake every time we hold a scalpel to somebody's skin. It's why we weigh up all of the risks before we give the green light for any surgery.' Douglas inches closer to me, rests the tip of his fingers on my mattress. 'Gordon, even when we weighed up the option of surgery for you this morning, we knew we were playing with fire… but now this,' he says, jabbing his finger at the notes on his clipboard, 'this makes our job all the more difficult. You have left us with little choice.'

I stare over his shoulder at Elaine. She meets my eyes for

the first time since she returned to the ward. I open my mouth to call out to her, but nothing comes out... I remain silent, my lips slightly ajar.

'Gordon, your heart rate is fluctuating too much. I warned you time and—' she says taking a step forward.

'So you're just gonna let me die?'

Elaine places a hand on Douglas's shoulder and stares at me, her pity eyes wide.

'I'm going to measure your rate at two p.m. again, Gordon. But... I mean, I don't know what to say... if it's not at a respectable level, it wouldn't be wise for us to continue with the procedures. And this,' she says, removing the phone from my lap, 'isn't going to help you maintain a consistent heart level, now is it?'

I swallow hard, then throw my head back onto the steel bedpost making a clang reverberate through the ward.

'What is a respectable heart rate level?' I ask in a sulky tone.

'Well, in truth, Gordon, you haven't been at a respectable level all morning, which is understandable given the circumstances,' Douglas says. 'Ideally your blood rate should be well below 100, but given the complications your heart is currently going through I would expect it to be about ten or twenty points higher – 120s maybe. Hitting the 150s is just not acceptable for me to carry out surgery on you.'

I turn my head to face him.

'So what you're telling me is...' I crease my brow at him, prompting that he should finish my sentence.

'Gordon, your bloods have got to be lowered significantly,' Elaine butts in.

'Gimme a number,' I say.

Elaine and Douglas stare at each other.

'If you maintain a level inside the 130s, we're still taking a risk, but it'd be a risk we'd be willing to take for you,' Douglas says.

I nod my head.

'Okay, okay. I hear you. So what do you want me to do…? I'll do whatever it is you suggest. I want to live. I've so much to live for. I can't die not knowing what happened to Betsy.'

Douglas reaches out a hand to me, places it on my chest.

'I know you will never forget your daughter, Gordon. But I need you to forget about the investigation into finding her today. The theatre is just emptying now and after it's cleaned up it will be prepped for your surgeries. I'll need you down there at three p.m., but only if you're surgery-ready. Lie back in that bed, breathe deeply and consistently, all the while focusing on a positive outcome.'

He pushes firmer against my chest, guiding me to scoot down in the bed until my head is resting on the pillow again.

'As I said to you countless time this morning, Gordon,' Elaine says, stepping closer. 'All you have to do is relax.'

She presses at the standby button of my phone again and then opens up my bedside drawer and places it inside.

'And keep that phone turned off, huh?'

I stare up at them both, nod my head and offer a thin smile.

'Whatever you say, guys. Honestly. I'm sorry. I don't know what I was thinking this morning. Just – Jesus, Mr Douglas, Elaine – save my life. I beg you.'

Douglas almost sighs, as if my begging for life has burdened him somewhat. Then he places his hand back on my chest.

'Elaine will check your rate in twenty minutes. If the results are in the 130s then I swear to you, not just on your life, but on mine too, that I will do all I can to keep you alive.'

13:40

Lenny

LENNY WRINGS HIS HAT BETWEEN BOTH HANDS AS HE WAITS. He tries to rehearse in his mind what he's going to say. He needs his story to have clarity, but he also needs to be swift. Time isn't on his side. He stares at the large clock above the reception desk again. 13:40.

He's muttering a 'fuck sake' to himself when he sees the group of journalists he's been staring at flitter away from the huddle. Then he sighs with satisfaction when he notices the large spokes on the wheels turn. They're coming his way.

'Frank, I'm so grateful,' Lenny says, pacing towards the wheelchair.

'Over there,' Frank nods, his voice gravelly and instantly intimidating.

Lenny points to a messy desk.

'Here?'

Frank wheels by Lenny, positions himself into the desk and then points to an office chair sitting behind the large plant pot.

'Grab that. You've got five minutes.'

Lenny wheels the chair towards the desk Frank is at,

squelching his nose up at the untidiness of it. He thinks about mentioning the amount of paperwork piled up, just to break the ice, but doesn't have time for small talk. Not today.

He parks his butt on the office chair, then stares at the back of the famous journalist's head. He's unsure whether Frank is ready to hear his story yet, but decides to offer it up nonetheless.

'My name is Lenny Moon. I'm a Private Investigator. I got a call from Gordon Blake at about ten a.m. this morning. He's in Tallaght Hospital; has to have make or break heart surgery at three this afternoon. Doctors are only giving him a fifty-fifty chance of making it out alive. He contacted me, begged me to do my very best to find out new information on Betsy before he goes under the knife. He doesn't wanna die without doing all he can.'

'Betsy Blake is dead.' Frank's voice sounds as if there are rusty cogs working it in the back of his throat; either that or he's smoked thirty cigarettes a day for the past hundred years.

Lenny gulps.

'Gordon Blake doesn't think she is,' he says, almost whispering.

Frank stretches his arm to reach for his mouse and then taps away at it. Lenny waits silently. And then waits some more.

'That it?' Frank says, turning to him.

'Oh,' Lenny says, shifting uncomfortably in the chair. 'I eh… thought you were looking for something on the computer for me.'

Frank shakes his head. 'Listen, I'm very busy today – is there anything else you have to add to your story?'

Lenny shifts again in the chair, lifting his left butt cheek before placing it back down, then does the same on his right side.

'I spoke with Detective Ray De Brun today, he says—'

'Ah, how is De Brun, haven't spoken to him in years?' Frank interrupts.

'Eh… fine, yeah, fine,' Lenny stutters, his eyes beginning to blink.

'You okay, kid, want me to get you a glass of water?'

'Fine, yeah I'm fine… the eh… oh the blinking, nah it's just a tic I have. Have had it since the very first day I was bullied at secondary school.'

Frank kisses his own lips, then returns his focus to his computer screen. Lenny looks around the office, uncomfortable. He's not sure whether or not to continue talking. He stares at the clock behind the receptionist and realises he just needs to get on with it.

'Gordon has to have a eh… an abdominal aortic aneurysm and aortic valve replacement. His ticker is fucked, almost ripped apart.'

Frank reaches both hands to his wheels and manoeuvres his chair back, and then to the side, so that he's face on with Lenny.

'Thanks for the info, kid, but to be honest; it's not much of a story. If he passes away, I'll get in contact with the hospital and we'll run a piece but y'know, we've got much more important matters to—'

'Who were all of the suspects in the disappearance of Betsy Blake?' Lenny bursts out, not giving Frank time to finish his dismissive sentence.

'Huh?' Frank grunts.

'De Brun said there were initially four suspects. He questioned and then ruled out Gordon himself, then he questioned both Alan Keating and Barry Ward before ruling them out. Gordon himself thinks Jake Dewey may have had something to do with Betsy disappearing, but the cops were never interested in him. However, when I spoke to De Brun this morning, he alluded there was another suspect. I wanna know who it was.'

Frank clears the phlegm at the back of his throat, then slaps both palms of his hands onto his knees.

'Kid, nobody took Betsy Blake. Cops found a car seven years later that had Betsy's DNA in it... and that DNA proved she was dead. I know the media – me in particular – reported that she was abducted for many years but the truth came out eventually. Ireland's biggest ever kidnapping case was never even a kidnapping case to begin with. Now, I'm really sorry, but if you don't have a story for me I'm gonna have to get back to stories I do have.'

Lenny stands, wrings his hat in his hands again, visibly agitated.

'Gordon Blake said he will pay me by leaving me his home in his will if I can make any breakthrough in Betsy's case before he goes under the knife...' Frank's eyes flick upwards, meeting Lenny's. 'Gordon never knew there was any other suspects other than Keating and Ward. If you can tell me who the other suspect was I'll give you all of the information on my investigation this morning, of all of my talks with Gordon. I'll go on the record and you can write about it in your next column. Gordon Blake tried to find Betsy right up until his death, ended up leaving the PI who last worked on it his million euro home in his will – it's a good story. And it's exclusive to you.'

Keville holds a balled fist to his mouth, coughs twice into it; the sound of his raw chest almost grotesque.

'He's going to leave you his house?'

Lenny nods his head, almost too frantically.

'Sit back down, kid,' Frank says.

He spins his wheelchair back into his desk, reaches for his mouse again, rolls it around an oversized mouse mat and clicks on it repeatedly.

'Jesus, is it that many?' he mumbles to himself. 'Wow, I wrote eighty-three stories on the Betsy Blake case over an eight-year period. Crazy.'

The excitement in Lenny's stomach turns up a notch, adrenaline slowly pumping its way towards his heart. Frank's playing along. He may well get the keys to that big house.

'Lemme ask you this question for starters,' Frank says. 'Do you believe Betsy is dead, or are you singing from the same conspiracy hymn sheet as Gordon Blake?'

'I eh...' Lenny pauses. He wipes his brow with his hat. 'If De Brun says she's dead, I guess she's dead. But I eh... my job is to just try to look into this a little further. If I can get information Gordon's never heard before, it would mean the world to him.'

'To you, you mean.'

'And to me.' Lenny nods his head. 'Yep.'

Frank leans his head back, stares up at the ceiling of the open office. Then he interlocks his fingers and rests them on top of his rotund belly.

'Betsy Blake was reported missing on the twenty-first of January 2002,' he says. 'I assumed, as soon as I found out that Gordon Blake had dodgy dealings with Alan Keating, that that scumbag had something to do with it. But as the days passed, I realised it couldn't have been him. Keating's a prick. A prick of the highest order – he's the reason I'm in this wheelchair. But he's no kidnapper. Gordon Blake didn't realise that his falling out with Keating was insignificant to Keating. Keating had bigger fish to fry. Just because Gordon refused to launder parts of Keating's cash was in no way reason for Keating to kidnap his daughter. So after the cops hit a roadblock, they looked into similar cases, see if they could form any link.'

Lenny's eyes light up. He removes his left bum cheek from the seat, takes out his notebook from his back pocket, folds his legs and then rests the notebook on his left inner thigh. He pops his pen, begins to scribble as Frank, still looking up at the ceiling, continues.

'There were zero other cases in Ireland. Young girls just don't go missing, do they? Not on our little island. But there were two other cases that intrigued De Brun – both in Britain; one girl who went missing in England, one who went missing in Wales. Eh... lemme see...'

Frank looks down, repositions his wheelchair back into his desk and reaches for his mouse again. He hums as he clicks away.

'Yeah – this case; a three-year-old, Sarah McClaire. She went missing from a park in Kings Heath, Birmingham in the summer of 2002, about five months after Betsy. The police were interested in that case because there was an associate of Gordon Blake who happened to be in both Birmingham when Sarah went missing and in Dublin when Betsy went missing.'

'Who?' Lenny snaps.

Frank turns around, offers a scowl to Lenny.

'Hold on, I'm telling you about the two cases.... the other one was only of interest to De Brun because the names were similar. Elizabeth Taylor. Or Betsy Taylor as her parents called her. Same name, similar profile to Betsy Blake, but nothing in it.'

'I think I remember that case,' Lenny says.

'Yeah, that got a lot of exposure because of her name. If you share the same name as a Hollywood celebrity, then you're bound to stick in the mind of people. Sub editors had a field day making up headlines for Elizabeth Taylor.'

'So, the only reason that was of interest to De Brun was because the name was the same?'

'Yep,' Frank says. 'There was nothing in it, only the name coincidence. Turns out, it seems Tommy Saunders was responsible for Elizabeth Taylor's abduction. No link to our Betsy at all.'

'Tommy Saunders, the serial killer?'

'That's the one,' Frank says, clicking at his mouse.

'But what about the link with Sarah McClaire, who was the associate of Gordon's who was also in Birmingham at the time she went missing?'

'It's not only that,' Frank says. 'This guy was also questioned in 1999 for possession of child pornography.'

Lenny's mouth falls open. His eyes widen too.

'No need to get too excited, Lenny. De Brun looked into him, all was innocent. Lots of people visit Birmingham and Dublin regularly; the two cities have major links. It's hardly a coincidence.'

'Who is it?'

'Listen to what I'm saying to you, Lenny. This guy didn't do it. Nobody did it. Betsy was knocked down by a car, was killed by accident and then—'

'Who?' Lenny says, his volume rising.

Frank shakes his head.

'Guus Meyer – Gordon's business partner.'

'Woah – Guus Meyer is a paedophile and they just let him go?'

Frank closes his eyes shut, the lines on his face deepening.

'You haven't listened to a word I've said, Lenny. I didn't say anybody was a paedophile, did I? I said he was caught in possession of child pornography on his computer. The cops looked into it and let him go, so I assume it was very minimal at worst.'

'I don't believe this,' Lenny says, standing up. He lightly curls his fist into a ball and punches dead air, adrenaline rising in his stomach. He's done it!

'And Gordon won't have known this?' he asks, shuffling his feet.

Frank shakes his head.

'Because of the sensitive nature of the findings, what-with the kiddie porn and all, it wasn't shared with anyone that Guus was a suspect in the Betsy Blake case. Listen, they brought him in, questioned him and let him go. So don't go getting your hopes up that you are about to solve anything. You're not gonna solve jack shit. I'm just letting you know who the fourth suspect was because your running around might make a good story on a slow news week.'

Lenny punches dead air again, in celebration. He really has done it. He's managed to get information Gordon would never have known about. The million euro gaff is going to be his. Well... if Gordon doesn't make it through his surgeries. Lenny spins in a circle, his mind racing.

'So Guus Meyer is not only somebody who views child porn, but he happened to be in Birmingham when Sarah McClaire went missing and was in Dublin when Betsy Blake went missing?'

Frank holds a long blink... irritation evident on his face. He says nothing.

'Where does Guus Meyer live?' Lenny asks when he finally stops fidgeting.

'Lenny, I told you our little chat was off the record. You can't go around accusing any—'

'And I agreed. I won't say you told me anything. I just want to speak to him.'

'Well, the answer to your question is: I don't know where Guus Meyer lives.'

Lenny sucks the dryness of the office air conditioning in as Frank turns back to his computer. He clicks at his mouse again, then types away.

'I'm going to write this story, the story of Gordon's investigation from his death bed, do you hear me?' Frank says. 'But I want to emphasise, I did not give you this information so you could go around accusing innocent people, I gave it to you because it will suit my story.'

'Yeah, yeah, of course.'

'Clontarf,' Frank says.

Lenny's eyes light up. He inches forward, to see what Frank has called up on his computer screen. Then reads it out loud over the journalist's shoulder.

'Number one Avery Place, just off the main Clontarf Road.'

He grips both sets of fingers around Frank's shoulders.

'You're a legend, Keville.'

EIGHT YEARS AGO

Betsy

I HAVE TWO NEW HOBBIES NOW. TWO NEW FAVOURITE THINGS to do. I still read. Lots. But I don't read what Dod told me are called fiction books much anymore. I read non-fiction most of the time now. But my new favourite hobby is to look out the window in Dod's bedroom. I see different things all the time. I ask him if we can look out the window instead of watching the TV. He agrees most of the time. Sometimes he lets me watch TV and look out the window afterwards. I like looking out the window because it gives me ideas to write my own books. Although, because I now like to read non-fiction I have started to write a book all about myself. I'm going to call it *Betsy's Basement*. And it will have me, Dod and Bozy in it. I will write about what I do every day down here. It will be a bit like the books I read now.

I think my favourite non-fiction book so far has been the one called *I Know Why the Caged Bird Sings*. I have learned lots of new words because of that book. It's about a young girl like me called Maya who felt she was trapped but then became a really good writer. She wasn't a good writer when she was younger and then she became really good because she read lots and lots. I hope the same thing happens to me. She had brown skin. I'd like to see somebody with brown skin. People with brown skin sound as if they'd be beautiful.

Another girl who I have read a non-fiction book about also has brown skin. Serena Williams. She is another woman who wasn't really happy when she was younger but then became really happy when she got older. She thinks women are the best. Better than men. So do I. She plays a sport called tennis. And is the best person to ever play it. I asked Dod if he could show me some tennis on the TV but we can never find it on any of the channels. We have tried to look for it a few times. He keeps buying me new non-fiction books because I ask for them now. I think he feels just as happy as I do when he gives me a new book. He buys me a new book almost every week. I read so fast.

My room is mostly taken up by the big shelf I have against the wall. It is filled with books. I counted a few weeks ago. I had ninety-five. And Dod has bought me four more since then. So the next one I get will be my hundredth book. I wonder what it's going to be. I hope it is about another strong woman. A woman who has a bad childhood but then becomes really, really happy. Because I think that is what is going to happen in my life. I will be happier when I'm older. I want to be a happy writer when I am an adult. Just like Maya Angelou.

I have started to write *Betsy's Basement* but it is not easy. It takes too long for me to spell out the words correctly.

I hop up onto my bed and pick up Bozy. Then I place him so he is sitting up against my pillow and say: 'Are you ready, Bozy?' I make him nod at me by using my fingers to push at the back of his head.

'This is the start of Betsy's Basement.'

I flick open my copybook.

'I was playing on my street one day while Daddy was

talking to somebody from work. It was a long time ago now so I don't really remember everything. I was four years old. I know that. Now I am thirteen years old. So it was nine years ago when it happened. But I was walking on a wall and then Dod just took me. He put his hands around my mouth and around my legs and just took me. He told me to be quiet. Then he put me in a car and he drove for ages and ages and ages. I was really scared. And I was really hungry. And then after ages he took me out of the car and into my basement.'

I look up at Bozy.

'What do you think so far?'

I think he likes it.

I just wish I could write much faster. That much has taken me two weeks to write. I keep spelling words wrong and then changing them. Maybe when I am older I will be able to write much quicker. I want to write loads of books. *Betsy's Basement* is just my first.

13:50

Gordon

I took a mindfulness class once. Wasn't for me. But I remember one instruction quite clearly; the five breaths per minute technique. Breathe in for six seconds, breathe out for six seconds. I've been trying to apply this since Douglas and Elaine left me a few minutes ago, but it's a difficult technique to maintain; especially when you have a multitude of stuff whizzing through your mind. I've tried leaning fully flat out on the bed, tried half sitting up with the pillow behind the arch of my back, tried fully sitting up while resting my head against the steel bed frame. But nothing seems to be helping me calm down.

I keep seeing Betsy's little face. I always imagine her as she was – four years of age; mousy brown hair, a dash of freckles across the bridge of her nose. I can never quite imagine what she would look like now. She'd have turned twenty-one last August. A bona fide adult. I'm pretty certain she would have ended up being something special. Guess I'll never know.

I press both shoulder blades firm against the bedpost, then close my eyes and attempt to concentrate on my six-second breaths. I'm refusing to even look at the bedside cabinet my phone is currently resting in. Poor old Lenny Moon out there running around for me when I don't even need him to anymore. But fuck it; he got a grand for his morning's work and, given his appearance, I'm guessing that's quite a lot of dosh for him. He'll be fine. Last thing I heard from him he was on his way to Jake and Michelle's house. I'd love to know how that went... but I can't turn on my phone, can't ring him. It'll only raise my heart rate again.

Six seconds in through the nose... six seconds out through the nose.

I can't stop my mind from swirling. It's too quiet. Maybe I need a little background noise to help me focus. I pick up the TV remote control, hold down the standby button.

Loose Women. Fuck that! Jesus, if there's anything that will raise my heart rate it's watching that shite. News. No! More news. No! Ah... a music channel. Maybe. But it's blaring out some awful hip-hop song that can barely be filed under the medium of music as far as I'm concerned. No! A crappy, dated American sitcom. No! Fuck it. I tap at the standby button again. The screen blinks off.

Six seconds in through the nose... six seconds out through the nose.

Christ, this is difficult. Not the breathing. The shutting off of my thoughts. I've always been a deep thinker. Have never been able to shake off my guilt. Even when I'm not directly thinking about Betsy, there's always a grey cloud circling my every moment.

I wonder what time it is. Without my phone I can't tell, but it's got to be coming up to two o'clock. That's when Elaine said she'd be back in to measure my bloods. Jesus... I may have only one hour left to live. And here I am, lying in an uncomfortable bed, doing my best to focus on six-second inhales and exhales. I blow out through my lips, making a rasping sound. The thought of what happens when you die flipping over in my head. I wonder what the fuck a God would say to me if I was to somehow find myself at the gates of Heaven this evening.

'Why did you never have faith in me, Gordon Blake?'

'Because you made it fucking impossible for anybody with half a brain to have faith in you, you long-bearded twat!'

I make myself laugh a little with that thought. The first time I've produced a moment of giddiness all morning. But the giddiness doesn't last long; the thought of dying and ceasing to be begins to hit me hard. I've never really been afraid of death itself; I've only ever been afraid of dying without knowing what happened to Betsy. It looks very likely that my biggest fear may become a reality in just a few hours time. I let out the saddest sigh I've let out in years. I can hear the self-pity within it.

Six seconds in through the nose... six seconds out through the nose.

The ward door opens while I'm finishing my long exhale. I stiffen my lips, look over at Elaine strolling towards me. She stares at me sympathetically, unsure of what to say. We've been quite open with each other throughout the morning, but right now she knows she's about to give me a quick test that will determine whether or not I'm guaranteed to die today. That's hardly an easy topic to raise. So, instead of talking to me, she nods slowly, then clenches her lips tight.

'So this is it?' I say.

Elaine remains silent. She almost looks as if she'd cry if she spoke. I think that's why she hasn't said a word. It's either that or the guilt she has felt for ratting me out to Douglas is eating at her. She holds up the blue tabs, presses them into my chest. Then she turns to her machine, presses at a couple of buttons and glances at me, her eyes blinking.

'Very best of luck, Gordon,' she says.

I reach out my hand, grab a strand of her hair and brush my fingers gently through it.

'Thank you, Elaine.'

She breathes deeply, presses another button and then holds her eyes firmly shut. She must be willing the digits to blink to something in the 130s as much as I am. I bend forward to stare at the small screen when it beeps and as I do, Elaine opens her eyes.

Bollocks. 142.

Elaine holds her eyes closed again, then opens them and tilts her head to stare at me. I fall back onto the bedpost, hold my hand to my forehead and for some reason begin to breathe in for six seconds, then out for six seconds. By the time I'm finished one breath Elaine is at the foot of my bed, unhooking the clipboard from the rail.

'One thirty-nine,' she says, scribbling. I remove my hand from my forehead, then smile up at her.

She walks towards me without saying another word, removes the tabs from my chest and then folds them neatly before hooking them to the machine.

'You are an angel sent from heaven,' I say, aware that such a statement totally contradicts the thoughts I had been stewing around my head just minutes ago.

She doesn't even look at me. She just swirls on her heels and heads for the door.

'I'll let Mr Douglas know he should begin to prep the theatre. We'll be going down in an hour, Gordon. You just continue to relax.'

14:00

Lenny

LENNY TOUCHES A BUTTON ON HIS PHONE, JUST SO THE SCREEN blinks on and he can see the time. Bang on two o'clock. One hour left. He clicks into call history, brings up Gordon's name and presses at it.

'Ah for fuck sake,' he says as he pushes at the glass doors of Independent House and walks out into the rain.

He stops, fidgets at his phone to recall Gordon, then looks up to the grey sky upon hearing the dead tone again.

'Please tell me they haven't taken him down to surgery already,' he says to the clouds.

He stands in against the wall of a newsagents as if that's going to protect him from the rain as he contemplates his next move. He knows he's taking a taxi to Clontarf, but he needs to let Gordon know what's going on. The whole point of finding out something new is so he can secure the million euro house. He tries calling one more time. Same frustration – dead tone.

He places the phone back inside his jacket pocket, zips it up and then paces towards Amien Street in search of a taxi. He bounces shoulders with one young woman, holds a hand up in apology as he walks away, then slaloms through two umbrellas coming towards his face.

'Ah for crying out loud,' he yells out as a woman stops in front of him, causing him to walk around her. The woman stares at him, shock at his over-the-top outburst evident on her face. Lenny doesn't react, doesn't apologise. He just continues to walk at a swift pace, head down, sheltering his face from the rain.

His mood has changed swiftly in the past three minutes. He had ran down the three flights of stairs of Independent House feeling elated at the thought of giving Gordon something new in the investigation. But now his blood was slowly coming to the boil; the thought he may never be able to communicate this news with Gordon settling in his mind as a high probability. He can't bear the thought of being that close to earning a million quid and losing it all.

'Taxi,' Lenny shouts out, holding his hand up as if he just leaped off a pavement in New York City. A silver Ford Focus screeches to a stop and Lenny – his clothes soaked right through, his woollen Sherpa hat heavy on his head – jumps in.

'Head for the Clontarf Road,' he says.

The taxi man eyeballs Lenny in the rear-view mirror as he resets his meter, then pulls out and sets off.

Lenny removes his hat, unzips his puffer jacket to allow him space to breathe, then lays his head back on the rest. He chews on his bottom lip, stewing. Blinks his eyes rapidly, stewing. Then brings the phone to his mouth and begins to chew on the butt of the cover, stewing. He remains in the same position, head back, as the taxi man finally drives out of the city centre and towards the coastal road.

'What's the number when you don't know a number,' Lenny says, shooting himself back into an upright seating position.

'Huh?' the taxi man says.

'Y'know when you don't know a phone number and there's a number you can ring that'll give it to you?'

'Jaysus,' says the taxi man. 'Who uses that shite anymore, sure can't you just search for any number on your phone?'

'Don't have Wi-Fi on this,' Lenny says shaking his mobile in the air. Then he leans forward. 'Can I eh... any chance you'd give me a loan of your phone for a minute? Need to get the number for Tallaght Hospital.'

The taxi man eyeballs his passenger in the rear-view mirror again, then removes his phone from the cradle and hands it back. As soon as Lenny has the phone in his hand, the sound of the doors locking sounds out.

'You're a star, thank you.'

Lenny scrolls through the phone, into the internet browser and types 'Tallaght Hospital' into the search bar.

The hospital's information flashes up straight away; address, phone number, fax number, an About Us page, visitor information.

'Gotta get me one of these,' Lenny whispers to himself. Then he picks up his own phone and begins to punch in the number.

As he's handing the phone back over the shoulder of the taxi man a friendly voice answers his call.

'Tallaght Hospital, how may I help you?'

Lenny double taps the bicep of the taxi man after handing back the phone, his way of thanking him.

'Yeah, I eh... I need to speak with a patient please. A Gordon Blake. He was taken in last night, has to have heart surgery today and eh... yeah, can I speak to him?'

'Sir, patients don't have phones in their rooms.'

Lenny falls silent, then blinks rapidly.

'How can I get a message to him?' he asks.

'Let me see... do you know what ward he's in?'

'Floor three eh… what is it, oh yeah – St Bernard's Ward.'

'Hold on one moment, Sir.'

Lenny clenches his fist, gives the air a little jab as the sound of elevator music pierces down the line. He stares out the window as he waits, taking in the greyness of the day. The taxi is splashing up rain spray, pedestrians are wobbling around with either umbrellas held high or hoods clenched tight. He begins to whistle along to the elevator music, his mood suddenly shifting. He's certain Gordon doesn't know that Guus Meyer was another suspect in Betsy's disappearance; feels confident that this information is enough to trigger the will he had been shown back at the hospital. He begins to imagine Sally's face when he finally tells her they have the keys to a new million euro gaff. Then he sits upright, chuffed with himself for picturing his wife smiling for the first time in God knows how long. He offers the air an uppercut this time, not just a jab, then beams a huge smile of his own, stretching it right across his face.

'I'm sorry, Sir, nobody seems to be answering up at St Bernard's Ward. Is there anything else I can help you with?'

Lenny lies back in the chair, his smile disappearing.

'I need to get a message to Gordon Blake, can you deliver it for me?'

The man on the other end of the line offers a subtle laugh.

'I'm sorry, Sir, but there is no way I would be able to do such a thing; the front desk here at the hospital is constantly busy. I can eh… can keep trying St Bernard's Ward for you… I do know the staff up there are extremely busy, but when a nurse finally sits at the nurses' station they will answer.'

'Yeah, yeah… keep trying,' Lenny says, bowing forward out of frustration, his head hanging through the gap between his knees.

The elevator music sounds again and Lenny lets out a deep sigh.

'Rough day?' the taxi man asks. Lenny looks up, meets the eye of his driver through the rear-view mirror.

'I'm not sure,' he says. 'Odd is the word I'd use for it. Could turn out to be rough, could turn out to be one of the best days of my life.'

The taxi man creases his brow in confusion.

'How's that then?' he asks, tilting his head.

'Putting you through now, Sir,' the man on the other end of the line says. Lenny raises his index finger, holding it up for the driver to signal that he will return an answer in time.

'St Bernard's Ward,' a woman says.

'Hey, I'm looking to speak to a patient there – a Mr Gordon Blake. I'm a eh… an associate… a friend of his.'

'We don't have phones in the rooms themselves, I'm afraid. But if you are looking for updates on Mr Blake's health, I can see if I can find his nurse – Elaine Reddy – to speak to you about his current condition.'

Lenny sits up straight in the back seat, reaches a calming thumb to massage his temple.

'He hasn't gone down for his surgeries yet, has he? Please don't tell me they've taken him down.'

'No… not yet. But soon. I think he's due to go down at three p.m. Again, Elaine would be the one to give you all of the details of Mr Bl—'

'Can you please enter his room, let him know Lenny Moon is on the line for him and that I'd like him to call me back on his mobile as soon as possible. Tell him I have news for him.'

'Eh… hold on one minute.'

There's no elevator music this time. No sound at all except for distant murmurs of a functioning hospital; muffled footsteps down hollow corridors, the odd beep.

He looks back up at the taxi man while he waits.

'I'm eh… I'm holding out for news on a house,' he says.

'I've either got it or I haven't... Still hasn't been made clear to me.'

The taxi man's brow creases again. He looks totally miffed.

'It's kinda complicated,' Lenny says, his attempt at straightening his driver's brow lines. He knows how ridiculous that sounds, especially as the taxi man is well aware that he is on hold at a hospital. Lenny turns his face, stares out at the greyness of Dublin again. He takes in the big terraced Victorian houses on the Fairview Road, imagines the faces of the happy families that must live in such comfort within them.

'I'm sorry, Sir, but Mr Blake said he's not able to make or take any more phone calls today, he's preparing himself for surgery,' the woman's voice says down the line.

Lenny feels his heart pinch a little. He hangs his mouth open, then folds himself right over – his head hanging well below his knees this time.

'Fuck sake!' he yells.

14:05

Gordon

I PICK UP THE PEN I'D LEFT RESTING AT THE SIDE OF MY BED, brushing the envelope I have addressed to Lenny aside. I wonder what he's up to now; how he's handling Michelle and Jake. It won't be easy. It always infuriated me that the cops wouldn't look into Jake for me. It's hardly just a coincidence that he came into our lives just as Betsy was taken. But it still doesn't add up that he took her. The only motive I've ever been able to come up with is that he would have wanted me and Michelle to split up... but why would he go to such lengths? I don't know. I've fuck all to go on. I'm pretty sure Jake had nothing to do with Betsy's disappearance, but what was I supposed to do... lie here in my last hours of life and do nothing? I bet Lenny's been trying to get hold of me. I'd love to turn my phone back on, see what he's up to. But I guess it's gonna be a case of him saying he questioned Jake and came to a conclusion that he had nothing to do with Betsy's disappearance.

I stare over at the envelope again, suck at my own lips. I don't know who I'm going to leave the house to if I die today. Probably nobody at this stage. The state will take it, do with it whatever the hell they please. Anyway, I'm not planning on dying. I'm going to get through these surgeries. I'm so grateful to Elaine... lying to Douglas for me; knocking a couple of digits off my actual heart rate. I owe it to her to just lie here and relax.

I grab at my book, rip out another blank page and without even thinking of how I'm going to construct this letter, I begin writing.

Dear Michelle,

Then I bring the pen to my mouth and begin to nibble on the top of it. I've so much to say to this woman. Half of it in an irate tone, half of it filled with adoration. How the fuck do I even begin to sum up what she's meant to me? Fuck it!

I know you and I have had our differences, but I don't want this letter to come across in a negative way.

If you're reading this, it's because I'm dead – that I didn't make it through my surgeries.

I guess I'm writing to you because I want to apologise for all of my faults. I know I was never the perfect husband. And it's pretty clear to everyone – you especially – that I was never a perfect father either. But I need you to understand that, while I have lived with the guilt of our dear Betsy going missing on my watch, I genuinely feel as if

As if... as if what? I lay my head back against the rail. What the fuck am I trying to say to her? I'm sorry, but it's not my fault? I don't know. I gurn in frustration, then come to the realisation that the process of writing a goodbye letter to

Michelle is not going to be as cathartic as I'd hoped it might be. It's only going to raise my heart rate even more. This wasn't a good idea. I place the pen back down on the bedside cabinet, then rub at my face with both hands, rubbing them up and down until the frustration I have running through my mind disappears.

The door opening causes me to take my hands down and when I do I immediately feel better. She's smiling at me. It seems as if we're friends again.

'Thank you so much, Elaine,' I say, as she makes her way towards me. She has both hands held aloft, palms out. I hold both my hands out to her too and we high ten.

'All sorted, Gordon,' she says. 'The team are going to operate. The theatre has been cleared of its last surgery and it's being prepped for yours now. Mr Douglas was deadly serious about not operating, but when I told him your bloods had just crept below the one-forties and that you were now being as restful as you possibly could be, he agreed to go ahead.'

I stare at her wide eyes. My little heroine.

'I may literally owe you my whole life by tonight,' I tell her.

She waves my compliment away, then points a finger at me.

'You can't tell anybody I fudged the numbers, you hear me? Even when you do survive, this has to be our little secret. I'd totally lose my job if that ever became known.'

I grab the hand that is pointing at me, turn it over and then bring it to my mouth to lightly kiss it.

'I promise I will never tell a soul.'

Elaine creases her lips into a friendly smile, then looks at the sheet of paper on my chest.

'Writing letters?' she asks.

I rub at my face; the reminder of me trying to justify

myself to Michelle making its way to the forefront of my mind again.

'The ex wife,' I tell Elaine. 'Problem is, I don't know what to say.'

'You never asked her to come up to see you, no?'

I shake my head. Can't bring myself to explain an answer. It's just way too complicated.

Elaine lets out a deep breath, her hand still being held by mine, and then eyeballs me.

'It's probably for the best,' she says. 'Let's just keep you relaxed, there isn't long to go.' She lets go of my hand, removes her pocket watch and then raises her eyebrows. 'A little less than an hour. I have to say, Gordon, you are in the best hands and—'

She looks behind at the door opening. Another nurse, dressed in a slightly different shade of purple scrubs, steps inside.

'Sorry, Elaine,' she says, 'but Mr Blake, I have a Lenny Moon on the line. He said he has something to tell you and wondered if you could call him back.'

I feel my heart rate instantly rise. What the fuck has he found out about Jake Dewey? I need to know.

'That's okay,' Elaine says, staring over her shoulder at the nurse. 'Mr Blake won't be taking or making any phone calls until he's come out of his surgeries, isn't that right, Gordon?'

She squeezes my hand. I look up to her, offer a thin smile.

'Eh... yes, I eh... I'm prepping for the surgeries now. I won't be talking to anybody.'

The nurse steps backwards towards the door.

'Of course, Mr Blake, sorry to have disturbed you.'

Elaine continues to squeeze my hand, then offers me a little wink.

'We're a good team me and you, huh?' she says.

I gulp as I offer her a fake laugh.

'You're the best,' I say.

'That's Saoirse; Saoirse Guinness – a new nurse. She'll put Lenny straight. You can speak to him after you wake up from the surgeries… okay? So, will we turn the TV back on?' she suggests casually, as if news from Lenny is insignificant.

I nod my head slowly, reach for the remote control under my sheets and hand it to her. She sits in the blue plastic chair, presses at the standby button and proceeds to click through the channels, asking me at every turn whether or not what's showing on the TV is something that interests me. I continue to just shake my head, even though I don't know what's on. I'm staring through the TV, not at it; my mind racing.

'Oh… that's all the channels,' she says eventually. 'Will I just leave something on? Pick a number.'

I smile with my eyes, wave my hand.

'I don't know… number three,' I say.

We both stare at the screen, a cheesy toothpaste advert showing images of an annoying-looking boy grinning from ear to ear comes on.

'Is Colgate going to help you relax?' Elaine says, looking to me.

I sniff a small laugh out of my nostrils, then tilt my head back as a thought comes to me.

'You know what would help me relax?' I ask.

'Go on.'

'Fruit Pastilles.'

'Fruit Past— sure you're supposed to be fasting.'

'I won't swallow them, just the taste… they'd, I don't know. I just really fancy some. I have some change here,' I say, reaching for my bedside cabinet. I open the drawer, shovel some loose change into the palm of my hand then hold it towards Elaine. 'Please,' I say, sounding a little bit like a pleading Oliver Twist.

Elaine twitches an eyebrow.

'If it'll help you relax.' She scoops the coins from my hand, then hands me the remote control. 'You find us something to watch. I'll be five minutes.'

I click at the buttons of the remote, not looking at the screen but at her as she leaves the ward. When she closes the door, I reach for the drawer of the cabinet again and grab at my phone. I hold down the standby button and wait for the screen to blink on.

'C'mon, for fuck sake,' I hiss at it. It seems to take an age for the phone to load up. When it does, I immediately click into my call history, then hold my finger against Lenny's number.

'Jesus, Gordon, what took you so long ringing me back?' he says.

'Never mind that; what's the news you have for me?'

SEVEN YEARS AGO

Betsy

MY WRIST CAN GET SORE FROM WRITING. I TWIST IT ROUND and round in circles until the pain goes away. Then I lift up my pen again and keep going.

I think my spelling is getting better. I am writing words a little bit quicker. I've been nearly a whole year writing *Betsy's Basement* and I am on chapter five. This morning I've been writing about the time I screamed when I was in the toilet upstairs. That was silly of me.

I wanted to die that day because I thought I would go to see Mummy and Daddy in heaven. Whatever heaven is. A lot of the books I read don't mention heaven. Maybe it's not even real. It makes me sad to think that I will never see Mummy and Daddy again. But I can't talk about it with Dod. Talking about Mummy or Daddy is one way to make sure Dod definitely turns into angry Dod. So instead of talking about it, I write about it in my story. Chapter one was all about me being taken by Dod. Chapter two is about how I used to keep really quiet in the basement when all of the people used to come visit Dod's house. Not so many people visit anymore. Chapter three is about me and Bozy and how we became best friends. Chapter four is about Dod letting me go upstairs for the first time. And now chapter five is about how I got beaten up by Dod for screaming when I was upstairs. I think my back is still not the same since that beating. It's sore when I wake up every morning. But even though all of my chapters are about me being here, in the basement, they always have a bit of Mummy and Daddy in them. Not that I can remember much about that time. But writing helps me remember. Or what it does is make sure I don't forget.

I can't wait to write the chapters about how me and Dod became really good friends again though. About him buying me lots and lots of books. About him letting me go upstairs to watch TV. And about him letting me look out the window from his bedroom. When I get to those chapters, I'm going to have lots of stories. Lots of stories about all of the different characters I see when I look out the window. There is a woman who lives across the street, in the house with the red door. I call her Mrs Witchety and she is a secret witch. She has fifteen cats and twelve brooms in her house. She is really funny. But scary too. I have so much fun when I am looking out the window and making characters up.

When Dod opens the door, I rest my pen down inside my book, then fold it over. I walk up the steps and hope Dod will let me look out the window today and not watch TV.

'Whatcha wanna do?' he asks when I get to the top of the steps.

I just look up at him.

'You wanna go upstairs, huh?' He makes a funny shape with his mouth and then nods his head towards the stairs. 'Okay, c'mon.'

We both walk up and as soon as I am outside his bedroom, I get down on my hands and knees and crawl around his bed until I am at the window ledge, Then I place my hands on the ledge and bring myself up so I can see out the window. I look straight away to Mrs Witchety's house but she's not outside, not today. Then I look up and down the street. Nobody's walking. This happens sometimes. Sometimes I can spend a long time looking out the window and not see anybody. Maybe today is going to be one of those days.

I look around Dod's bedroom again. There isn't much in it. A big bed and two really big wardrobes. I often wonder what's in the wardrobes. But I have never asked.

'Dod.' I say his name really slowly.

'Yes, Betsy?'

'Do you not have lots of books in your room like I do in my basement? Are they in these wardrobes?'

He laughs a little. That makes me feel good. I was worried he might turn into angry Dod for asking him about his wardrobes. He walks over to the far side of his bed and then opens a drawer.

'Here are all my books,' he says.

I'm not sure what he is showing me. It looks like just one book, but it's grey and skinny. When he brings it closer I notice that it isn't a book at all. There are no pages. I make a funny face at him and he laughs again.

'It's called a Kindle,' he says.

I keep the funny look on my face.

'I have over a hundred books on here. He presses at a button. A light comes on and makes it look like a really small TV. He turns it around so I can watch. 'See all these,' he says, 'they are all the books I have on here and I can choose to read one anytime I want.'

I'm a bit confused. But when I point my finger at one of the books, it opens. Chapter one appears on the screen.

'That's magic,' I say.

But I'm still confused.

'I buy books and they just download on to here.'

I give him my funny face again.

'Tell you what, you take a look at this. The books I read are a little old for you, but take a look through the Kindle. I've a tiny bit of work to do. So I'm going to go downstairs. I'll give you twenty minutes up here, okay? Keep your head down, Betsy.'

I look up at him and then nod my head slowly.

'Okay, Dod.'

He's never left me up here on my own. I think he thinks that I'm becoming a big girl now. A bit like a grown up. I'll be fourteen next month. I smile to myself when he leaves the room. I feel really happy that he thinks I can be left alone up here.

I take the Kindle from him and begin to press at the screen. Into one book called *War and Peace* and then another one called *Anna Karenina*. There are lots of big words in these books. Dod is right. I don't think I'd be able to read these. But this is so much fun. I can't believe all of his books are in here. Mine take up so much room in my basement.

I crawl back towards Dod's wardrobe so I can sit with my back leaned up against it and continue to play with his Kindle. I would love one of these. Except I think I would miss the smell of the paper from books. One of the first things I do when I get a new book is to flick the pages under my nose and breathe in the smell. I bring the Kindle to my nose, try to smell it. Nothing. It smells like nothing.

I stare over at the drawer Dod took the Kindle from. Wonder what other magical things he has in there. But I shouldn't look. I'd get myself into so much trouble. If I don't keep my head down, Dod will definitely turn into angry Dod. And that's the last thing I want. I look towards the window, then towards the drawer again. Then the window. Then the drawer.

I place the Kindle on top of Dod's bed and then crawl. I do it really, really slowly. When I reach his drawer I pull it open and then place my hand on his bed so I can pull myself up a little bit. I look inside. There are some pills that look like sweets and an old watch. I hold up the watch and stare at it. The hands aren't moving. It must be broken. I put it back inside, then close the drawer really slowly, making sure there is no noise. Then I crawl back over to the wardrobe I'd been sitting against. My heart thumps a little bit. That was naughty. I probably shouldn't have done that. But I can't help myself. I pull open his wardrobe. See lots and lots of clothes. There are lots of shoes in the bottom of it, lots of shirts hanging at the top. Then I pull open the drawer at the bottom of his wardrobe. Lots of papers. I flick through them to see what they are all about. But there's too many of them. I lift the top one off and then sit with my back to the wardrobe and begin to read it.

In big black writing at the top, it says "DNA confirms Betsy Blake is Dead".

14:15

Lenny

A SLITHER OF ORANGE IS THREATENING TO RID THE SKY OF ITS greyness by the time Lenny steps out of the taxi, but the sun has a lot of work to do if it wants to make itself known over Dublin today. The rain is still falling, but only lightly now. Lenny stands outside the uneven wooden railing of Guus's house and just stares at it. It's a big detached house, yet it's unkempt; the grass in the garden overly long and peppered with litter, the windows dusty and smeared. Lenny stiffens his nose at the contrast of what he's seeing. In order to live in this house – especially around here – you'd have to be worth a good few quid. Why couldn't a rich man afford somebody to at least make their home look good?

When he finally takes his eyes from the garden, Lenny feels his phone vibrate in his pocket. He flips it over to see who's trying to reach him.

'Ah for fuck sake!' he rages, stamping on the pavement. He sighs deeply, then presses the answer button.

'Hey, sweetie,' he says.

'How's work?'

'Eh… grand. Y'know, the usual.'

'You seemed quite busier than usual earlier when I rang you.'

'It's been a bit of a different day alright, sweetie. I'll tell you all about it when I get home.'

Sally makes an interested huff sound down the line.

'Okay cool. Will you be coming by the house to pick me up before the meeting or will I see you at the school?'

Lenny opens his eyes wide, then squelches his entire face in to an ugly gurn. He places both hands over the phone, holding it away from his face, them mouths a quiet 'bollocks' to himself. He lifts one hand from the phone, stares at the screen to catch the time. 14:17.

'I eh...' he stutters as he blinks rapidly. 'I eh... got caught up in a job. I don't think I can get to the boys' school for three p.m.'

He winces in anticipation of Sally's response. But he doesn't get one; both ends of the line deathly silent.

'Sweetie,' he says eventually.

'You've let me down. No, no... hold it: you've let us all down. Me, Jacob, Jared.'

Then a dead tone sounds.

Lenny kicks the pavement again. He immediately begins to fumble with his phone, then holds it back to his ear, a ringing tone sounding.

'Go on... explain yourself then,' Sally says upon answering.

'Sweetie... I can't tell you exactly what is going on right now. I will when I get home, but I'm on a very delicate job that I can't discuss over the phone.' Silence. Again. 'It's good news, baby. I got big money for this gig. A guy gave me a grand just to do a tiny bit of snooping but it's ended up with me out in Clontarf now and I'm just not going to get back in time for the school meeting. I'm sorry. I really am.'

'The grand that was transferred into the account this morning?'

'Yeah... yeah, that's it,' Lenny says.

'You told me that was for some older job.'

The line goes dead.

Lenny thumbs his phone, calls the home number again. No answer. Tries again. Same result. He stares at the big old house in front of him and then tips his head back, all the way back so that the light rain begins to fall against his mouth. He's unsure what to do; whether to take a taxi back home or to follow through on his investigation. Sally has always been his priority, always will be. He should go home, give up the ghost. He spins around, faces the coastal road and begins to nibble on the butt of his phone. He thinks about his wife, about his two sons. About their sad existence.

'Fuck it,' he says, bringing his phone down to thumb at it again.

`Sweetie I'm really sorry. Please don't do anything stupid. I'm doing this job for us... for the whole family. Trust me. Call me back when you can. I love you. x`

Then he spins on his heels and heads straight for the rickety wooden gate in front of him. He's beyond intrigued now, the thought of making an impact in Ireland's biggest ever missing person's case overriding the concerns he has for his wife. He can barely bring himself to imagine what kind of attention he would get if he solved – in the space of a few hours – a mystery that has plagued the country for seventeen years.

Instead of heading for the front door, he walks to the side of the house, towards an old Volkswagen Beetle, the grass growing thick around all of its deflated tyres. He cups his hands to stare in through the window but sees nothing but darkness. Then he paces around the back of the house, notices that it's even more unkempt than the front. The grass must be at least three foot in height, going all the way up to Lenny's waist.

'Jesus, this place could be so fucking gorgeous,' he whispers to himself.

He walks further into the back garden, wading through the blades of grass and then peers in through the back window from a distance, noticing a massive, modern kitchen. He squints again – not sure what to make of the place. But he's enjoying playing detective; his heart rate working at a pace he seems to revel in. He rummages through the long blades, picks up some litter, examines it as if he's doing something worthwhile and then releases it from his fingers. He picks up dirty ice pop wrappers, empty plastic bottles, a broken picture frame with no photo inside it, an old oil-stained T-shirt and then the arm of a doll.

'What the fuck?' he says, staring back at the house. His pulse quickens. He wants to examine further, to go deeper into the mass of land at the back garden, but decides he needs to get inside. He's not going to find Betsy out here. If Guus Meyer has her, he has her locked up inside his home. Lenny puts the doll arm in his jacket pocket, creeps back through the grass, past the Beetle and then finds himself at the large front door. He looks for a bell, can't find one. The only thing noticeable on or around the door is a sign reading: 'No unsolicited mail.' Then he clenches his fist and rattles on one of the door panels. Nothing. He knocks again. Nothing. Lenny paces backwards to take in every window of the front of the home, to see if any curtains are twitching. But the house seems dead.

'Bollocks,' he says to himself. He contemplates ringing De Brun back, letting him know he's outside Guus Meyer's house and that he is growing in certainty that she may be inside; the arm of a doll enough evidence to suggest Betsy wasn't killed by a car on the day she went missing; that she's been holed up in this gaff all that time. But he knows he'd be laughed at. De Brun would have to be here in person to comprehend the creepiness of it all. It's only when Lenny looks up to allow more rain to fall on his face that he realises it has stopped raining.

Then his jacket pocket begins to vibrate. He parts his lips, sighs a little and then reaches for his phone, mindfully preparing himself for his apology to Sally. But it's not Sally ringing. Lenny's eyebrows rise as he jabs at the answer button.

'Jesus, Gordon, what took you so long ringing me back?' he says.

'Never mind that; what's the news you have for me?'

Lenny pauses, takes a deep breath and then composes himself.

'There was another suspect in Betsy's disappearance – somebody De Brun never told you about.'

Lenny can hear the shuffling of bed clothes, assumes Gordon has got out of bed and is now on his feet anticipating news he has waited seventeen years to hear.

'Who?' he says.

'Now hold on, Gordon... I want to know that you will abide by the deal we made a few hours ago. If I am to give you information on Betsy's disappearance that you've never heard before, you will leave me your home in your will.'

'Who?'

'Gordon, do we have a deal?'

'Who the fuck is it?' Gordon says, his voice rising in both volume and frustration.

'Gordon – I need you to—'

'Of course you can have my fucking home if I die... tell me who the other suspect was. It's Jake Dewey, isn't it? The cops always told me they didn't look into him, but they did, didn't they? The dirty fucking—'

'Gordon, it's not Jake Dewey. Dewey didn't have anything to do with Betsy's disappearance. I spoke with De Brun and then to Frank Keville, do you know who he is?'

'Frank Keville, the journalist guy?'

'Yep... he told me there were four initial suspects in the case. You were one. Keating and Barry Ward the others.'

'And?'

Lenny pauses, and for the first time imagines how Gordon is going to take this news; that his best friend and business partner for many years looks likely to be the person who abducted his daughter. Then the green door creaks open and a man, dressed in a crisp white shirt, peers through the crack.

'Who, Lenny?' Gordon continues to bark down the line.

Lenny holds the phone down by his side, stares at the stranger.

'Who?' Gordon continues to yell.

'What'sh going on – why are you shnooping round my property?' the stranger asks with a broad accent.

Lenny holds the phone back up to his ear, just in time to hear Gordon speak.

'Guus... Guus... Is that Guus Meyer?'

SIX YEARS AGO

Betsy

'Hmmmm. That was good,' I say to Bozy as I put down my copy of a book called *Agatha Christie: An Autobiography*. She was an incredible woman. I must read some of her books sometime. I don't really read too much fiction these days, but I'd love to read some of hers.

Some of the words in her autobiography were a bit difficult for me. But I managed to read it all and thought it was really good. I just wish I could write as many books as her.

I climb down off my bed and sit against the wall and pick up my copybook. I flick it open to where my pen is – right at the start of chapter 21. Chapter 20 was all about me seeing out of Dod's window for the first time. Chapter 21 was supposed to be about the stories of the people I see when I look out the window. But I was thinking last night that I should begin to write about the newspaper articles I find up in Dod's bedroom instead.

I look up at the crack beneath the door at the top of the steps and when I am sure that Dod is nowhere near, I go over to my shelf, pick up my *Harry Potter and the Philosopher's Stone* book and open it. Then I pull out the newspaper article I took from Dod's room two nights ago. I read it again. It's an article about how a detective called Ray De Brun has been under pressure to find me. At the top of the newspaper page it says the date was sixth of September, 2006. I went missing in January 2002 according to another article. This isn't the best one I've read. And it doesn't have any pictures of me either. It's just a small bit of writing down the side of the page with a headline that says: De Brun Feeling the Heat.

It is weird when I see pictures of myself in the newspaper pages. I never think they look like me. But I guess it is difficult for me to remember what I looked like when I was four years old. It always seems to be the same picture; me with a little smile on my face wearing a navy jumper. I don't remember that jumper at all. I don't remember much about who I was or what I did before Dod took me. I just know that he took me and that there is a big detective out there looking for me. I really want to read all of the newspaper pages Dod has in his room. But it is not often that he leaves me alone up there. When he does, I open that drawer under his wardrobe, take one of the newspaper articles out and shove it down my pants. This is the fourth newspaper article I've taken and I think I found them for the first time nearly a year ago. I like reading them, even though they scare me a little bit. They also make me hate Dod a little bit because he took me from Mummy and Daddy. But then he will just walk into my basement and hand me a brand new book. And suddenly I don't hate him anymore.

He can be so good. And yet he is so bad. I guess that's why there is a good Dod and an angry Dod.

I hear the key turn in the door and then it swings open. Oh no. I put the newspaper article inside the Harry Potter book and snap it closed really quickly. This is the first time

Dod's come down to the basement without me having a newspaper article I've stolen from him hidden safely. I hear my heart thump louder than it normally does. I stay silent, don't even look up at Dod when he comes down the steps. I don't know where to look or what to do.

'Hey – what's wrong with you, moody pants?' he says. I finally look up at him and then shrug my shoulders. He probably has a little present for me. I should be feeling excited about it. But I don't. I feel really scared. I stare down at the Harry Potter book, then back up at him.

'I've got you a little something,' he says.

I get to my feet, walk over towards him.

'Close your eyes, put out your hands.'

I do.

'No peeking.'

And then he puts something into my hands. It feels a little cold. Hard and cold.

'Okay, and open.'

A Kindle. A Kindle!

'Is this for me?' I ask.

He laughs.

'You betcha.'

I wrap my arms around his waist and hug him really hard.

'Thank you so much, Dod.'

He laughs again, tosses my hair with his hands.

I look up into his eyes and smile a really, really big smile.

'Well, I figured we wouldn't have much room for many more books down here.'

He turns around and points at my shelves.

'How many do you have now?'

'A hundred and thirty-three,' I say.

'Well a hundred and thirty-three in this,' he says, touching the Kindle I have snuggled into my chest, 'won't take up a whole wall of your basement, huh?'

I laugh.

'Ah… and this one still is one of your favourites out of all one hundred and thirty-three, isn't it?' he says.

'Huh?'

My heart thumps when I look to him.

He bends down and picks up my *Harry Potter and the Philosopher's Stone*.

'Y'know – I know I'm an old man at this stage, but I really should try these out.'

He smiles, looks at me. Then his smile goes away.

'What's wrong with you, Betsy? Looks like you've seen a ghost.'

I hug my Kindle, step back a few steps and just nod my head. My heart sounds like a train. Ka-chunk, ka-chunk, ka-chunk.

'Betsy. Betsy.'

He calls out my name as he takes a step towards me. I try not to look at the Harry Potter book in his hands. But I can't help it. He holds a hand to my forehead.

'Your temperature seems fine. Why don't you just hop into bed? Take some rest today. Maybe you can read your Kindle. I have two books loaded up on it for you. I can teach you how to download newer ones too. I've set up an account for you.'

I sit on the edge of my bed. Dod then lifts my feet, turns me into the bed and pulls the sheet up over me.

'Do you not like the Kindle?' he says. 'Hold on – you just want books, huh? You prefer paper.'

I don't say anything. I just stare straight ahead.

'What's wrong, Betsy? Why have you gone really quiet?'

I'm not quiet. My heart is being really loud. Really, really loud. Ka-chunk, ka-chunk, ka-chunk.

'You'd rather read a paper one like this, huh?' he says wiggling my Harry Potter book.

Then I see it fall out. The newspaper article floating slowly from my Harry Potter book, and sailing in the air until it finally reaches the ground. I stay still.

Dod crouches down, picks it up and opens it. Then he stares right at me. As if he wants to kill me.

14:15

Gordon

I sit up sharply, whip the sheets away from me and throw my legs over the side of the bed.

'Who?' I say.

'Gordon, do we have a deal?'

My palms begin to sweat. I suck a sharp breath in through my grinding teeth.

'Who the fuck is it?'

'Gordon – I need you to—'

'Of course you can have my fucking home if I die! Tell me who the other suspect was. It's Jake Dewey isn't it? The cops always told me they didn't look into him, but they did, didn't they? The dirty fucking—'

'Gordon, it's not Jake Dewey,' Lenny says and then my world seems to almost stand still. 'Dewey didn't have anything to do with Betsy's disappearance. I spoke with De Brun and then to Frank Keville, do you know who he is?'

My eyes flicker around the ward.

'Frank Keville, the journalist guy?'

'Yep... he told me there were four initial suspects in the case. You were one. Alan Keating and Barry Ward the others.'

'And?'

The line pauses. For way too long.

'Who, Lenny?' I bark.

Silence again.

'Who?'

Then I hear a quiet voice. A voice I haven't heard in years. The Dutch lisp still strong.

'Guus… Guus… Is that Guus Meyer?'

My eyes widen. I pace around the room, my feet slapping against the cold floor.

'Yes, Gordon. I'm at Guus Meyer's home. I'll ring you back in a few—'

'You will in your bollocks ring me back… I wanna know exactly what's going on.'

For some reason I find myself in the toilet cubicle, then outside it. I perch on the end of my bed, then pace over to the far wall. I can't stay still. My whole body is sprinting just as quickly as my mind is.

'Gordon, I know this has come as a major shock to you. But please just calm down. I am going to get answers and then I am going to ring you straight back.' I hyperventilate down the line, can actually hear my heavy breaths reverberate back into my own ear. 'Gordon, just get that will signed and I will deliver on my promise. I am about to have news for you that you have never heard before.' The line goes dead.

I lean back against the wall, slide down it until my ass is sitting on the cold floor. I don't think it takes long for my head to snap out the spin it's been in. My eyes focus on the bed rail in front of me. I lift the phone back up to my face and press at Lenny's number. I remain focused on the bed rail, my eyes in no way interested in even blinking. Bollocks! The phone rings out. I get to my feet, try again.

'Answer the fucking phone, Lenny,' I pant just as my ward

door opens and Elaine walks in. Her face contorts seeing me strolling around with the phone to my ear.

'Gordon!' She paces over to my bedside cabinet, drops a tube of Fruit Pastilles on top of it, then folds her arms under her tiny breasts and sighs at me.

I hold the phone down by my side, hold her stare before I finally speak up.

'Elaine, my PI found something new. My best friend, can you believe it? He thinks my best friend took Betsy.'

Elaine doesn't react; she stands still, her arms still folded. The silence is almost deafening, both of us deep in thought.

'I need to ring him back. I need to ring him back.'

I bring the phone to my face to redial and just as I go to press on Lenny's number Elaine finally makes a move, stepping towards me and grabbing my wrist.

'Mr Douglas will not go through with your surgeries if you make that call,' she says. She's gripping so hard it actually hurts. 'You promised me you would keep that phone turned off, promised me you would relax. I'm trying to keep you alive, Gordon Blake. Whatever your PI has to say to you, he can say it to you after you recover from your surgeries.'

I hold my eyes tightly closed. And as I do, I sense Elaine leading me over to my bed. Without questioning her, I arch my bum cheeks on top of the mattress and then lie down.

'I need you to witness me signing something,' I say.

She doesn't reply.

'In fact I need you and some other person to witness me signing something, can you do that?'

She stands back after draping the sheets over me.

'Elaine?' I say, turning to her, opening my eyes.

'Gordon, I need you to relax. There is barely any time left until you are taken down for surgery.'

I close my eyes again, then shift down in the bed until my head is resting on the pillow.

Guus. Fucking Guus. No. Couldn't be. I can't get my head straight. My thoughts keep jumping. Is this why the cunt hasn't spoken to me in years? Jesus, Gordon, get your act together. Think, for fuck's sake!

I feel Elaine grab at my left hand as I continue to stew in thought. She feels for my pulse. I don't pull away. I just let her do what she needs to do as I think this through. Guus Meyer took my Betsy?

'Just breathe, Gordon,' Elaine says, her thumb pressed against my wrist. Then I feel her face near mine; she breathes in deeply, then out deeply.

'Follow my breaths,' she whispers.

I do. I sync my breathing with hers. It slows my thinking.

'In just over half-an-hour, you are going down for major surgery. You need to survive these surgeries.' Elaine sounds like one of those meditation tapes. 'In order to survive those surgeries, you need to be calm. Your heart rate needs to be consistent. Keep breathing.'

I imagine myself on the surgical table, Douglas slicing his scalpel into me, ripping my chest open. Fucking hell. I'm going to die. I'm going to die in the next couple of hours. My eyes open wide. I whip the sheets off me again and jump out of bed, almost pushing Elaine aside. I still have the phone gripped in my hand. I tap at it, call Lenny's number. It rings. And rings. And rings. Then cuts off.

'Gordon Blake, I swear if you don't lie down right now I am going to advise Mr Douglas to cancel your procedures.'

I don't answer Elaine; I just pace around the room, look at the phone's screen and press again at Lenny's number. I know I look like a madman, almost running around, but I don't give a fuck.

'Gordon please!' Elaine shouts. She stops me from pacing in circles and grabs me around the waist. I can hear the tone ringing out again as she tries to wrestle the phone from my hand. We end up in a scrum in the middle of the ward, both of us tumbling to the floor.

Then the door opens. I look up, under Elaine's armpit, and expect to see Mr Douglas standing there with his clipboard, shaking his head. But it's not him. I relent, release the grip on my phone and allow Elaine to take it. Then I scramble to a standing position.

'Michelle,' I say, stretching a big smile across my face. I wipe both of my hands down the front of my T-shirt and walk towards her, leaving Elaine sitting on the floor. 'What are you doing here?'

FIVE YEARS AGO

Betsy

THIS IS THE WORST CHRISTMAS EVER. DOD JUST PUT EXTRA money on my Kindle account as a present. That was it. No box to unwrap. No funny hats to wear. No silly songs to sing. I've been down in the basement all day. Dod upstairs. We barely speak to each other these days. Not since he beat me up back in February. He threw me against the wall. Slapped my arms, my stomach, my back, my legs. He was really angry. Really, really angry. His face was purple.

He doesn't let me upstairs to watch TV anymore. Doesn't let me go to his bedroom to stare out the window. I miss staring out the window the most. I loved to see other people.

But I know it's all my fault. I shouldn't have been stealing newspaper articles out of his drawer. Even if they were newspaper articles about me.

The worst thing about it all is that Dod feels really disappointed in me. I don't think he loves me anymore. I don't even know if he likes me. He probably wishes I was dead.

The other times he beat me up, he always felt bad about it. He would come back down to my basement the next day and tell me how sorry he was. But ten months on from the last beating he gave me, he still hasn't said sorry. And I think that's because he is not sorry. He feels I deserved the beating. And so do I. I'm the one who should be saying sorry. I have tried to say sorry lots of times since, but Dod doesn't say anything back.

The only time I really see him these days is when he lets me upstairs to wash in the toilet room and then on some days I go to the kitchen to cook dinner for us. But I don't eat with him in the TV room. I have to take my dinner down here and eat it all by myself. I thought he would have let me upstairs to eat today of all days. But no. I'm here doing nothing. He's up there doing nothing. This is the saddest Christmas I've ever had.

The thing that I'm most sad about is that I will never get to see the rest of those newspaper articles. I wanted to find out so much about them for my book. I only ever got to read four of them. I found out things I never even knew about myself. I didn't know my second name. But now I know that. I didn't know the date I was taken. Now I know that. I didn't know that I had a big detective looking for me. Now I know that. I wonder if he is still looking for me. The first article I stole said that I was dead. So maybe they've given up.

I've written all of this into my book. *Betsy's Basement* now has thirty-three chapters. The last seven chapters have all been about characters I made up that I saw when I was looking out of Dod's bedroom window. So the book has changed. It has turned from a non-fiction book to a fiction one. Some days I think it's all just rubbish and other days I think it is good. I've been writing it for three years. But the problem is, I don't know how to end it. I don't know what way the story should finish.

I pick up my copybook and wonder what I should write about today. But I'm not really in the mood. I'm bored. Or tired. Maybe both. I stretch my arms way above my head and then let out a big yawn.

Worst Christmas ever.

Bozy has the right idea. He's all snuggled up under my sheets on the bed. I yawn again. Fuck it, I'll join him. There's nothing else to do.

I lift up the sheets, grab at my Kindle which is lying under them and then snuggle into Bozy.

'This is a bad Christmas, Bozy,' I say. I use my two fingers to make him nod back at me. Then I give him a big kiss.

I roll back over, turn on my Kindle and go straight into the bookstore. I have twenty-five euro in my account now. I click into non-fiction books and scroll through the list. I've read most of the ones I want to read. Nothing else really interests me. So I click out and into the fiction list. Nothing really on this list interests me either. I think this year has been my worst year for reading. I just haven't been interested in reading too much. I haven't really been interested in anything.

Ever since Dod beat me up, I've just wanted to do nothing but lie on this bed. I feel really sad. Really, really sad. So sad, I'd rather not be alive. Being alive and having all these sad thoughts makes me wish I didn't have any thoughts at all. Being asleep is now my favouritist hobby. It would probably be better if I was always asleep.

I press the home button on my Kindle. Only because I don't know what else to do. A little box flashes up that I've never seen before.

Software update required.

I click on it and then loads of writing comes up. It says 'Terms and Conditions' up the top, but when I try to read it I get confused. I don't know what any of it means.

By the time I get to the bottom of the page it asks if I

would like to continue. I am about to press 'Yes' when I see another box below.

`Chat with one of our representatives now.`

So I click that. And then a blank box appears. I don't know what to do. I try to find something that will let me click away from it, but I can't find anything. Then some writing appears.

`Hi, my name is Sana. How may I help you today?`

I stare at the message. Then a little keyboard appears. I hit at one of the keys and it shows up in the box.

My heart begins to get faster. Wow. This is amazing. I can talk back to Sana. This will be the first time I've spoken to anybody other than Dod since I was four years old. That'll be a whole thirteen years next month. I breathe in and out really fast. Then in and out really slowly.

I wiggle my fingers in front of my face and then begin to type back to Sana. Slowly. Really, really slowly.

`Hello, my name is Betsy Blake.`

14:20

Lenny

Lenny blinks rapidly after hanging up the call.

'I'm so sorry about that,' he says to the man in the doorway. 'That was eh... that was your old mate on the phone – Gordon Blake.'

'Gordon? What the hell were you two talking about?' Guus says, looking dumbfounded, his eyebrows almost coming together above his narrow eyes.

'Guus, would you mind if I came in to speak to you for a few minutes?'

Guus looks behind him, into his hallway, then back out at Lenny.

'I'm a busy man. What'sh going on?'

Lenny stares at Guus, assumes he certainly doesn't look the type to kidnap a kid, though he's under no doubt that his home looks exactly like the type of house a missing kid would be kept in. It's eerie. Creepy. Something's not right about this place. He can't quite work out why Guus would be so well refined in his appearance, yet his home is a total mess.

'I just need ten minutes of your time. I have some bad news about Gordon.'

Guus's eyebrows are still narrowing when he steps out from his front door and stands aside.

'Ten minutesh,' he says, pointing his hand towards his dark hallway. Lenny inches forward, then stalls to look Guus square in the eye. He nods a silent thank you before walking past him. As he does, his phone begins to ring. He looks at the screen, sees Gordon's number, then hits a button that silences the call and places it back inside his jacket pocket. He sucks on his own lips as he takes five steps down Guus's floorboarded hallway, sparks of adrenaline beginning to rise from the pit of his stomach. This is the rush he's been chasing his entire career. This is proper fucking investigating.

Lenny stops and looks back at Guus closing the front door. When it's fully closed, the hallway falls into total darkness. Lenny's knees almost buckle as Guus's slow footsteps edge closer to him. Then he flinches slightly when he feels Guus raise an arm. Click. The entire hallway lights up. Lenny straightens his neck, lifting his head away from his shoulders and then takes in his surroundings. He's immediately drawn to a door at the end of the hallway. A door that must lead downstairs. A basement. The perfect place to hide somebody.

'I eh... I'm sorry to say,' Lenny croaks, 'that Gordon Blake may only have hours left to live.'

Guus's eyebrows straighten and his pupils grow wide.

'You're fooking kidding me.'

'I'm afraid not, Guus. He has to undergo major heart surgery that he may not wake up from.'

'Jeshus fookin Christ,' Guus says, bringing his hand to his mouth. 'All the fooking shtress and strain he's been under for so many years... I'm not surprised.'

The hallway falls silent but for the buzzing inside Lenny's jacket pocket. He ignores it while staring into Guus's face just inches away from his own. Lenny taps Guus on the shoulder, offering condolences in an attempt to come across as initially supportive. He figures it may be best to endear himself to his suspect before finally pushing at his buttons.

Guus turns his wrist over, checks the time.

'Please,' he says. 'Let'sh go in here... would you like a cup of tea?'

Guus leads Lenny through a doorway before turning on another light. The kitchen is a beautiful white; modern and bright. Lenny creases his brow, confused by the contrast of the interior of the home compared to the exterior.

'Please. Two sugars, drop of milk.'

As Guus makes his way towards the kettle, Lenny paces the kitchen, taking in all of his new surroundings. He stares at the framed abstract artwork on the walls, then picks up the salt and pepper shakers from the table as if inspecting them. He's acting how he assumes a detective should act in these circumstances.

'So... what'sh wrong with Gordon exactly?' Guus asks.

Lenny places the pepper shaker back on the table, then looks up sheepishly at his suspect.

'He has to have abdominal aortic aneurysm surgery at three p.m. today. The procedures he has to undergo carry major risks... surgeons are only giving him a fifty-fifty chance of making it out alive.'

Guus shakes his head and then blows out through his lips, making a raspberry sound that stops just as the kettle comes to the boil.

'That man never caught a break his entire life. Do you know him well?' Guus asks as he begins to pour.

'I eh... only met him for the first time this morning.'

Guus stares back over his shoulder at Lenny, his

eyebrows creasing inwards again. He makes his way to the fridge, pulls out a bottle of milk and when he realises Lenny isn't following up, he asks another question.

'You just met him today? Are you from the hoshpital or something?'

Lenny clears his throat.

'No, Guus. I'm a private investigator.'

Lenny maintains his stare after he says that, he doesn't even blink. It's his attempt at acting cool, composed, calm. He thinks back to Alan Keating and how brilliantly the gangster handled confrontation earlier this morning. He's trying to act nonchalant, as if he's in control of both the pace and the tone of the dialogue.

'A private inveshtigator?'

Lenny just nods but then loses his cool persona when Guus walks towards him with a hot mug.

'Oh, oh, oh fuck that's hot,' he says as he takes the mug from Guus.

'I'm shorry. Let me cool that down for you,' Guus says, turning around and then grabbing at the bottle of milk.

He pours some into Lenny's mug, then sits at the table opposite and begins to sip his own brew.

Lenny pulls out a chair of his own, sits on it and then stares across at Guus, wondering how he should approach the conversation. He takes a deep breath, then dives straight in.

'I'm investigating the disappearance of Betsy Blake.' He stares at Guus's face as he says this, determined to find a glimmer of guilt. All Guus does is tip his head back in surprise, then forward again.

'Betsy's disappearance? Does Gordon still think Betsy is alive?'

Lenny clears his throat again. He's finding acting like a

cool investigator particularly difficult. It just doesn't seem to come naturally to him.

'You don't think she is?' he asks, before sipping on his tea.

Guus offers half-a-laugh, a tiny snigger that sneaks out of the side of his mouth.

'Nobody believesh she is alive, surely,' he says. He stares over the rim of his mug at Lenny. His eyes change; his pupils growing large. He swallows, then gasps. 'Hold on, does Gordon genuinely shtill think Betsy is alive?'

'Yep,' Lenny replies. 'Gordon is convinced she is; that somebody abducted her.'

Another laugh sneaks out of the side of Guus's mouth. Lenny swirls his jaw; the laugh grating on him.

'Well... he must be the only person on the planet to think tha—'

'He's not,' Lenny says placing his mug back down on to the table. 'I think it too.'

Guus opens his mouth ajar.

'But I thought the cops concluded Betsy was killed in a car accident. The DNA in the back of a car they found shuggested she was dead, no?'

Lenny coughs again, then shifts uncomfortably in his chair.

'That's one theory, yes,' he says. He flickers his eyes up to the ceiling, reminds himself that he should stay cool, stay composed, stay in control.

'I don't believe it,' Guus says, shaking his head. 'You're telling me the cops got it wrong, made it up?'

'It's possible the cops came to a conclusion under pressure to close the case. They never found anybody or anything relating to Betsy. There was a lot of heat on them.'

Guus pushes back his chair a little, then leans more forward, his elbows resting on the table.

'Cops don't do that kind of shtuff in Ireland,' he says. 'That doesn't make any sense at all.'

'Well, we've looked at the evidence of the car theory and none of it adds up,' Lenny lies. 'So we are looking again at all of the original suspects. We feel something went under the radar.'

Guus laughs; not with humour, with discomfort. He stands up, spins around and then grips the back of the chair he had been sitting on.

'This doesn't make any... I mean... I eh... I don't know what to say.'

Lenny stands up, almost matching his suspect for height.

'Well, you can start by telling me where you were when Betsy Blake was abducted.' He lifts his mug from the table, stares over the rim at Guus as he sips from it. He notices Guus's face crumble, his eyes darting left and right.

'Not this shit again,' Guus says. 'I told the cops when they questioned me that I was here, working from home, ash I normally am, when Betsy was taken.'

'And do you have any witnesses that can confirm that for you?' Lenny asks.

Guus washes the palm of his right hand over his entire face; swiping it right, then left.

'Listen, the cops have been through all this. I didn't take Betsy... of course I didn't. What would I be doing taking a four-year-old girl?'

Lenny shrugs his shoulders.

'Well... you tell me,' he says.

Guus squints, then shakes his head.

'What does that even mean?'

Lenny falls silent, stares up to the ceiling in search of an answer to the question posed. He realises he may be taking his cool detective persona past a place of no return. Guus's right; that question doesn't make any sense. If he keeps acting ambiguously, he's either going to be run out of the house, or run out of time. He tilts his head back upright, places his mug back down on the table and then eyeballs his suspect.

'I'm intrigued,' he says, 'why is the inside of your home so immaculate yet the outside is eh...'

'Unkempt?'

Lenny nods his head once, then awaits an answer.

'I don't like people coming to my home. Shimple as that.'

'Hold on. You own this massive house that you must have spent an awful lot of money on, have it looking supreme inside, but on the outside you make it look...'

'Unwelcome.'

Lenny squelches up his nose. 'Why?'

'I mostly work from home, like to be left alone. I don't like attention. Lotsh of different reasons. I don't live in the garden, I live inside the house. This ish where I'd rather spend my money, my time, my efforts.'

Lenny squints.

'You got something to hide?' he asks.

'You mean apart from the young girl I have hidden in the basement?'

Lenny blinks rapidly. His cool persona dissipating. He doesn't know how to react to what's just been said. He wonders why Guus kept such a straight face as he said it. He tries to shield his eyes with his hand, to hide his blinking tic, but he's aware Guus has already sensed that the investigator has been stumped.

'Lenny, if that's all the questions for now, I'd like to get back to work. Tell Gordon I'm shorry to hear of his condition and that I hope he makes a full recovery.'

Guus walks towards the kitchen door, holds it open, readies himself for Lenny to move. But Lenny remains where he is.

'I have another question for you, Guus.'

Guus brushes his hand through the air, signalling that Lenny should fire away.

'When is the last time you maintained your garden… gave it a good clean up?'

'Holy shit – are you a PI or a horticulturisht?' Guus says, a creepy laugh seeping out of the side of his mouth again.

'I'm a PI, and I'd like you to answer the question.'

Guus sniggers.

'Probably seven or eight years ago. When I first moved in, I looked after it. It was messy when I moved in, I gave it a good going over and then decided I preferred it looking dilapidated because nobody used to call to the house when it was dilapidated, so I've let it grow out since.'

Lenny sits down, stares right through the man standing across from him.

'So you cleaned up the whole garden when you moved in?'

Guus shrugs his shoulder.

'As best I could, yesh,' he says.

Lenny smirks, adrenaline starting to rise in his stomach again. It was moments like these he'd had ambitions of experiencing for years – ever since he was a teenager. He reaches inside his jacket pocket while eyeballing Guus.

'So if you cleaned up your garden, why did I find this in it today?' he says, sliding the doll's arm across the table.

Guus stares down at the plastic arm, squints to work out what it is, then looks back up at Lenny before creasing into laughter.

'Sure you could find anything out there. There's lotsh of shit in my garden.'

Lenny sucks in both of his cheeks, then nods his head slowly.

'But you said you cleaned up the garden after you moved in.'

Guus sighs, then strolls back to the kitchen table and sits down. He rubs his hand over his face.

'I really don't have time for this shit,' he says. 'Lishten, I gave the garden a once over when I moved in. My once over is fooking nothing. I cut down some bushes, trimmed parts of the garden. There is a whole load of shit out there that is probably lying there years. I don't fooking know. What are you suggeshtin? You're going to have me arrested because you found an old toy in my garden? Is this all you've got?'

Lenny stops himself from blinking; consciously stretching his eyes wide open. But he goes quiet, moot, as he tries to think of where he can go to from here. He thinks about the door in the hallway that leads down to the basement, then flicks his entire face when his next question pops into his head.

'No, that's not all I've got, Guus,' he says.

Guus hangs out his bottom lip, shakes his head a little.

'What... you've got a teddy bear in the other pocket?' The volume of his laughter goes up five notches after he says this. Lenny doesn't wince though. He doesn't feel intimidated. He knows what's coming next.

'No – no more toys. Just records.'

'Records?' says Guus, still laughing.

'Yep. Records of your online activity – records of your fascination with kiddie porn.'

Gordon

MICHELLE DOESN'T ANSWER MY QUESTION. SHE JUST LOOKS AT me, then shifts her gaze to Elaine on the floor. Shit. Elaine. I turn around, offer her my hand. She allows me to help her to her feet.

'I am so sorry, Elaine,' I say. She keeps her gaze away from me as she steadies herself. What the fuck have I done? This young woman has done nothing but help me all morning.

'What's going on?' Michelle finally pipes up. She removes her handbag from her shoulder, stares at me with wide eyes.

I hold my eyes tight closed for a few seconds, try to let everything wash over me.

'Myself and Elaine here just had a little disagreement about how much time I've been spending on my phone; it's nothing to worry about, Michelle.'

Elaine walks by me, heading for the doorway Michelle is standing in.

'No, no... wait,' I call out, holding a hand across her. 'Please.'

She stands frozen. Then stares at my ex wife.

'Gordon, let the nurse go,' Michelle says.

246

I take my arm away, then clasp both of my palms together, as if I'm in prayer.

'Elaine, Michelle... please,' I beg. 'Listen to me, both of you – I have something astonishing to tell you.'

Neither of them look at me, they're too invested in each other's faces; both of them wondering what the fuck I'm rambling on about.

'Please,' I beg again, 'hear me out for two minutes.'

Michelle walks by both of us, places her handbag on the blue plastic chair and then sighs.

'What have you got to tell us, Gordon?' she says.

I look at Elaine, wait on her to turn around. She does. Slowly. I reach for the door, slap it closed, then make my way back towards my bed.

'Just give me a sec,' I say scratching at my temple. I want to get this out right but I have to let it all sink in. I perch on the side of my bed, then look up at both women. Michelle is a little drenched, her hair slightly matted to her shoulders, but she still looks good, still attractive. Even if there is strain splashed across her eye set. Elaine looks pained, disappointed. Disappointed in me, I guess. I need to speak up.

'You'll never guess what I've just heard,' I say, then stop to gulp. 'Guus Meyer – he took Betsy.'

I look down on the floor, afraid to witness the reaction of Michelle. I can sense her looking over at Elaine and rolling her eyes. But there's silence. A very strange silence. As if I didn't say anything at all.

'I had a private investigator dig deep into Betsy's disappearance and he found out that Guus was involved. He's out in his house interviewing him now. I couldn't just lie here and die without... without...' I hold my hand up to my face, try to stop the tears from spilling out of my eyes, but it's a hopeless task.

Elaine's the first to react. She takes three steps towards me, places her hand on my shoulder and helps me to lie down flat on the bed. I use my feet to scoot myself backwards, so that I'm sitting up, my back against the bed rail.

I know Michelle is silent, but I can hear her thoughts. She thinks I'm a fucking madman. That I'm making this all up.

'Gordon,' Elaine whispers towards me, 'I have to go now to speak with Mr Douglas about your surg—'

'No, no,' I say, panicking. I pinch at Elaine's scrubs, hold her sleeve between my clenched fingers. 'Please – you can't do that. These surgeries have to go ahead. You can't just let me die.'

She stares at me, her pity eyes larger than ever. She looks as if she's going to cry too.

'We had a deal, Gordon. You said you would relax and now—'

'Can somebody tell me what the hell is going on?' Michelle screeches out from behind Elaine.

I swallow down some tears, hold both of my palms out to face the two women.

'Elaine,' I say slowly, 'this is Michelle – my ex-wife.'

Elaine purses her lips at Michelle, then nods before turning back to me.

'Gordon is in need of emergency surgeries on his heart. He is due to go down for these surgeries in about twenty minutes, but that's totally dependent on his heart rate remaining stable.'

Michelle folds her arms, stares at Elaine, not at me.

'Is it true that he only has a fifty per cent chance of surviving these surgeries?' she asks.

Elaine sticks out her bottom lip and then nods her head slowly.

'I'm afraid that's the ratio,' she says. 'The more stable his heart rate going into these surgeries, the more his chances of survival rise. But... but...' she stutters.

'But he hasn't been able to remain stable because he's been cooking up conspiracy theories about our daughter's disappearance,' Michelle says.

Elaine confirms Michelle's assumption with a slight sigh and a shrug of her shoulder.

I hold my hand to my face again, my head thumping from all angles; both temples, the crown, the tops of my eyes. I have to stop Elaine from ratting me out to Douglas. I have to tell my wife that our daughter might be found today. I have to get on to Lenny, see what the fuck he's found. Jesus Christ. Where do I even begin? I swing my legs over the side of the bed again and attempt to stand. But Michelle steps between me and Elaine, holds her hand to my chest.

'You're going nowhere,' she says, bossing me about just like she used to. 'Are these surgeries at three o'clock?' she asks Elaine.

'They were supposed to be, but...' Elaine purses her lips again. I'm fucking sick of her pursing her lips.

'Please,' Michelle says rubbing at the side of Elaine's arm with her other hand, 'make sure the surgeries go ahead. He's too young to die. I'll see to it that he relaxes now and when he makes it out of the surgeries I'll make sure he's looked after.'

I actually feel my heart almost mend. Nobody has said anything nice to me in years. Jesus, I miss Michelle so much. I place my hand on top of the one she has resting on my chest.

'Thank you,' I say. She doesn't respond. She's more interested in what Elaine has to say than what I have to say.

Elaine pinches the bridge of her nose with her index finger and thumb, stares down at her feet.

'I'll give you two five minutes alone. If you can do your

best, Michelle, to steady him ahead of surgery, that'll at least give him a fighting chance.'

She looks at me, says nothing, then heads for the door.

I take Michelle's hand, place it aside before planting my feet on the floor.

'Elaine,' I say, walking towards her. She turns around. I take two steps then throw my arms around her and breathe in her hair. 'I'm so sorry.'

She leans off me, purses her lips right in my face, then spins around and walks out the door.

Michelle reaches out for my elbow, helps me back to my bed.

'Chelle,' I say, settling my back comfortably against the bed rail again, 'I hired a PI called Lenny Moon – he's—'

I stop talking when Michelle holds her eyes shut and sighs through her nostrils. I've already pissed her off and I haven't even finished my first sentence.

'I know,' she says, opening her eyes. 'He paid me a visit. Gordon, you need to listen to me now. You have to calm down, your life depends on it.'

'But he has informa—'

'Gordon, stop!' she raises her voice.

'Michelle, look, it makes sense. Guus fucking Meyer. Of course he took Betsy; it meant I would lose interest in the business, that he would be able to take it over.'

Michelle places her hand over my mouth.

'Gordon, honestly, you need to stop. You need to let it all go.'

I try to talk but only a mumble comes out, so hard is Michelle's hand pressed against my lips.

'Listen to me, and listen to me carefully, okay?' she says, craning her neck so she can stare straight down into my eyes. She places her cold hands either side of my face, holding my head still. 'Betsy. Is. Dead.'

FIVE YEARS AGO

Betsy

I FEEL REALLY SAD WHEN I STARE BACK AT SANA'S MESSAGE.

How may I assist you, Betsy Blake? Do you need help downloading the latest software update?

I thought she might know who I am. Thought she might know the girl who has been in the newspapers and on the news on the TV. It takes me ages to type back to her.

Do you know me?

I stare at the screen. I can't wait to see what she says back. I tap my fingers against the back of the kindle until her reply comes up on the screen.

I'm sorry. Would you like help downloading the latest software update?

Ah fuck, no, no, no!

'I don't think everybody watches the TV and the newspapers,' I say to Bozy. Bozy just stares back at me. I'm not sure what I should type back to Sana. I hang my fingers over the letters for ages. Hitting buttons and then deleting them.

Betsy; are you still available to chat?

```
Here   are   the   details   for   the   software
update.
```

I try to read everything Sana has sent me but it doesn't make sense. It is really long. Really, really long.

```
Betsy,  you  haven't  answered  in  a  long
time.   Please   get   in   touch   with   our
representatives  on  1800  852  852  should  you
need further assistance.
```

'No, no, no,' I shout as I type at the keyboard and hit send.

```
Hkjsuy sihkh
```

I just wanted to type something. Anything to let her know I'm still here. 'Oh, Bozy,' I say, climbing back up to my bed beside him. I keep the Kindle on my lap.

```
Betsy  -  please  call  the  helpline.
Goodbye. And Happy Christmas.
```

The Kindle screen goes blank. I let out a big, big breath and then cuddle into Bozy. I feel really sad that Sana has gone. But I also feel really excited. That was the first time I've spoken to anybody other than Dod since I was four. I decide I must practice how to type, in case that message thingy ever comes up again. Next time, I'll be ready.

I press at the screen of my Kindle. The box that Sana's words were on is gone. There are just words saying:

```
Software update needed.
```

It won't let me go to the page where all my books are. This Christmas is getting worse and worse. I have nothing to do. I crawl out of bed, walk over to my book shelves and look at all the books on there.

'No. Too baby-ish. No. Too baby-ish. No. No. No. No. Hmmmmm. No.'

I keep saying no at every book I see. Then I let out a really big yawn and when it is finished I feel tears in my eyes. I fall down onto my knees and let the tears pour out. Then I bang my hands onto the floor. I just want to get all of the sadness out. Maybe if I get it all out, I might feel happy again. I was stupid robbing Dod's newspaper articles. Because I was the happiest girl I ever was when he used to let me upstairs to look out his window. And now here I am, in my basement doing nothing all the time. If I'm not sleeping, I'm yawning. Every day seems to go really, really slowly.

My crying gets louder and louder as I lie on the floor. I can feel my whole body shake as I cry. Then the key rattles in the door.

'Betsy, Betsy, what's wrong?' Dod walks down the steps quickly. I don't raise my head to look at him. I'm still bent over on my knees with my head on the floor.

His arms lift me up.

'What's wrong, sweetheart?' he says.

He takes my hands away from my face. Then he rubs his fingers under my eyes, wipes up some of the tears.

'This,' I say, then cry again. 'Is. The. Worst. Christmas. Ever.' I sob in between each word until my sentence comes out.

He holds me close and suddenly I don't feel so sad anymore. This is the first time he has hugged me in ten months, since he beat me up for finding the newspaper article.

After a really, really long hug, Dod lifts me up a bit and puts me on the edge of the bed. Then he sits beside me.

'It's been a pretty shit Christmas for me too,' he says.

I look up at him.

'I'm so sorry, Dod. I am sorry for everything. I shouldn't have taken your newspaper articles. I was really bad. You were right to get really angry and beat me up. I will never do anything like that again. I promise. I promise. I promise. I just want us to be friends. I hate it when we don't talk.'

Dod puts his arm around me and drags me into him. Then he kisses the top of my head.

'Those articles weren't about you,' he says. 'That's another little girl. And… I hate it when we don't talk too. I want us to be friends.'

I get away from his arm and look at him.

'The newspapers weren't about me?'

He laughs a little bit.

'Betsy; I've told you this before. You weren't the little girl taken. Your Mummy and Daddy died, so I had to look after you. You know this. I told you this before.'

I don't think I believe him. I remember him taking me. I remember being on the wall and walking and then Dod putting his hand on my mouth and around my legs. He took me when I was looking at my Daddy. My Mummy and Daddy weren't dead when he took me. But I really don't care. I hold up both my arms and then wrap them around Dod. I need him to be my friend. I hate living if I'm not friends with Dod. The days are really, really bad when we aren't friends.

'I love you, Dod,' I say.

He kisses the top of my head again.

'I love you too, Betsy.'

We hug for ages. Then after he lets me go, he picks up the Kindle.

'Ah, you need a system update,' he says. 'Let me sort this out for you. Why don't you come upstairs with me. There's a Christmas film on the TV, you can watch that while I fix your Kindle, huh?'

I smile at him. Then I grab his hand and we both walk up the steps. This is the happiest I've felt in a long, long time.

'Happy Christmas, Dod.'

14:40

Lenny

'WHAT THE FOOK ARE YOU TALKING ABOUT. KIDDIE PORN?' Guus snaps, narrowing his eyes again.

Lenny clasps his hands together atop the table, then nods his head slowly.

'Don't just sit there nodding,' Guus says. 'Tell me what you mean by kiddie porn?'

Lenny's cool demeanour begins to wear away again. He just can't stay consistent with it; it keeps coming and going. He begins to blink rapidly, then shifts uncomfortably in his chair. He didn't get enough information from Frank Keville to follow through on his claims; he was in too much of a rush. Is not sure where to take the conversation from here. He coughs lightly into his hand.

'Yes. I have it on good authority that you were charged with possession of child pornography.'

'This ish unbelievable,' Guus says. He stands up again, spins in his kitchen, his hands on his hips. 'Not this shit again.' He pauses, facing away from Lenny and takes in three long breaths. 'I've been through this with the cops. I have never had any interest in child pornography. And this was all proven. I was just checking on paedophilia, to see what is classed as paedophilia exactly... because I myshelf was sexually abused as a child. I was doing research for my own sanity.' Guus spins back around, faces Lenny. 'I put my laptop in to be repaired one day, next day I know the cops are at my door wanting to talk to me.'

Lenny looks sheepishly up at Guus.

'And?'

'What do you mean 'and'?' They fooking let me go because it was nothing. They looked at the computer – nothing. I wasn't watching child porn, I was researching paedophilia. That'sh it. Then when Betsy went missing, they dragged all this shit up again because they had nothing elshe to go on... they questioned me about Betsy for four hours in Kilmainham Station before they realised I had nothing to do with it. They said they'd never tell anyone I was a shuspect because the links to my paedophilia search were so sensitive and so innocent... Now, here you are, dragging all this shit up again.'

Lenny rubs at his own temple, still unsure whether or not to believe everything he's just heard.

'How did you find out that I was questioned about Betsy?' Guus asks, his face turning stone cold.

Lenny shifts in his seat again.

'I can't divulge that information.'

Guus paces towards him, crouches down so he is face on with the investigator, their noses just centimetres apart. Lenny can taste his stale breath.

'You have fooking nothing on me.'

Lenny holds his eyes wide open, determined not to produce his tic with his suspect in such close proximity. They eyeball each other, seconds passing without either of them blinking. Then Lenny's jacket buzzes, causing them to break the standoff. Guus leans back to an upright position.

Lenny gulps, then removes his phone from his pocket. Gordon. When the ringing stops, he checks the time on his screen. 14:49. Jesus – Gordon only has eleven minutes. Lenny stares down at his own feet resting under Guus's table and tries to think everything through. The end goal is securing the house. He's got to call Gordon back before his surgeries.

'Guus, let's take a time out. Two minutes for us each to calm down. Then I have one more question for you and once that's answered I'll be out of your hair.' Guus doesn't say anything, he's too busy circling his kitchen floor, his anxiety evident. 'I just wanna make a quick phone call, get all my ducks in order and then we can rule you out of our investigation. Am I clear?'

Guus shifts his eyes sideways, to look at Lenny. Then he nods his head.

'As long as it'sh to rule me out,' he says.

Lenny stands up, nods his head at Guus as he passes him and then makes his way out of the kitchen. He looks right, takes in the door of the basement again, wonders what's behind it, before turning left towards the front door. When he's outside, he palms his phone, presses at Gordon's number. The call is answered before he even hears a dial tone.

'Lenny, what the hell's going on?' Gordon snaps down the line, though he sounds as if he's whispering it, as if somebody might be in earshot that he doesn't want listening in.

'I'm at Guus Meyer's house,' Lenny says, almost in a whisper himself. 'Guus was a suspect for De Brun back in the day, Gordon. They never told you about him because of some sensitive information relating to the cop's interest in him. But I'm questioning him about all of that now and I'll have answers for you in the next few minutes. I'm going in to search his house now.'

'Are you telling me Guus took Betsy?'

Lenny stares back at the house.

'That's what I intend finding out.'

'They're coming to get me for my surgery in a few minutes. I don't have much time, minutes…'

'Gordon, I promise you I will ring you back before three o'clock. Guus's house is odd. *Very* odd. There's something not quite right about it. He has a basement that I wanna get inside. After I check it all out, I promise I will ring you back. And I'll have answers for you. Now… are you keeping your promise to me?'

Lenny bites softly down on his bottom lip in anticipation.

'Lenny, I gotta go. Ring me back!'

The line goes dead.

Lenny stares at the phone in his hand, then takes a long, deep inhale. He clicks into his text messages, re-reads what he sent to his wife earlier. Then he taps at his buttons again.

```
Please get back to me. I'm so sorry,
sweetie. I'll be back home soon and will
tell you everything about my crazy day.
Don't do anything stupid. I love you. x
```

After the text is sent, he eyes the hall door again, then walks towards it and pushes it open. When he closes it behind him, the whole hallway falls into darkness again. He walks slowly, his shoes tip-tapping against the floorboards, then calls out.

'Guus.'

No answer.

'Guus.'

Lenny steps backwards, his heart thumping when the light switches on.

'Lishten,' Guus says appearing right beside him. 'I don't know where you got your information from, but it'sh not on, you coming here to my house and opening up old wounds.

I'm shorry Gordon's health is in a bad way, but I would like to be left alone now.'

Lenny holds a palm out, to signal to Guus that they need to calm tensions down.

'I promised Gordon I would give this my best shot. I told you before I went to make a call outside that I had one last question for you – do you mind?'

Guus stiffens up his nostrils, then turns around and walks towards the kitchen again. He opens the door, flicks on the light and awaits Lenny.

Lenny turns his head left, stares at the basement, then follows Guus into the kitchen. Guus has his arms folded, is leaning the arch of his back against his kitchen countertop.

'Go on,' he says.

Lenny blinks, and as his eyes refocus he notices the time on Guus's microwave oven. 14:53. He's gotta get a move on.

'The cops weren't only interested in you because somebody had once reported that you searched for... paedophilia, I guess, on your laptop, there was another coincidence.'

Guus shrugs his shoulder towards Lenny.

'Sarah McClaire,' Lenny says, and as he says it, Guus's eyes close. And stay closed.

'Same shit, Lenny,' he says, his fists closing into a tight ball.

Lenny doesn't let up. He knows he doesn't have the time.

'You happened to be in Birmingham when Sarah McClaire went missing, you happened to be in Dublin when Betsy Blake went missing. There were searches of paedophilia on your laptop—' he spits all of this out of his mouth like a rap verse.

Guus finally opens his eyes, takes a step forward, stopping Lenny's flow.

'The fooking cops have been through all this with me. I

am in Birmingham about six or seven times a year. My business requires it. This is nothing new. You have nothing new. You are just dragging up old shit. I was cleared. The cops cleared me. How fooking dare you come back in to my home and drag all this shit up again.'

Lenny holds his hand across his own face as he blinks in rapid succession. He tries to reassure himself he's doing the right thing, that he is conducting a huge investigation just as he always dreamed he would. He's got his suspect rattled. Surely that's a good thing. He's doing a stellar job. He pays himself a compliment inside his own head, reminds himself to stop blinking, that he's winning here.

'I wanna check your basement,' he spits out.

Guus baulks his head backwards. He looks as if he's aged ten years since Lenny first saw him twenty minutes ago.

'The fook you will.'

Lenny blinks again.

'Well if you want me to remove you from the investigation, you will let me see what's down there.'

'I'll tell you what's down there. A fooking washing machine and boxes of files from work. Who the fuck do you think you are coming into my home and demanding to look around? You will do no such thing.' Guus walks towards Lenny, his index finger pointed. He jabs it back and forth at Lenny's chest. 'I think I'm a better investigator than you, Lenny, you know why? Because I've learned more about you in the past twenty minutes than you've learned about me. You know fooking nothing about me, nothing that the cops haven't already questioned me on. But y'know what I've learned about you?' Lenny starts to shake a little. He takes steps backwards, driven by Guus's jabbing finger, finds himself in the hallway, up against the wall. 'I've learned that you don't have a fooking clue what you're doing. You came to my home acting like some kind of big shot inveshtigator.

Please. You're not an inveshtigator. You are a fooking bluffer. You thought you could catch me out by bringing up my old Google searches, by bringing up Betsy, by bringing up Sarah McClaire. Hey... why not ask me about Elizabeth Taylor too? The cops asked me about that one back in the day as well. Ooops, did you forget about that one? Or did you just not know that bit of information? You're embarrassing. You're not an investigator, you're a clown. I'm sure Gordon only hired you becaushe you were the cheapest option. Are you really that shtoopid that you thought you could solve the Betsy Blake case in just a few fooking hours?' Guus laughs out of the side of his mouth again.

'I... I,' Lenny stutters, his bottom lip shaking. Guus has him practically pinned up against the wall, his finger digging into the centre of his chest. 'I just want to clear you from my investigation, that's all. Quickest way is for you to let me see what's in the basement, then I'll be on my way. On to the next suspect.'

Guus looks away from Lenny, stares towards the basement door.

'No.'

'Guus, listen to me. Gordon doesn't have long left. Minutes. He just wanted one last sweep of the investigation so he could clear his mind before his surgeries. Don't let him go down for his surgeries thinking you had something to do with Betsy's disappearance. What if he dies thinking you took his little girl?'

Guus removes his finger from Lenny's chest, then reaches his hand around the back of his own neck and starts to rub at it.

'Well that's all your fooking fault isn't it? Gordon didn't know I was a sushpect until you somehow found out today and told him.'

Lenny gulps. He doesn't know what to think. Maybe he

did fuck up. Maybe he shouldn't have told Gordon that Guus was once a suspect. It probably wasn't his place. What if Guus is totally innocent; that he really was just researching his own abuse as a child, that he really does visit Birmingham six times a year. But what if… what if he isn't innocent? What if Gordon's best mate took Betsy in 2002; has been hiding her in his basement ever since?

'Guus,' he says, holding the stare of his suspect. 'Let me see the basement, then I'm outta here.'

'Uuugh,' Guus rages, punching the wall just behind Lenny's head. He snarls, breathes deeply right into Lenny's face. 'You know what; fook you.'

Guus walks away from Lenny, allowing him to breathe properly for the first time in minutes. He'd felt smothered.

He straightens the collar of his yellow jacket, then watches as Guus walks up the hallway, towards the basement door. He stretches up, on his tip toes, takes a key that had been resting atop the door frame, then places it into the keyhole and turns it. The door creaks open. Lenny walks slowly towards him, notices Guus's hands are clenched tightly.

'You first, hot shot,' Guus says.

THREE YEARS AGO

Betsy

I TAKE DOD'S PLATE OFF HIS TRAY, PUT IT ON TO MINE, THEN place my tray on top of his empty one and make my way to the kitchen.

'Thanks, Betsy, that was lovely,' Dod says.

I made a chicken stir fry in sweet and sour sauce. It was a recipe I got from a cookbook by a chef called Jamie Oliver. I liked it too. I just think next time I can make it even nicer. I can add a bit more spice. I read the four cookbooks Dod has bought me over the past year or so and pick out ingredients that Dod will go and buy from the shops. He calls us a 'team' now. I agree. We're a really good team. Dod hasn't been angry in nearly two years – not since we made up on that great Christmas day.

I get cookbooks and other nonfiction in actual paper books. But I use my Kindle for all fiction stuff. Dod always has money in my account. I just download some great books with the push of a button and get reading. I am really happy that I am back reading fiction these days. It makes me sad to think that I didn't really read fiction for a few years. I hope everybody reads fiction; reading a book like that takes you away from real life. It makes you have adventures.

'I'll wash up,' Dod says, following me into the kitchen. 'You go and watch the TV. You like that cooking programme.'

I smile back at him, hand him over the dirty plate I was about to dunk in the sink.

'Thanks, Dod.'

The show he's talking about is called US Masterchef. Loads of different people cook dinners and desserts to try to win their own restaurant. I love it. As I'm walking out of the kitchen I notice the back door on the other side is slightly open. Dod opens it sometimes if I'm cooking to let the steam out. Looks like he forgot to close it today.

I decide I better not go near it. I don't want to upset Dod. So I just continue to the TV room, pick up the remote control and turn the volume up.

I really like the chef Gordon Ramsay. He shouts at the cooks all the time. But he knows what he is talking about. I have four of his cookbooks. Dod says he is going to buy me his latest one when it comes out in November.

I read non-fiction during the day and fiction at night. Last year, I asked Dod to buy me a copy of The Bible because religion and God kept appearing in my books. Some of the characters in my books prayed a lot and I wanted to know what God was all about.

The Bible's a big book. A really, really big book. And the way it is written means it is tough to read. But I got through it all in the space of one month. I wasn't sure whether it was a fiction book or a non-fiction book when I asked Dod to buy it for me. But I know now. It's definitely fiction. It has a talking snake at the start of it and then after that it is all about a man called Jesus who grew up in a place called Nazareth. In the story it says his mother, Mary, got a visit from an angel who made her pregnant from God. Then when Jesus grew up he was able to perform magic. A bit like Harry Potter. I still can't understand why some people think it is a non-fiction book. They must be really stupid.

It's the same with my book; Betsy's Basement. Some people might think it is fiction, some people might think it is non-fiction. But I'm not sure who is ever going to read it. Maybe people will only read it after I'm dead. It is still in my copy book, in the bottom drawer of the cabinet beside my bed. I have often thought about asking Dod if he would like to read it. But that's not a great idea. He is likely to get upset, or angry. I have only written the truth in it about Dod. Most of the things I write about him are nice things. But he might get angry about me writing about the beatings he has given me in the past. And about the newspaper articles. It makes me a bit sad that I won't be able to share it with anyone. Especially him.

I laugh when Gordon Ramsay spits out one of the cook's dinners into a bin.

'Christ, that's raw chicken,' Gordon says. 'It's redder than your cheeks.'

I giggle so loudly that Dod pops his head around the door.

'Gordon cracking you up again?' he says as he dries his hands with a tea-towel.

'He always does,' I reply.

'Okay... Betsy. I'm just gonna run upstairs to hang up some of my clothes. Are you okay staying here, or should I put you back down in the basement?'

I'm sure my eyes are really wide. I can't see them of course, but I think I can actually feel them getting bigger. Dod has never given me this option before. Ever. Anytime he's not with me, he puts me back down in the basement and locks the door. I even wonder if he is messing with me, testing me. I decide to take the test.

'I'd like to watch the end of this,' I say nodding over at the TV.

'Thought you might,' he says coming over to me. He kisses me on the top of the head. 'I trust you, Betsy, okay? Don't do anything silly.'

I look at him.

'Course I won't.'

Dod winks at me then turns around and I hear him run up the stairs.

I lie back on the sofa and watch as Gordon calls more cooks up to him at the top of the room before he samples their dinners. He high fives the next cook and tells him that his chicken is cooked to perfection. But just as he is about to put the next cook's dinner in his mouth, the silly voice over man says 'next time on Masterchef'. Uuuugh. I hate when it does that. I'll have to wait till tomorrow to find out what happens. I pick up the remote and begin to press at the buttons to see what is on the other channels. I don't see anything that I'd like to watch. Then I remember. The back door is open a bit.

I put the remote down and walk slowly into the hall. Really, really slowly. I don't want Dod to hear me. If he sees me, he will go crazy. I tip-toe towards the back door and when I get there, I push at it gently. It doesn't creak. It just opens up silently.

The brightness of the outside almost blinds me. I have to close my eyes. When I open them I am amazed. I've never seen the back garden before. The grass is really long. Really, really long. It's probably up to my waist. At least. But it's beautiful. Really green and beautiful. Birds are chirping in the big tree over in the next garden. The sun is really high in the sky, and there is a little breeze that is making the grass look as if it is waving at me. The wind feels so nice on my face. It makes me stand still. I would love to stay out here for the rest of the day. I breathe in some of the wind up my nose, then let it out really slowly. I can taste it at the back of my mouth. It's so nice. The nicest breath I have ever taken.

As I breathe in again I stare at the fence that separates our house from the next door neighbour. I bet it's about my height. I wonder if I could climb over it.

I let my breath out really slowly again. These breaths taste so nice. While I am tasting it at the back of my mouth I hear Dod speaking to me. 'I trust you, Betsy.' He says it three times. I open my eyes, turn around and step back inside. I close the door as slowly as I can without making a noise and then tip-toe straight to the basement and back down the steps.

14:45

Gordon

'SHE'S NOT FUCKING DEAD!' I SCREAM. BUT ONLY INSIDE MY head. I remain still, until Michelle removes her hands from either side of my face. Then I open my eyes, stare up at her. She's almost in tears, her eyes glazed over. I wanna hold her, whisper sweet nothings in her ear – tell her how much I miss her, how much I miss Betsy, how much I miss us. But I don't. I just lie flat on my back and let my mind wander in a million different directions. Guus? Guus? The fucker won the lottery after Betsy was kidnapped. He took over the company, bought a massive big house out in Clontarf. The cunt had motive. It all makes sense. I want to grab at my phone, ring Lenny back. But I remain still, Michelle towering over me. She wipes a tear from the corner of her eye, then takes one step back, removes her coat and hangs it across the back of the blue plastic chair.

'I'm really sorry you are going through this, Gordon, I really am,' she says. I continue to stare up at the ceiling, not sure whether I should be listening to Michelle's voice or the one inside my head. 'I sincerely hope you get through this, get yourself together.' She sits in the blue plastic chair, scoots it a little bit closer to me and then grabs at my left hand, gripping it between both of hers.

It's been years since Michelle and I have sat in the same room, let alone held hands. I feel so grateful that she's come up to see me just before my surgeries, but she's hardly going to tell me all is forgiven; she's hardly going to say all of this wasn't my fault. I curl my fingers, gripping her hands in a sign of gratitude.

I wouldn't mind talking it all out with her; tell her she's a fool for buying De Brun's theory; tell her she was a fool for leaving me at my most vulnerable time; tell her that my failing heart is most likely all down to her. But there's no value in me spending my final ten minutes on earth arguing with my ex wife. My mind shifts again. Guus? I begin to hear his smarmy little face scream out to me. 'I took your daughter. *And* your fucking business.' He keeps saying it, over and over again before he produces that horrible, snidey fucking laugh he has. 'I took your daughter. *And* your fucking business.' He's still repeating it as I solemnly stare over at Michelle. He's still repeating it as I decide to strike up small talk with her.

'How's life?'

She offers a vacant huff of a laugh.

'We don't need to talk about me,' she says.

'No… no I want to,' I offer up. 'I need the voices in my head to stop. Let's just talk… like adults. Honestly. How have you been?'

'Shit,' she says, producing a short snort of laughter out of her nose. Jesus, how much I've missed that laugh. 'I mean, the banks have let us all go, I've no job for the first time in my adult life. The twins are causing trouble in school. I mean…' she stops. 'I mean… I guess it's nothing compared to… compared to being sick. But… life's just… well life's just shit, I guess.'

Wow. Michelle hasn't opened up to me in years.

'I'm sorry to hear that,' I say. 'Y'know when I found out ACB were closing down, I was going to call you, tell you how sorry I was to hear you'd lost your job, but...' I shrug my shoulder and nod my head. She knows what I mean.

'Thank you,' she pouts at me.

She lets out a small sigh, then releases her hands from mine.

'I eh... need to visit the rest room. I need to wipe my eyes, freshen up,' she says.

She points to the door inside my room and I nod to confirm to her that it is indeed a toilet cubicle. Then, as she disappears behind the door, I grab at my mobile phone, press at Lenny's number as quickly as I can.

Fuck! It rings out. I begin to type a text; to get him to ring me back straight away. While I'm typing, I notice the time. 14:49. Fucking hell. I might only have eleven minutes left to live. I'm re-reading my text and am about to send it when the phone begins to buzz in my hand.

'Lenny, what the hell's going on?' I snap down the line, though I snap it as quietly as I possibly can.

'I'm at Guus Meyer's house,' he says. He's whispering too. 'Guus was a suspect for De Brun back in the day, Gordon. They never told you about him because of some sensitive information relating to the cop's interest in him. But I'm questioning him about all of that now and I'll have answers for you in the next few minutes. I'm going in to search his house now.'

'Are you telling me Guus took Betsy?' I can actually physically feel my heart rate rise, but at this stage I really don't give a shit.

'That's what I intend finding out.'

'They're coming to get me for my surgery in a few minutes. I don't have much time.'

'Gordon, I promise you I will ring you back before three o'clock. Guus's house is odd. *Very* odd. There's something not quite right about it. He has a basement that I wanna get inside. After I check it all out, I promise I will ring you back. And I'll have answers for you. Now… are you keeping your promise to me?'

I stare over at the envelope resting on my bedside cabinet, then hear somebody outside my room. They begin to wrestle with the handle of the ward door.

'Lenny, I gotta go. Ring me back!'

I manage to hang up and then hide the phone under my sheets before the door fully opens. Bollocks!

'Gordy, Gordy, I found her. I fuckin found her. I know where Betsy is!'

I stare up at him as if I'm staring at a ghost.

He moves closer to me, right to the edge of my bed, then leans over and stares into my eyes.

'Have you got that copy of your will – leaving your house to me? If you have it signed, I'll tell you where she is.'

I remain schtum, stunned. Then my eyes go wide when I hear a rustling in the cubicle. Oh fuck. Michelle. The door snaps open and out she strides. Straight towards him.

'You fucking scumbag bastard,' she screams, clawing at his face. I can actually see rows of cuts form under his eyes.

'Fuck you. Fuck you. Fuck you, Alan Keating,' she howls. She's on top of him, slapping, punching, scraping.

I throw my legs over the side of the bed, and ready myself to pounce on Michelle; to take her off Keating. But then the ward door opens wide. It seems as if the whole of the bloody surgery team are there. Each of them open-mouthed at what they're witnessing, Elaine front and centre of the group. She looks up at me, then back down at the two wrestlers on the floor.

14:50

Lenny

LENNY FEELS HIS WRIST BEGIN TO SHAKE A LITTLE, WHICH IN turn makes his entire hand, even his fingers, shake. He takes the first step down, more wary of what's going on behind him as opposed to what may lie in front of him. He takes another step down, then another – walking towards the darkness. The light from the hallway behind him is all that guides his next step. He inches an ear towards the dark, the deathly silence making his heart sink a little.

As he reaches the bottom of the steps, he flinches upon hearing Guus's arm shoot up behind him. He turns around, elbows up, ready to defend himself.

Click.

Guus has pulled at a hanging light switch. Lenny doesn't take the time to sigh a relieved breath; he just swings his head back around, takes in the basement. Boxes. More boxes. An old washing machine. More boxes. Shelves with boxes on them. He swallows hard, then holds his hands up, palms out, as if to signify some sort of an apology. Or maybe it's just disappointment. He's beginning to think Guus isn't involved at all. Yet why does he always produce that snidey laugh that screams 'guilty'? Lenny looks back and sees Guus shrug a shoulder, a sly grin on his face.

'Wanna check she's not inside any of the boxes?' he says, then delivers that horrible laugh out of the side of his mouth again.

Lenny holds two fingers to the centre of his forehead and bows his head a little. Heat rises within him, as if his blood is coming to boiling point.

'Betsy! Betsy!' he shouts from the top of his voice.

He brushes Guus aside, runs past him and back up the steps.

'Betsy Blake. I'm here to save you. To bring you home!'

He sprints in to the living room opposite the kitchen. Then darts back into the hallway and into a large dining room. Back out into the hallway. Up the stairs.

'Betsy! Betsy!'

Into one bedroom. Then another. A bathroom. Another bedroom.

'Betsy!' he ends up in the middle of the square landing; his voice echoing off the walls and back into his own ears. As he hears himself calling Betsy's name, his face cringes. He takes two steps backwards until his back leans against the wall. Then he slides down it slowly into a seated position, and sinks his eyeballs into the caps of his knees.

'What the fuck am I doing?' he whispers into his crotch.

Then footsteps sound out. Slowly coming up the stairs towards him. He doesn't look up. He feels too ashamed, too embarrassed.

Guus shuffles towards him, then slips down into a seated position, their shoulders almost touching. Nobody says anything; Lenny's frustrated breathing the only sound between them.

'I'm so sorry,' he finally mumbles.

Guus lets out a soft sigh.

'I think old Gordon has made you jusht as deluded as he is,' he says.

Lenny almost edges to peel his eyes up from his knee caps, but stops himself. He can't bring himself to look at Guus. He's never been more mortified at any point in his whole life.

'You didn't really think I took her, did you?'

Lenny doesn't answer. He can't find the words to justify his madness. He just closes his eyes firmer, forces them deeper into his knee caps. He begins to question whether or not he genuinely believed Betsy was here. He actually can't remember. The past ten minutes have been a bit of a blur. A cringe runs down his spine, making him shudder.

Guus nudges his shoulder against Lenny's.

'Look, maybe you got carried away, but it's not all your fault. You were just doing a job.'

There's a hint of sympathy in Guus's voice. Lenny can't understand why he'd be sympathetic, certainly doesn't think he himself would be that sympathetic if somebody ran around his house calling out for a missing girl.

Lenny lets out a grunt; a real frustrated ugly yelp. Then he shakes his head as he wonders why the hell he thought he could solve a seventeen-year-old mystery in just five hours.

'Cops questioned me seventeen years ago and let me go within a few hours,' Guus says, interrupting Lenny's swirling mind. 'I was in Birmingham alright when Sarah McClaire was taken, but I was in a meeting with twenty-five other people. I wasn't anywhere near the area that poor girl went misshing from. And when Betsy went misshing, I was on a phone call here to a client of mine. The cops know all this, I had alibis that were proven to be correct within minutes of me being questioned. I don't know what elshe to say to you… it wasn't me who took Betsy. In fact, nobody took her, well nobody abducted her. She was killed when a car hit her, her body taken and disposed of somewhere. I thought everybody in the country knew that. Well, everybody except Gordon. It'sh kinda why we had to buy him out of the company. Gordon went... well, Gordon went a bit mad. The guy's nuts, Lenny.'

Lenny shakes his head one more time, then finally peels each of his eyes from his knee caps. He raises his left hand a little, rests it on Guus's knee.

'I'm sorry.'

Then he rises up, manages to get himself safely to his feet without stumbling despite his head still spinning. He rests his palm against the wall for balance, takes a deep breath, then he reaches down to Guus, pats him on top of the head and apologises again. He staggers towards the stairs, trudges down each step as if he's got major back problems and then finds himself out in the hallway.

'Listen, when you talk to Gordon, pass on my best wishes, and tell him I mean that genuinely,' Guus shouts down the stairs.

Lenny doesn't answer. He wrestles with the zip of his jacket pocket, then whips out his mobile phone and checks the time on the top of his screen. 14:58. He told Gordon he'd ring him back before three; told his wife he'd be at the school for a meeting at three. He thumbs the buttons on his phone.

'Priorities. Priorities,' he mumbles to himself as he opens Guus's front door and steps out, finding himself in the messy garden once again. He looks up as the tone rings. And rings. The sun is starting to dominate the sky, a light blue winning out against the grey.

'Bollocks,' he says when the tone rings out. 'Please answer, sweetie.'

He rings again; breathes in some fresh air through his nostrils as he waits. It rings out. He thumbs his way into his text messages.

Sweetie. I'm getting a taxi home right
now. I'll be with you soon. I'm so sorry
about today. I'll tell you all about it
when I get home. Love you. X

Then he scrolls into his contacts list, presses at another
number as he walks up Avery Street towards the main
Clontarf Road.

'Hello, Lynck Cabs.'

'Hi, I need another taxi please. I'm on the Clontarf Road,
I'll be waiting just outside The Yacht pub.'

'No problem, Sir, we'll have one with you in less than ten
minutes.'

After Lenny hangs up, he edges the phone closer to his
mouth, begins to nibble on the rubber cover as he tries to
straighten his thought process. He can't put this phone call
off much longer. He tilts the screen towards his eyes. Checks
the time. 15:00. Then he looks up to the sky, squints at the
brightness.

'Fuck it,' he says, then thumbs at his phone again, holds it
to his ear. It rings. And rings. Until finally a click confirms
the call has been answered.

'Thank fuck, Lenny,' Gordon says, almost panting down
the line. 'They're bringing me down to theatre now, what
have you got for me?'

ONE YEAR AGO

Betsy

DOD TURNS OFF THE LIGHT IN THE BACK HALLWAY AND THEN inches towards the door. When he opens it, he steps out, looks around at the back of the houses behind us, his head turning left, then right. Then left, then right again. He turns to me and curls his finger to let me know I can follow him. He does the same thing every time.

I pull at the door really carefully to step out and immediately breathe in through my nose to taste the fresh air in the back of my throat. It's the first thing I do every time Dod lets me out the back. He's been letting me do this for nearly a year now. I couldn't stop thinking about that time I sneaked out and really, really wanted to ask him to let me outside. But I didn't know how I could ask him without letting him know that I had sneaked outside once while he was upstairs. So when he asked me what I wanted for my nineteenth birthday last year, I told him I would love nothing more than to breathe in some fresh air. He really didn't want to do it, but after he turned out all of the lights in the back of the house, he realised nobody would be able to see us. We just have to stay quiet, that way nobody will ever know we are here.

He lets me out here every Saturday night. Just as a treat. He always stares at me as I take long breaths up through my nose. We stay here until Dod feels as if it's too cold, then we go back inside. Saturdays are always fun. There's always something good on the TV whatever time of the year. We like to watch *Strictly Come Dancing*. And when that's not on, there might be *Britain's Got Talent*. Or *Saturday Night Takeaway*. Ant and Dec are really funny. I think I might fancy Dec. He has a really pretty smile and everything he does makes me laugh. He doesn't have to do much. He might just look down the camera or something like that and it makes me giggle.

I don't have to cook on a Saturday. Dod orders Pizza. We get pepperoni, chicken tikka and green peppers on our pizza. It's so yummy. It'll probably arrive in about ten minutes' time.

It's cold tonight. I put my arms around Dod's waist and lean my ear in to his chest as I breathe in the air.

Every time I'm outside here I think about the first time I sneaked out. I often imagine what I would have done if I had have jumped over the fence. I could have screamed at the neighbours and started to bang on their back door or windows. But I'm so glad I didn't. Life is good now. I am a really happy girl. Or woman, seeing as I'm going to be twenty soon. That'll mean I've been here for sixteen years. Some of those years were really bad. Some of them really good. Like this year. The best year I've ever had.

I squeeze Dod a little tighter.

I read – once – in a book called *Dear Octopus*: 'the family, *that dear octopus from whose tentacles we never quite escape, nor in our innermost hearts never quite wish to.*' That really made so much sense to me when I read it. It made me think of Dod.

He is my family. My entire family. The most important person in the world to me. I'd be lost without him. I don't want the neighbours. I don't want Mrs Witchety across the street. I don't want anything or anyone anymore. I just want Dod.

'Come on, Betsy, let's go inside,' Dod says as he releases his arms. I smile up at him, then follow him in.

Dod heads straight for the kitchen after he's locked the back door. I can hear him get the pizza slicer from the drawer. I go into the TV room, pick up the remote control, switch the channels until I find BBC.

'Come on, Dod, it's almost starting.'

He arrives with the pizza slicer just in time. The catchy title music begins to play and Dod shakes his shoulders at me. I laugh really loud at him trying to dance. I can actually hear myself laugh and it fills me with a real happiness. Then he holds his hand out to me.

'No,' I say, giggling.

'Come on!'

So I do. I grab his hand. And as the professional dancers begin their routine on the TV – as they do at the start of every *Strictly Come Dancing* show – me and Dod join them on the dance floor. He spins me around as we both laugh. Then he tries to pick me up to do a lift. But I seem to be a bit too heavy for him. We fall into a heap on the floor and can't get up because we are laughing so much. In fact I'm laughing so much that I feel tears come out of my eyes.

There's no better feeling then tears of laughter. Laughing seems to be the only reason I produce tears these days. I'm so lucky.

I'M NOT SURE MICHELLE HAS EVEN NOTICED THE PRESENCE of five other people in the ward as she continues to claw and slap at Keating. I sit on the edge of the bed and just watch as two male members of Douglas's surgical team grab at my ex wife's armpits, lifting her off the old prick. Keating staggers to a standing position, his face already swollen, scrape marks visible under his left eye.

Elaine, still in the doorway, removes her hand from her face and stares at me, her lips ajar.

'That woman is a psychopath,' Keating calls out.

'Me? *You're* the fuckin psycho,' Michelle shouts.

They're both hushed; one man in a white coat standing between both of them, his arms outstretched.

'This patient,' he says pointing at me, 'is due to undergo major heart surgery now. The last thing he needs is his heart rate rising prior to these procedures. How dare the two of you act in such a manner.'

'She just fucking hopped on me, started—'

'Shut up!' the man in the white coat screams. The whole

ward falls silent, no more squabbling, no more murmuring from those standing in the doorway.

'Mr Blake, what has been going on here?'

As he asks that question, three security men arrive in the ward, shuffling their way past the surgical team.

'He,' I say, pointing at Keating, 'just powered into this ward making up all sorts of false accusations about my missing daughter. My wife – ex wife – was only protecting herself, protecting us. Take him away.'

Two of the security men step towards Keating and force his hands behind his back.

Keating just snarls at me, shrugs his shoulders.

'Worth a try, wasn't it?' he laughs as he's led away.

'And, miss,' the other security man says, 'you'll have to come with me too.' He places his hand on her shoulder, moves her around so she's facing the door.'

'Hold on, hold on,' Michelle says, turning back to face me.

The security man looks at me. I nod. But as he lets go of Michelle's shoulder to allow her to come to me, Elaine walks into the centre of the room, between me and my ex wife.

'Wait!' she says, then gulps. 'It's not clear if Gordon will be going for his surgeries now.'

Out of the corner of my eye I can sense the rest of the surgical team cringe in the doorway.

'Elaine,' I call out. She doesn't react. 'Elaine!'

She walks towards the rest of her team, and as she's about to leave the room with them, she turns back. 'Give us two minutes,' she says.

The security man remains with Michelle and me; my ex-wife looking like she's about to throw up, her face paling more and more with every passing second.

'I'm so sorry, Gordon,' she says. 'I'm so sorry.'

She drapes herself over me. I breathe her in. It's been so long since I've done that.

'It's not your fault,' I whisper into her ear. 'I've been causing drama in this ward all morning.'

She leans off me, sucks wet droplets of watery snot back up her nose, then wipes at her soaked face.

'Hey, you really beat the shit out of him, huh?' I say laughing. She tries to laugh too, but it just causes her snot to fall back out of her nose.

I swallow hard, then I stare at the closed door, wondering what the fuck is going on outside. The team are literally discussing whether or not my life is worth saving. I guess it's bizarre that that isn't even at the forefront of my mind right now. I look at the phone in my hand, will it to ring. Come on, Lenny. What the fuck have you found?

The door bursts open, Elaine leading the other five people in to my ward.

'Okay, Gordon, we're going to take you down now. Mr Douglas has the theatre set up; he's awaiting your arrival.'

Two of the team approach the rail behind my head, one of them kicking out at something under the bed. Then I feel myself floating, being wheeled towards the door.

'Gordon, Gordon,' Michelle calls out. She grabs my hand. 'You're going to make it through, I know you will.' She leans in to me, kisses my forehead. My mind begins to spin, swirl, do backflips. I'm going for make-or-break surgery. My ex wife is fucking kissing me. Guus Meyer took Betsy. What the fuck has gone on this morning? It feels as if I've woken up in the middle of the most surreal nightmare fathomable.

'You won't be needing this,' Elaine says, grabbing the phone from my hand.

I shout out but she doesn't care. She hands it back to Michelle who is now sobbing in the doorway of my ward as I am wheeled away from her. I turn over on to my belly, stare backwards and watch Michelle. It almost feels as if I'm being wheeled away in slow motion.

Then Michelle begins to wave at me. She's running. Getting closer.

'It's ringing,' she says. 'It's ringing.'

Elaine tries to stop her from giving me the phone, but I swipe at it.

'Thank fuck, Lenny,' I say as I hold Elaine at arm's length. 'They're bringing me down to theatre now, what have you got for me?'

The silence between me asking that question and Lenny answering is almost torturous. I can actually hear my failing heart beat loudly in my ears.

'Gordon, Guus didn't take Betsy,' he says. The sound of my heart thumping suddenly stops. As if it no longer wants to beat. As if it no longer feels a necessity to keep me alive.

'What do you mean?'

'Gordon, she's not there. Guus had nothing to do with her disappearance.'

Elaine grabs at my wrist.

'Gordon, you need to hang up that call now.'

The surgical team push me into a large elevator. I don't even hang up on Lenny, I just hand the phone over to Elaine and lay my head back on the pillow, my mind splintering in a thousand different directions.

Bollocks. Lenny didn't get me any answers. Why the fuck did I get my hopes up? I think about the envelope I left back in my ward. Fuck it. It doesn't matter anyway. I'm going to survive these surgeries. I *have* to survive these surgeries. I need to know what happened to my Betsy.

I grab at the sleeve of Elaine's scrubs.

'I need to get through this,' I say. She sighs quietly, then purses her lips at me. 'Please tell me Douglas is going to carry out the surgeries. Please!' I'm almost crying through my begging when the lift door opens and I'm wheeled out. Elaine doesn't answer me, she just stares straight ahead.

I'm wheeled down a long corridor and then around a corner towards another long corridor. The colour has disappeared from the hospital. No greens or blues or yellows. Everything is just white here; either white or clear glass. As the team and I are buzzed through a double doorway, I see him. Douglas.

'What took you all so long?' he asks.

The surgical team look at each other. Except Elaine. She's too busy staring at me.

'Sorry, Mr Douglas, but we had an issue with the bed, it wouldn't wheel. We had to find another one.'

Douglas tuts loudly, then motions, with curled fingers, for the team to wheel me into his theatre.

'We're all ready here,' he says. 'We need to do this asap.'

When I'm wheeled through, a member of the team places his hand around my back, moves me up into a sitting position. Then the T-shirt I'm wearing is taken from me, my arms reaching up so it slips up over my head. I stare around the room, almost blinded by the brightness of it all.

'Ready, move,' somebody says beside me. Suddenly I find my whole body being lifted and then placed down on another bed. Possibly my deathbed. Douglas is dictating orders to his team, but I can't really make out what he's saying. My mind is racing too much. My whole life seems to be flashing before my eyes. My parents, my school friends, my horrible fucking teachers, my first job, meeting Michelle. Betsy. Betsy. Betsy.

'Gordon, Gordon?' Douglas says, removing me from my thoughts.

'Huh?'

'Do you understand everything I've just said to you?'

I arch my head back a little, strain my eyeballs to look up at him. I've no idea what he's just said to me, but I just nod anyway.

'Okay, so take one deep inhale.'

I do. And as my lungs are filling, he places a mask over my mouth and nose.

'I'm going to ask you to count backwards from ten. By the time you do, you'll be asleep, okay?' I nod again. Then Douglas nods at me, prompting me to start. I look around, find Elaine, then hold a hand out towards her. She grabs on to it, squeezes my fingers.

I take in another deep breath as I close my eyes. Then I begin to count.

'Ten… nine… eight… seven… si—'

YESTERDAY

Betsy

ANOTHER BLOODY SOFTWARE UPDATE. THIS SEEMS TO HAPPEN about every three months now. A box flashes up offering me the chance to:

Chat with one of our representatives now.

I just click the tiny 'x' on the corner of that box and then continue to download the new software update. I don't need to 'chat' with anyone. Downloading the latest Kindle update is easy. Dod showed me how to do it.

I couldn't live without my Kindle. It's one of the best inventions ever. I have nearly two hundred and twenty books inside this skinny little machine. There's no way I'd be able to fit all of those books in this basement. Not unless I slept on top of them. Dod still buys me my non-fiction books in paperback form. I'm currently reading about a president of America called Barack Obama. He was the first ever president of America with black skin. I don't know why I always seem to relate to people with black skin. I think it might have to do with the fact that they were held as slaves for so long until they fought their way to a better life. Maybe I can relate to that in some way. Obama seems to be a real modern-day hero. I'd like to say that it would be great to meet him but I really don't have much interest in meeting people anymore. It used to be my dream to meet somebody… anybody, but I've learned to love my life. It might be restricted; I don't ever leave this house, except to breathe in some air out the back garden, but I have everything I could ever want. I have all my books. I have Bozy. And I have Dod. What more do I need?

I love Dod so much. He is so many different things to me; a best friend, a parent, a partner, a cook, a hairdresser, a TV critic, a book critic. Sometimes we read the same books and then discuss them afterwards. We both read *Dreams From My Father* at the same time, although he finished it way before me. Then afterwards, over dinner, we discussed what we both love the most about Barack Obama. We also both read *The Hunger Games* books at the same time and then discussed them. I think Dod liked them more than I did. We've also watched the movies. They're crap in comparison to the books.

The software update finishes and I click back into the book I was reading: *The Fault in Our Stars*. It's very sad. Very, very sad. But it is so gripping. I only downloaded it yesterday morning. Am nearly finished it already.

'You should read this one, Dod,' I say.

He looks at me, then squidges his nose.

'Doesn't seem like my cup of tea.'

A small laugh comes out of my nose.

'You're just afraid you'll cry.'

He makes a face at me, then continues to paint the wall of my basement. He's so good at looking after me and my little room. I asked him to paint it light blue, so that it looks like the sky. He bought some paint yesterday and began the job today. The smell is a bit strong, but I don't mind. It will look great when it is all done.

Dod's going to buy me two plants as well that I can put in the corner of the basement, just so I can bring a bit of the outside into my inside. We still go out the back, with the lights turned off, every Saturday evening before our Pizza arrives. The smell of fresh air is still a joy for me. We whisper when we're out there; about anything and everything. It's normally the best twenty minutes of my week. But anytime spent talking with Dod is always great. He is so clever.

I stare at him as he runs a paint brush up and down the far wall. I think he has lost some weight in the past months. I asked him if he was doing more exercise.

'No. Apart from running around seeing to your demands!' he said to me laughing. He says I have him under my thumb, that I totally control him. He might be right. I don't know. I just know that we love each other. And that neither of us would change a thing. We don't even hold any secrets from each other.

Well, apart from *Betsy's Basement*. I still haven't told him about it. I'm not sure how he would react to reading it. I think it's a great book. I really do. It's a hundred per cent non-fiction now. I got rid of all of the fictional stuff about neighbours who I made up. The whole book now is about my time spent here. It's like a memoir; a bit like the Obama book in a way, a bit like the brilliant book I read last year: *Angela's Ashes*. That kinda thing. Somebody in the future will find it. Somebody will read it and know the full truth about my life in this house. And I will continue to add to it. My life is far from over. I'm only twenty-one. Have lots of years left. My spelling and my writing improves all the time, but it's still not perfect. I'm sure there are still lots of mistakes in it, but I really like *Betsy's Basement* and think whoever does find it in the future will really enjoy reading it. I might even become famous. Only I won't know. Because I will be dead.

I sniffle up a tear that almost falls out of my eye as I

continue reading *The Fault in Our Stars*. I always know if a book is good or a bad depending on how it makes me feel. Once it makes me feel anything – happy, sad, angry, afraid – then I know it's good. It's the writer's responsibility to make the reader feel... feel something. This book is definitely making me feel something: sad. But that's a good thing. The writer has done her job. I hope whoever reads *Betsy's Basement* feels something. But I don't want them to just feel sad even though there are sad bits in it. I want them to feel happy too. And angry. And afraid. Because they are all the feelings I have had while I've been writing it.

'Ohhh,' I need a glass of water,' Dod says as he scrambles back to a standing position.

'I can get one for you,' I say.

He shakes his head.

'Don't worry about it. I wanna take a little break. I don't feel too good. I'm a little light-headed from the fumes, I think. I'll be back in ten minutes. You just keep on reading.'

I smile back at him and watch as he makes his way up the steps. He doesn't seem to be walking like he normally does. He's holding on to the wall for balance as he makes his way towards the light in the hallway.

Then he just drops; his whole body slapping against the floorboards in the hallway.

FIVE HOURS LATER

20:00

Lenny

LENNY CRUNCHES ANOTHER PLASTIC CUP IN HIS GRIP, TOSSES IT into the bin and then interlocks the fingers from each of his hands around the back of his head. He lets out another sigh and then begins to pace the corridors. Again. Slowly. Really slowly. He's not going anywhere, but he's sick to death of sitting in the waiting room. He can't fathom why the plastic seats in these waiting rooms are always so uncomfortable, as if they're designed to itch people's arse cheeks. He has studied each face he's come across during his repeated walks, but none has matched the pretty girl in scrubs he'd seen in Gordon's ward this morning.

He grinds his teeth again, the day's events constantly nagging away at him, then squirms. He's furious with himself that he spent much of his day running around strangers' homes shouting out Betsy Blake's name – as if she was just gonna magically poke her head out from behind a curtain after seventeen years.

'I'm a fuckin idiot,' he whispers to himself as he continues to walk, his hands still interlocked behind his bald head. It's not the first time he's mumbled that sentence in the past couple of hours.

He's frustrated with himself over a number of things, but none more so than the fact that he put Sally on the backburner. He'd never done that before. He got so wrapped up in his job that he let Sally down. He's promised himself – and her –countless times over the past hours that he will never do that again.

Still, despite the cringe-worthiness of his day, it may all work out wonderfully for him in the end. As far as he's aware, Gordon said he was leaving his home to him in his will; it was practically the last thing he said as he was being taken down for surgery. Wasn't it? The day's been such a blur, Lenny isn't entirely sure what was said. Though, if he learned anything since he arrived home and researched the Betsy Blake case, it's that it wouldn't be particularly wise to trust anything Gordon Blake says. Yet, despite that, here he is – back at the hospital, desperate to find out if that will Gordon wrote in front of him was left on his bedside cabinet before he was wheeled down for his surgeries.

The first thing Lenny did when he arrived back at the hospital was to go up to St Bernard's Ward; into the room Gordon had been lying in all morning. But there was nothing in it; nobody in the bed, nothing in or on the bedside cabinet. Lenny has begun to wonder if he's being equally as deluded as he was earlier in the day, thinking Gordon would leave him his house. But he couldn't just sit at home not knowing for sure. He felt he had to be here, he had to find out. Intrigue was controlling him.

He told Sally everything. It took quite a while for it all to sink in and for her to understand what had gone on during his morning, but once the penny dropped that Lenny was doing everything for his family – for her and the boys – she held her arms out, invited him in for a hug. They held each other for about half an hour, until the boys finally asked why dinner was taking so long.

When Sally released him from their long embrace, Lenny made his way to their pokey dining-room and wiggled the mouse of the home computer, making the screen blink on. He researched the Betsy Blake case as thoroughly as he possibly could. Every minute of reading made him squirm even further into his seat. He never thought he could be so gullible.

Everybody he spoke to during his investigation; from Alan Keating and Barry Ward to Michelle Dewey – Betsy's own mother – to Ray De Brun, the lead detective on the case, Frank Keville who reported on the case for a decade and even Gordon's former best mate Guus Meyer – they all told him Betsy was dead. And yet he still raced around thinking he could find her. The internet informed him there's no doubt about it: Betsy Blake's DNA was found inside that car back in 2009. And that DNA did indeed confirm she was deceased. Unless the cops are unfathomably dirty and had somebody in the lab ensure their findings matched up to the theory, then there's absolutely no doubt about it: Betsy Blake is dead.

The penny dropped within Lenny that Gordon Blake must have just gone crazy after he lost his daughter, and couldn't bring himself to admit that she was gone forever. But that's exactly why Lenny is here – because Gordon Blake *is* crazy. Maybe, just maybe he was crazy enough to leave a small-time investigator he barely knew a million euro house in his will.

Lenny lets out another deep sigh as he turns another corner, into another corridor that looks identical to the other thirty he's strolled down over the past hour and a half. He spots another water cooler, decides to fill another plastic cup just to break the monotony of his corridor walking. He holds down the small white tap, and when the cup is only half-filled, he stops and tilts his head sideways. He can hear a familiar voice; a voice he was talking to earlier today. He takes one large step back, just so he can peer around the corner. Michelle. She's nodding her head, in conversation with a nurse. Michelle's eyes look heavy, as if she's been crying. Maybe Gordon didn't make it. Though maybe she's been crying because Gordon *did* make it. Their relationship is so toxic, Lenny's not quite sure what way Michelle would react to any result of Gordon's surgeries.

Lenny's eyes stretch wide and he instinctively takes a step forward, out of her sight, when Michelle glances her eyes towards him.

'Bollocks,' he mutters to himself. The conversation around the corner stops dead. Then the sound of heels stamping their way towards him echoes against the walls.

She doesn't say anything when she's directly behind him, but he can feel her eyes burn into the back of his head. After blinking rapidly, he finally spins around, widening his eyes in mock surprise.

'Michelle, how did Gordon get on?'

She holds his stare, snarls up the butt of her nose at him.

'You should be fucking ashamed of yourself,' she says. Then she trots away, her heels clapping against the tiled floor again. Lenny tucks his chin into his chest and waits for the cringing to stop running down his spine.

'Eh... Mr Moon, am I right?'

He lifts his chin, sees the nurse Michelle had just been speaking to approach him slowly. She holds a hand out to his bicep and pats it gently.

'I'm really sorry to tell you that Gordon Blake passed away during his procedures this afternoon. His... his heart rate was too high, making the surgeries all the more complex. Plus he produced about six massive blood clots after the procedure had begun; a couple of which entered one of his lungs. I know it's no consolation right now but he slipped away under heavy anaesthetic, so wouldn't have felt any pain.'

The nurse continues to pat at Lenny's bicep, continues to try to console him but he's barely listening anymore. All he wants to know now is whether or not Gordon left behind an envelope with his name on it; whether or not he is now the owner of a million euro gaff. He nods solemnly towards the nurse, trying to act as if he's desperately saddened.

'If you would like to meet with any of our grief counsellors, I can put you in touch with them...'

Lenny stiffens his face, then blinks before composing himself.

'Did he eh... did he leave anything for me?'

The nurse purses her lips, then shakes her head really slowly.

Shit!

'Not that I'm aware of,' she says, 'But I didn't clear Gordon's ward. I know all of his possessions were brought to our family storage room – would you like me to check them for you?'

Lenny nods. Probably a little too eagerly. But before he's even stopped nodding, the nurse slips her hand around to the top of his back and begins to guide him back down the corridor.

Lenny can sense that the nurse is interested in talking, perhaps she's intrigued by the life of Gordon Blake – she must be if she found out he was the father of Betsy Blake. But they don't talk as they take a lift down to the ground floor, and don't talk as they stroll down a long corridor to reach a small reception area.

'Hi, Tanya,' the nurse says, 'Gordon Blake, the patient we

lost on the table today, his belongings were taken down here a couple of hours ago…'

'Oh yeah,' Tanya says, turning her back and entering a pokey room to the side of her reception desk.

The nurse reaches out another hand to Lenny's bicep, pats at it. But he can't bring himself to look at her, he's afraid he has guilt written all over his face. She thinks he's saddened by the news she's shared with him, she has no idea he is bubbling up inside with excitement.

'It's not much,' Tanya says, standing in the doorway. She holds the door open, nods for Lenny to enter.

'I'll leave you to it,' the nurse says. 'I'll be back up on floor three if you feel you need to come talk to me, okay?'

Lenny barely reacts, he's too busy staring inside the pokey room. He paces forwards, bypasses Tanya in the doorway and stares at a plastic bag resting on a small white fold-down table.

'That's everything we took from Mr Blake's ward,' says Tanya. 'I'll leave you to it.'

When she closes the door, Lenny looks to the ceiling first, as if he's praying to a God he doesn't believe in. Then he takes one deep breath, still staring up at the ceiling, and steps forward to spread the bag wide open.

He removes a T-shirt and a pair of shorts before spotting a small brown envelope. He snatches at it, spins it around in his hands.

Fuck yeah!

For the attention of Lenny Moon.

He rips the envelope open with his thumb, and unfolds the paper inside it. There are two sheets of paper. But it's the very first sheet that makes his heart thump loudly. It *is* the will. And it's made out to him.

This is the will and testament of Gordon James Blake.

I hereby wish to leave the home, addressed 166 South Circular Road, Inchicore, Dublin 8, Ireland to Leonard Moon.

It's signed by Gordon and signed by two girls – one named Elaine Reddy, the other Saoirse Guinness. Lenny's eyes almost glaze over with joy. The guilt he had been feeling has dissipated, the cringes that were flittering up and down his spine all afternoon forgotten. He and his family are now rich. In bricks and mortar at least.

He places the first sheet aside, sniffles up the tears that threaten to fall, then continues to read.

Lenny, if you are reading this it is because I have passed away.

Yes – I did, as promised, leave you my house.

I hope you enjoy living in 166 South Circular Road. I certainly didn't. Too many dark memories.

You'll find a girl in there when you go in. Elizabeth Taylor. Betsy Taylor. I took her when I was travelling around Europe ten months after my Betsy was taken. Even on this day – my dying day, I guess – I'm not sure what possessed me to snatch her. I guess I just wanted to replace my daughter.

I stopped for lunch in a small town in Wales during one of the last days of my travelling and was amazed when I heard a man call out the name 'Betsy'. I stared at her. Couldn't keep my eyes off her. She didn't look exactly like my Betsy – not in the face – but she had the same brown hair. Was a similar height. Similar age. I followed her and her family for hours, staring from behind bushes, around corners. Suddenly she started walking on the wall I was hiding behind while I was trying to look at her. And I don't know what came over me. I just wanted her. I thought my pain would disappear. I stood up and grabbed her.

But she was never my Betsy. I didn't know what to do with her. Whether to treat her like a daughter, like a friend, like a partner. I tried all of those hats on, none seemed to fit. Not until the final few years when we both realised we couldn't live without each other. But she'll have to live without me now, I guess.

I love her very much. I looked after her; she's well nourished, well read. I guess that's the best I could do.

I must have apologised to Betsy a thousand times over the years. Guilt kept eating away at me. Give her one last hug and one last apology from me before she's sent back to her real home. And tell her I'm going to miss her. Just as much as I've missed my own Betsy.

Sincerely,

Gordon Blake

TODAY

Betsy

I'M WORRIED. REALLY, REALLY WORRIED. I HAVEN'T BEEN ABLE
to read for the past twenty-four hours. I can't concentrate. I
keep seeing Dod with his eyes rolled into the back of his
head. He was breathing funny. And his tongue was hanging
out of his mouth. I kept calling his name, louder and louder
each time. Right into his face, right into his ear. It was
working. A bit. He would respond by making funny noises,
but I wasn't sure what he was trying to say to me. So I rooted
through his pockets, took out his phone and fumbled with it
until I could find some numbers. Then I dialled 999 and
waited.

'I need an ambulance,' I said. 'Dod needs to go to hospital.'

The girl on the other line asked me for the address. I ran
to the door.

'Number one-six-six,' I said.

'One-six-six where?' she asked.

My eyes went wide.

'Dod… Dod,' I screamed. I slapped him across the face.
Did whatever I could to wake him up. To make him talk.

'One-six-six. One-six-six.' I repeated the number into his face over and over again. Then I watched him swallow hard and his eyes turned more normal.

'South Circular Road.' he squeaked out of his mouth. Then his eyes rolled back again.

I keep playing it over and over in my head. Him looking like he was about to die; me making the phone call; me letting the ambulance man and woman come into the hallway; me watching as Dod was put on a stretcher and wheeled out of the house.

I feel so alone. And very, very sad. I cried most of last night. And this morning. I've had to creep outside the back door; just to breathe in some fresh air. I know Dod would be angry that I did that during the daytime, when a neighbour could see me. But I needed the fresh air. Desperately needed it.

I'm back in the basement now, under my covers with Bozy on my chest just waiting to hear Dod come back through the front door. I wipe my hand over my face and let out a big sigh. I think all of my tears have dried up. The crying has stopped.

I sit up in the bed and look at my Kindle. I'm really not in the humour of reading. My brain won't let me concentrate on the story. All I can think about is Dod. About how he collapsed when he reached the top of the stairs yesterday. The noise of his body slapping on the wooden floor.

Then I look to my right, to my bedside cabinet, whip the duvet off me and pull it open. I reach inside and take out my copybook. Betsy's Basement. If I can't read because I keep thinking of Dod, then maybe I can write, because I'll be writing about Dod. I click at my pen and then begin to scribble a new chapter. Chapter 115. I chew on the top of the pen, wonder what to call this chapter.

Dod goes to hospital.

And then I begin to write it. I write about him painting my room, then needing a glass of water, then falling onto the floor at the top of the stairs. Sometimes when I write the name Dod, my 'o' looks like a small 'a'. He told me once, not that long ago, that he asked me to call him Dod because it sounded like the word Dad. But then he said he was only messing. I'm actually not sure if he was or not though. Then I write about me calling the ambulance and about the ambulance man and woman coming into the house. I write about how odd that was for me. I hadn't spoken to anybody but Dod for seventeen years. The woman asked if I'd like to go in the ambulance with them. I looked out the door, stared at the big bright yellow ambulance with blue lights flashing on its roof, and then shook my head.

'I shouldn't go out,' I said. Then I asked her to look after him as best she could. I write about that too. And about me crying all night.

This is the fastest I've ever written. And the longest. I've probably been writing for the past two hours. Maybe three. Then I stop suddenly. I think I hear a key in the hall door.

I slap Betsy's Basement shut and look up the steps. The hall door creeps open and my heart thumps really fast with relief. Ka-chunk, ka-chunk, ka-chunk. A big smile stretches right across my face. Dod. Dod is okay. He's safe. He's home.

I place Betsy's Basement and my pen on top of my cabinet, grab Bozy, and we both make our way to my steps. But I stop suddenly because I get confused. I think Dod's brought somebody home with him. I'm sure I can hear people talking up there. I stand at the bottom of the steps and try to listen. Then the basement door opens and I see a shadow of a man. It's not Dod. Then a woman appears. Then another man. He's not Dod either.

All three of them walk slowly down the steps, one of them shining a torch towards me. I squeeze Bozy tight. Really, really tight.

THE END

DID YOU SPOT ANY OF THE CLUES TO THE END TWIST?

WELL, AUTHOR DAVID B. LYONS GOES THROUGH THEM DURING this exclusive Q&A.

You can watch it in the link below. Get ready to kick yourself!

www.subscribepage.com/betsyblakeq&a

THE TICK-TOCK TRILOGY

Whatever Happened to Betsy Blake? is just one book in a gripping trilogy of books all told in real time. The Tick-Tock trilogy can be read in any order.

Midday
by David B. Lyons

Whatever Happened to Betsy Blake
by David B. Lyons

The Suicide Pact
by David B. Lyons

ACKNOWLEDGEMENTS

My first thanks – as always – go to my wife without whom none of this would be possible. There isn't room for moping if you live with Kerry Lyons – every minute has to be appreciated. She's an inspiration every day.

This book is dedicated to our daughter Lola. Within it, I hope to teach her a valuable lesson: see what happens when little girls don't stay by their daddy's side forever? You're never leaving home, Lo. But don't worry; we live with somebody who won't let us mope.

I'd also like to extend a thank you to my ma, Joan, and my sister, Debra, for no fucking reason whatsoever once again. I've started thanking them in acknowledgements and I guess that needs to continue for tradition's sake.

A huge thanks goes to Barry O'Hanlon and Hannah Healy who helped me refine this book as I was writing it. And also to Margaret Lyons, Rubina Gomes and Livia Sbrabaro who read very early drafts and offered fantastic constructive notes. I'd also like to mention the great Andrew Barrett who has helped me through my journey in more ways than his humbleness will allow him to admit.

Thank you also to Niamh Mehigan who provided me with great research insight into Gordon's medical condition. I appreciate you giving up your time to help me.

And to my editor, Maureen Vincent-Northam, who dotted the Is and crossed the Ts with her razor-sharp eye.